IRA SILVER LINING

IRA SILVER LINING

ISBN: 978-1-7350632-0-1

Authors Note: *Ira Silver Lining* is a work of fiction. Characters, places and incidents are the product of the author's imagination. Any real names or locales used in the book are used fictitiously.

Cover Image by Lesley Nash
Edited by Meghan Stoll
Book Design by Nonon Tech & Design
Bio Photo by Mae Lizama

IRA SILVER LINING

By

Shane Finkelstein

Dedicated to the memory of Doug Rittner.
And to Memaw, Mom & Dad
for all your love and support

1

Ira Silver's feet were tucked inside an empty wooden box screwed to the top of a six-foot ladder. The day before, it had held a couple of toddlers begging for beads at the parades that passed in front of Ira's house on St. Charles Avenue.

It was Ash Wednesday and Ira was using a cane to clear the beads caught in the branches of a giant oak tree. He stretched as high as he could for a long strand of pink pearls while sweat dripped down the sides of his flushed cheeks and the hair on his back clung to his dirty faded undershirt.

Behind him, the broken iron gate scraped against the slate walkway. He caught a glimpse of Charlie hurrying to the front door and barreling her way into his home. She was wearing those shoes again, the ones with heels so high they added four inches to her petite frame.

Ira had a lonely life until Charlie came into it. He was a man of many routines, insignificant rituals that blended one day into the next: his morning coffee, walks along the avenue, Saturday mornings with Mother. Until Charlie's arrival, no one noticed those routines, and if Ira had failed to awaken one day, he worried that weeks would have passed before the mailman discovered the macabre stench seeping through the mail slot.

After Charlie slammed the wooden door shut behind her, another hot flash of pain seared through Ira's right ankle. It was so intense that he reached down to grab his foot, causing the ladder to wobble back and forth above the overgrown lawn. He swung his good leg back over the top of the ladder to reach for the second step but missed it entirely. Instead, he dropped the cane and tumbled down the ladder, crashing into a trash bag full of stuffed animals, Chinese trinkets, toilet paper, and hundreds of strands of cheap beads.

Ira patted his body for broken bones. Filling his emptied lungs, he felt a twinge in his back that left him unable to rise. Behind him, he heard the rusty gate swing open again, this time so forcefully that it sounded as if torn off its hinges.

Ira, still lying on the ground, craned his neck to see the profile of a man stomping up his brick staircase. The man wore aviator glasses resting on a crooked nose and had dark stubble covering a square jaw and a head as shiny as a glazed donut. He was dressed in dark blue jeans, a white button-down dress shirt, and a black sports coat. The rolls of skin on the back of his neck reminded Ira of a shar-pei.

The man pounded his meaty fist against the wooden door, twisted the doorknob several times, and then knocked again. Ira took a deep breath and rolled himself on all fours onto a patch of dirt. After two more wheezing breaths, he ended up on his knees brushing the dirt off his palms and eyeing the back of the man on his porch.

"Charlie, open the damn door," the man yelled.

Now upright but still gasping, Ira leaned against the trunk of the old oak tree. Though only twenty yards away, the man seemed not to notice him. He reminded Ira of a secret service agent or a bouncer on Bourbon Street. His thick neck twisted to the right to the sound of the streetcar clacking up the block.

He pounded on the door one more time, then dropped his fists and yelled, "You better show up tomorrow."

"Can I help you?" Ira asked in a cracked voice.

When the man caught sight of the speaker, he stared him down like a salivating pit bull at the dog park. "What are you looking at?"

Ira lowered his eyes and cowered behind the trunk of the oak tree until the man had bounded down the staircase, swung open the gate, and followed the streetcar in the direction of the French Quarter. He rummaged among the trash bags until he found his cane and limped across the lawn. Leaning hard against the rusty wrought-iron banister, he inched his way up the six stairs and stopped beneath the portico.

He took one last glance over his shoulder to make sure the man wasn't coming back before grabbing the knob of his front door and turning it back and forth. Locked, with his keys inside. He gently knocked but heard nothing. He knocked louder, slapping his palms first against the wood then against the beveled glass panes on each side of the door. He yelled Charlie's name, but she didn't answer.

2

Charlie was short for Charlene, or at least that's what she told Ira. At work she went by Rose because of the tattoo stretched across her pasty inner thigh. She was from Gulf-port, Mississippi, a senior in high school—just past eighteen, or so she said. She spent her weekends in New Orleans, stripping at one of those empty dive clubs on Iberville between Chartres and Decatur.

They had met on the streetcar on Christmas Day. She was sleeping with her knees tucked up into her stretched-out T-shirt, her head resting against the cold hard window. When she opened her blue eyes, she caught Ira staring. Ever since his divorce, he was always staring at pretty girls. They had become like foreign objects to him. Usually they would sneer or snicker, sometimes flutter an evil eye. This girl was different. She stared back at him and cracked a slight smile before Ira turned away, looked into his lap, and started biting his fingernails.

At Ira's stop, the blonde-haired girl got off too and followed from about twenty yards back until he ducked beneath the entryway to his home. A few seconds later, he heard an incessant knock pestering the front door. Peering through a crack, Ira asked, "May I help you?"

"Let me help you," Charlie answered with a raspy voice and a sly grin on her little face. Without waiting for an answer, she pushed the door open, brushed past Ira, and plopped herself onto the sofa in the front room. With heart pulsing and cheeks flushed from the home intrusion, he hurried to the kitchen to catch his breath and fix a pot of coffee.

When Ira returned she was asleep, sprawled face down into the cushions with one hand brushing the pine floor. He smelled her pungent odor of sweat and cigarettes mixed with the remnants of vanilla perfume. It was late afternoon when Charlie burst into his life, but it wasn't until early the next morning when she began to stir once more. He spent the entire rest of the day checking to see whether she was still breathing, listening for the faint sounds of her snoring. It had been years since one of Ira's own kids had fallen asleep on that couch, and the sight of Charlie's motionless body brought back some of those long-forgotten memories.

As the sun rose on that cold December morning and the shadows crept up the cracked walls, Charlie moaned and cursed before noticing Ira in the rocking chair. "Why you didn't wake me?" she grumbled.

"You looked tired," he said.

"But I must have missed work," she said. "They ain't gonna let me work tonight."

"You can stay here, if you'd like."

"You gonna pay me?"

"For what?" Ira asked.

"My time."

"I don't have any money."

He saw Charlie's eyes circle the room, looking at the chipped crown molding along the high arched ceiling. The lush velvet curtains covering the massive windows were torn at the top, the floral couch had stained cushions, the rug beneath her feet showed frayed edges and discoloration marks from a recent coffee spill. The room was shrouded in darkness, interrupted only by a beam of natural light shining through an oval stained-glass window perched above a dark wooden staircase.

"Got anything to eat?" she asked, turning back toward Ira, who was staring at the floor now.

"I have French bread," Ira said, fidgeting with his hands.

"That it?"

"And jam."

Ira hurried into the kitchen and exhaled for the first time since Charlie had opened her piercing blue eyes. It was the first time in years anyone had been in his home aside from the boys on their last spring break. He grabbed the French bread off the Formica countertop and flexed his fingers, crushing the top of the bread a bit, testing it for freshness. He had picked it up the day before at the Leidenheimer Factory on Simon Bolivar Avenue, where he went twice a week to schmooze the receptionist into giving him two-day-old bread before they tossed it. He usually froze one and ate the other with little packets of jam he got from the nearby Best Western.

When Ira returned to the living room, Charlie was looking at herself in the mirror, trying to mat down her crazy spiked hair. She asked, "Got any eggs? I'm starving."

"I do not."

"Coffee?"

"A pot is brewing," he said.

"Yes," she said, watching him through the reflection in the mirror, "I smell it."

"Would you like to take a shower?"

"With you?" she said, as she rubbed black eyeliner off her eyelid with her thumb.

Ira felt his cheeks turn the color of the Chinese flag. He spun his head around to avoid eye contact. "That's—that's—that's not what I meant."

"I could use a hot shower," she finally said, flashing a crooked-toothed smile.

"There's no hot water," Ira stammered.

Charlie ended up showering, drinking three cups of coffee, and leaving before dinner, but she returned shortly after dawn, pounding her fists against the front door. She was drunk, her eyes red and glossed over and her cheek showing signs of a light bruise. She stumbled past him with that same fetid odor, went straight to the couch, and fell asleep the instant her head hit the cushion. Ira wrapped a knit blanket over her body and removed her damp flip-flops from her feet—beautiful, porcelain feet with hard dirty yellow calluses on the soles. He then wiped a tear from the corner of his eye.

That was pretty much their routine every weekend over the past three months. Ira never knew exactly when the knock would come, but he found himself strangely intoxicated by the anticipation of this young girl tramping through the door and making herself at home in his huge empty house on St. Charles Avenue. She hadn't stolen anything and hadn't brought anyone back with her.

Sometimes she even contributed a few bars of soap or miniature shampoos, most likely culled from a stranger's hotel room. He was never happy thinking about her wild nights, but taming Charlie would have been like domesticating a tiger cub in a halfway house.

Most of their mornings together, Ira sat in his recliner and watched her breathe heavily through her tiny pug nose while he read his library books. Sometimes after she woke up they headed down to the New Orleans Hamburger and Seafood Company and grabbed a free ice cream cone from the self-serve station by the front door or free samples from Yogurtland, but more often than not she was like an outdoor cat that returns home to sleep whenever it feels like it. Though he never told Charlie, having someone to look after gave Ira a sense of purpose he hadn't had in years.

She never liked to talk about her life, about what she did all night in the French Quarter. Whenever Ira asked about it, she quickly changed the subject. She had never mentioned her family or her friends or whomever she lived with. One time she alluded to a boyfriend in Gulfport, some guy that worked in an auto body shop and drove a motorcycle. She didn't patter on about school or the prom or anything else a normal high school senior would. Their conversations were more insipid. They talked about the streetcar, about the ever-present construction, or about the way some flowers bloomed in the morning and others only opened at dusk. She was a perfect companion in loneliness—though on the opposite end of life's trajectory—contemplating how to survive in a material world without seeing a future past tomorrow.

3

With the big bald man no longer in sight, Ira dragged the bags of beads across the lawn and plopped them on a weedy patch near the front gate. Covered in dirt with back aching, he wanted nothing more than to find out who the stranger was that came looking for Charlie. He gingerly returned to the ladder, folded it up, and laid it against the side of the house. Ira once had quite the collection of ladders when his kids were around, but these days he had little use for them. This one had been left in front of his house against the black wrought-iron fence, where some inebriated father had forgotten it on Fat Tuesday. At some point, he would roll it up to the hardware store and try to sell it for a few extra bucks.

The searing pain that had befallen Ira on the top of the ladder was another gout flare-up. After pestering neighbors on the neutral ground for leftover burgers and beer during the first couple of night parades, Ira had felt that familiar burning sensation devouring his left foot. It was like smoldering charcoal crystallizing around the bones of his ankle. He had awoken still drunk on Saturday morning, begging Charlie to skip work and roll him in a little red wagon down to Touro Hospital on Prytania Street. Touro during Mardi Gras was an unpleasant place to be; it was six hours of undignified dealings with miscreants and drunks before Ira was finally allowed to see a doctor, only to be told that he was not sufficiently impaired as to receive free medical care. Luckily for Ira, Charlie stayed around to wheel him back home before she left for work that evening.

Ira took it easy the rest of the weekend, only leaving his house in the mornings and when parades were over to empty the beads out of the fishing net he had fastened to a lawn chair. The beads would be collected and sorted, stuffed in trash bags, and donated to the Krispy Kreme in Metairie in exchange for a few dozen glazed donuts. When Ira's parents had lived there—and to a lesser extent when his ex-wife Lin and the kids were around—friends and friends of friends used to congregate on the front lawn and use the bathroom, but it had been years since he had opened his home to those ne'er-do-wells.

"Charlie," he yelled. "Open the door. I'm outside."

His calls and knocks went unanswered for what seemed like forever. He checked the side door and even battled the interminable weeds along the side of the house to check the back door which faced the dilapidated shed in the backyard. They were all locked, so Ira gave up and went back to his routine. He limped the nine blocks to the Best Western next door to Superior Grill for the fresh pot of CC's Coffee brewing in the lobby. During Mardi Gras, a police officer had guarded the door and checked for wristbands all week. Now he was gone, and despite his disheveled appearance, Ira would be able to enjoy his free coffee without harassment.

Ira waded past a throng of tourists rolling overstuffed suitcases through the lobby, snuck past the front desk manager, and spied two pieces of king cake in a cardboard box next to a coffee urn. More than likely, these would be the last of the carnival season, so he took them both, ate one, and wrapped the other into a plain white napkin before gently dropping it into the front pocket of his khaki Dockers for safekeeping.

Ira glowered at the little eight-ounce coffee cups on the counter instead of the usual twelve-ounce, but the coffee was hot, and he wasn't paying three dollars a cup like people do at the CC's on Magazine Street. Sipping his first cup, he stood against the wall and observed haggard-looking strangers donning beads and rolling over-stuffed suitcases through the lobby. He used to enjoy talking to tourists and hoped one of them would make small talk, but they rarely did. He wasn't some celebrity chef or revered trumpet player or even a popular dude with a couple hundred Twitter followers. To their eyes, he was just a peculiar little man who looked older than his fifty years with stooped shoulders, a high forehead, and sneakers so worn that the soles had lost their bottom layer. Ira knew his was an appearance that more closely resembled that of the dozens of homeless men who lived under the interstate than of a homeowner residing on the grandest avenue in New Orleans.

Before heading out, Ira grabbed a copy of the *Times-Picayune* off the front counter. The desk clerk had already returned from church and wore a smudged ash mark in the center of his forehead. Ira nodded at him, then couldn't help but stare at the charcoal-grey cross signaling his devotion to Jesus Christ. The desk clerk frowned back at Ira. He wasn't sure whether it was because his forehead was ash-free or because he was mooching freebies from the hotel again. Either way, Ira was used to that frown; it followed him everywhere.

Normally, Ira would have walked from there to the Jewish Community Center, but in his current condition, he decided to hop on the streetcar. He swiped his transit card and paid the forty-cent disability fare before finding an empty seat next to a large woman wearing curlers and a shower cap and staring out the window. The smell of her oaky perfume forced Ira to hold his breath and grumble incoherently until she turned and asked him what the trouble was.

"It's the boys," he scoffed. "The boys will be here tomorrow."

The JCC had always been the epicenter of Jewish life in Uptown New Orleans. Mother had kept the family's lifetime membership active even though she hadn't stepped foot in the place since well before Father died. She thought Ira worked out at the gym and wanted him to keep in shape, still hoping he would one day make the acquaintance of another woman—this time a Jewish one. On occasion, Ira might go for a dip in the pool or use the sauna, but more often than not, he went for a hot shower or to watch TV.

In the men's locker room, Ira wrapped himself in a damp towel and nestled into a black leather couch in front of a flat-screen TV showing highlights of the latest sporting events. He had no taste for sports, so he commandeered the remote control, turned on CNN, and watched the ticker scroll the latest news across the screen. The place was bustling with middle-aged Jews working off their decadent failures of the past few weeks. Grabbing a pencil from his locker, Ira returned to the couch, spread the newspaper across his lap, and started in on the day's crossword puzzle.

Ira knew most of the people that worked out at the gym: mothers in Lululemon who dropped their kids at preschool and spent two hours toning flabby bodies, balding men with hairy backs sweating on treadmills, senior citizens curling five-pound weights under the watchful eye of a personal trainer. Everyone there was trying desperately to turn back the tides of time.

Resigned to the body that God had given him, Ira barely bothered. Instead he sat on the couch with the news ticker streaming through his peripheral vision and struck up three or four banal conversations, most of which featured a tale of Mardi Gras debauchery.

Marc Cohen, an advertising rep for the weekly rag, *The Gambit*, walked out of the shower naked but for a towel draped around his neck. "What's up, Silver?" he said with a condescending smirk, his penis flapping around in the stale air. "You going to the grand opening of Flesh on Saturday night?"

Ira took his eyes off Marc's penis. This was the first he was hearing about the Flesh opening. He used to get invitations to such high-falutin events, but now he had to talk his way in by flashing his business card and claiming the invite got lost in the mail. "Yeah, of course," he answered.

"Yeah, right, Ira. You don't have any juice. You ain't getting in there."

"Fuck off, Cohen. No one reads *The Gambit* anymore either."

Marc let out a huge belly laugh and pointed at Ira. "Yeah, whatever, dude. See you at Flesh."

Ira was the founder and publisher of *The New Orleans Jewish Monthly*, a once mildly thought-provoking and moderately successful local magazine. While the newspaper industry spiraled downhill back in the late nineties, Ira continued publishing his magazine, grinding it into the ground on a depressingly slow track toward insolvency. First, he fired his delivery driver and delivered the route himself. Then he let his one sales rep go, followed shortly thereafter by his editor-in-chief. One by one, the writers jumped ship. His monthly became a quarterly, and distribution went from twenty-five thousand a month to five thousand a quarter. With the extra time between issues, Ira had no difficulty writing all the articles and designing the few remaining ads himself. But there hadn't been a new advertiser in the paper since the fall. Ira blamed the lack of interest on the Internet and the average person's inability to retain focus for the duration of a thousand-word article. Instead, he spent most of his time tweaking a sentence or a paragraph from the manuscript that had consumed his mind for the better part of the past decade.

Without an agent, the prospects for publishing his manuscript had become increasingly unlikely and, with the newspaper barely clinging to life, Ira needed to find other ways to survive. As cash sales dwindled toward zero, he relied more and more on the Crescent City Trade card. Ever since he stopped printing monthly—right after Hurricane Katrina—most of his existing advertisers could be talked into bartering for an ad. Ira loved that trade card; it just about kept him alive. There were over a dozen restaurants in the uptown area that accepted it, though he was banned from a couple because he never left a tip.

With lunchtime approaching, Ira decided to check back home. He exited the side entrance of the JCC and heard the glug and whine of the streetcar coming to a stop at the intersection of Jefferson and St. Charles. He hurried after it, begging the conductor to hold the door for a few extra seconds so he could board. Though Charlie sometimes slept the entire day away, Ira hoped she would have woken by the time of his arrival. It was time to tell her about the impending visit of the Silver offspring.

4

When Charlie zoomed through the door that morning, she didn't even notice Ira de-beading the tree. He hoped that she woke at some point and had the presence of mind to unlock the door because he wanted nothing more than to sit in his rocker, read the rest of the paper, and listen to her snoring on the sofa until she came to again with that awkward twisted grin she always began the day with.

Last Friday, Charlie had announced she was on spring break and would be staying the entire week in New Orleans. Apparently, Mardi Gras was a boon for the local stripping industry and Charlie had made just over two thousand dollars since her arrival. Ira had spent that same time fretting over how to tell her that she had to vacate the premises. He couldn't imagine his boys finding out about a teenage stripper living in his run-down house. They wouldn't understand.

The door was unlocked, but when he opened it, Charlie wasn't there. The kitchen was empty, as were the bathroom and office. He called her name a few times, hearing a slight echo bounce off the hardwood floor. A small pile of her dirty clothes lay next to a chipped mahogany end table.

Climbing the dark staircase, Ira called her name again. As far as he knew, Charlie had never been upstairs, but he began to pick up her scent as he opened his bedroom door. The room was undisturbed, the door to the bathroom still closed. Ira walked unsteadily down the hallway checking the kids' bedrooms, but only a layer of dust greeted him behind each door.

He was about to concede and head back downstairs but got another whiff of her perfume. It was definitely coming from his bedroom, so he opened the door again, called her name, slowly walked toward the bathroom, and tapped lightly. No answer. Opening the door a crack, Ira saw Charlie's naked body submerged in the bathtub with just her nose and nipples peeking above the waterline. The first thought that crossed his mind was that the man had come back and killed Charlie in his house and he would be blamed and spend the rest of his life in Angola Prison. That thought made Ira smash the door against the wall and stumble forward into the bathroom. Charlie shot up so fast that water splashed over the tub's edge and onto the aqua-colored floor tiles.

"Ira!" she screamed, as he stepped back and slammed the door shut, apologizing like a teenage boy who was caught masturbating under the covers in his bedroom.

"You—you're not supposed to be up here," Ira stuttered loudly through the door.

"Sorry," she yelled. "I thought you wouldn't mind."

"I guess it's alright," he said, clutching his chest. "Sorry I walked in on you."

"Give me a minute to put some clothes on. I want to take you to lunch."

"You want to take *me* to lunch?"

"I'm hungry, Ira. And I'm tired of your jelly sandwiches."

"You don't have to do that," he said.

"It's all good," she said. "Made serious bank last night."

"Save your money, sweetheart."

"No, really," she said, "I'm aiming to take you out. Where should we go?"

Ira tried to think about the last time he went out to eat with someone. He couldn't remember. He guessed it was Mother, before the dementia, before the fights about who would pick up the tab. Ira was so used to eating alone, he couldn't even think of a place to go. Still standing behind the door, he said, "You pick. It's your money."

"I don't know. I ain't never been no place fancy. Maybe we should go to Ignatius. I hear they got good gumbo."

"I like gumbo."

"You ain't got to order just gumbo. You can get whatever's on the menu," she said.

Ira waited behind the closed door and took a breath, thinking about the menacing man that had followed Charlie home. He had no doubt she knew it hadn't been Ira pounding on the front door earlier, but he was afraid of getting all up in her business. "Was that your boyfriend that stopped by earlier?"

"My boyfriend?" she asked sarcastically.

"Yeah, you know. The bald guy that followed you home."

"That ain't my boyfriend, silly."

"Well, he didn't seem too friendly, if you ask me," Ira said.

"Friendly?" Charlie paused. "I reckon not."

"Maybe you shouldn't bring him back here again."

Ira heard Charlie stand up in the bath and turn on the shower. "Uggh," she screeched. "Why you can't get some hot water in this place? I had to boil water from the stove for a goddamn bath."

"I'm sorry," Ira stuttered. "Sewer and Water Board turned it off."

"Well no shit, Ira. Why didn't you just pay the water bill?"

"I paid the bill," Ira said. "But when they came back out to turn it on, hot water heater never started back up."

"Ever get somebody to look at it?"

"I can't afford that. Plumber's, like, seventy-five bucks an hour. And then they steal from you and break things and tell you that you need a new this and a new that. Next thing you know, I'm out four hundred dollars. I don't have four hundred bucks. I don't even have forty."

"I ain't believing you live in a house like this and don't have forty bucks, but whatever. Get ready for lunch and I'll be out in a minute."

Ira heard Charlie turn off the shower. She was singing "Carnival Time," as everyone tended to do after hearing it so often over those past few weeks. He chuckled and whistled along while he changed into a wrinkled white dress shirt and headed downstairs to wait for her.

5

A heavyset young girl in a sundress stood behind the counter eyeing Ira and Charlie as they walked in. "Sit wherever you want," she yelled.

Two rows of small wooden tables and blocky worn chairs lined the wall to their right. Cracks ran through the black and white one-inch-square tiles under their feet. They settled into seats at a table near the front window.

It was just past two, and Ira and Charlie occupied the only table in the restaurant. Despite several servers chatting behind the counter, no one came to greet them. The pair just sat there staring at people walking down the street. "No one's coming over," Charlie whispered.

Ignatius on Magazine Street used to be a coffee shop where Ira would spend his days drinking free refills and writing stories for the magazine or working on his manuscript. It became a de facto office when he needed to interview an intern or conduct a sales meeting. Then Benny, the owner, closed up shop, moved his little eatery from up the block into the premises, and chased the freeloading coffee drinkers out of the dining room.

"They must know me," Ira answered. "I used to be a regular here."

"I think they're talking shit about us."

"Don't be silly," Ira said. "I know the owner."

"I'm hungry," she complained, her voice rising to a more audible level.

Ira shushed Charlie as one of the waitress's shoulders sagged and a look of disgust crossed her face. She rounded the bar and ambled toward them with her eyebrows furrowed and lips pouted. She dropped two menus on the table and huffed, "Sorry, kitchen wasn't ready."

"Whatever," Charlie shot back.

"Benny around?" Ira asked.

"Benny doesn't work afternoons," the waitress said. "Might be up at the Rue on Carrollton."

"Can you tell him Ira Silver is here?"

The waitress hesitated, then shrugged her shoulders and rolled her eyes. "I'll be right back with your waters."

"Do you have any specials today?" Ira asked.

"Let me check," she said, as she spun around and gruffly trudged back to her girlfriends.

"What's with the 'tude?" Charlie commented.

"What do you mean?" Ira asked.

"Didn't you notice her attitude?"

"I'm used to it."

"Why? They don't act like that in the Quarter. Is that some kind of Uptown thing or what?"

Ira shrugged. "What are you getting?"

"Don't know. Haven't looked yet. I need a damn beer, though."

"You can't order a beer. You're not twenty-one."

"You can get one for me," she said with the grin of a seven-year-old in a candy store.

"I can't do that."

"Sure you can. As long as you're my legal guardian, you can order me a beer."

"I'm not your legal guardian."

"How would they know?" she said.

"They're looking at us like you're a hooker and I'm your sugar daddy."

"Well, thanks a lot, Ira. I'm guessing that means I look like a hooker. Just order me a Coors Light, would you?"

The waitress finally reappeared with their waters and said, "Did y'all decide?"

"You never told me the specials," Ira pointed out.

"The soup of the day is chicken tortilla. The fish of the day is red fish."

"What's that come with?"

"Veggies."

"What about drink specials? Do you have any two-for-ones?"

"No."

"No drink specials on a Wednesday?"

"Not that I know of," the waitress said, dropping her shoulders and shaking her head.

"You take the Crescent City Trade card?" Ira asked.

"The what?"

"It's a barter card."

"Never heard of it." The waitress spun towards the girl who had greeted them and yelled, "Tracy, ever heard of a Crescent Card?"

"Crescent City Trade card," Ira corrected.

Tracy yelled back, "No!"

"Don't worry about it, Ira," Charlie said. "I told you I was buying."

Ira crossed his arms over his gaunt belly and let out a sigh. Charlie ordered a fried shrimp po'boy and French fries. Ira ordered a bowl of gumbo and—pressed by a harrumph from Charlie—"Oh, yeah, a Coors Light please."

They sat for a minute or two in silence, Charlie fingering the rim of her water glass, staring dreamily out the long windowpane. "I like it here," she said.

"Ignatius?" Ira asked with his eyebrows arched.

"No, can't stand this place. I like New Orleans."

"Maybe you should find your own place. You can't stay with me forever."

"Why not?"

"Because it's not normal, a young girl like you living with an old man like me. People might start wondering."

"You ain't that old," she said. "Besides, I been with men older than you."

"Don't talk like that."

"You're such a prude."

"I am not a prude. Just don't like hearing stuff like that."

"Like what?" Charlie challenged.

"Like you being with old men," he said. "It makes me feel bad."

"Maybe you can be my sugar daddy then," she said with a giggle.

"That why you stay with me?" Ira asked.

"'Course not, silly. You ain't got nothing but that run-down house. What kind of sugar daddy would you be?"

The waitress dropped the beer on the table in front of Ira and he slid it over toward Charlie. A snarl crossed the waitress's lips before she departed back to her girlfriends.

Ira lowered his eyes toward the center of the table and whispered, "I guess I should tell you that my kids are coming to visit this weekend."

Charlie paused. "What you getting at?"

"I'm saying… I'm thinking, um, that probably, you know, it wouldn't be a good idea for you to be here… being around my boys. They're young and impressionable and, and might get the wrong idea, might not understand, um, what, you know, we have… me and you."

Charlie leered back at Ira, her deep blue eyes flecked with yellow piercing through the air between them. It occurred to Ira that if she were holding a cigarette, she would have taken a drag and blown the smoke in his face. Instead, she picked up the bottle, tongued the rim before sucking down a few slurps of beer, and said, "You embarrassed by me?"

"Embarrassed? No. But—" Ira stopped. He couldn't think of the right words. All kinds of thoughts raced through his mind. He just knew, deep down, that there was something not right about their relationship, but every moment spent with her was as intoxicating as a case of expensive champagne. And introducing her to his three young sons seemed as good of an idea as leaving the boys alone in a room with that same case of booze.

She finally broke the awkward silence. "I hear you. Loud and clear. Maybe you're right. I need to find a place with some silk sheets and hot water. You need better sheets, you know that Ira?"

A group of loud tourists bounded through the front door. They were graciously greeted and seated by the heavyset girl who then brought them to a table in the back corner. The other waitress startled Ira and Charlie by slamming the bowl of gumbo in front of Ira. As she walked away, Ira said, "Got any French bread?"

Without turning around she answered, "Yeah."

They waited again, the only sound a Johnny Cash song piping through the speakers. Ira wanted to apologize, but maybe it was time to let her go. He opened his mouth to speak, but the waitress interrupted the moment again by tossing a white paper bag on the center of the table. Before she walked away, Ira looked up and said with a smirk, "Tabasco. And perhaps a spoon, if that isn't too much to ask."

Instead, the waitress replied with a snort out of her nose that sounded somewhere between bothered and hysterical. She grabbed some napkins, hot sauce, and a spoon off the counter and hastily handed them to Ira.

"What's your problem, bitch?" Charlie snarled.

The waitress took a step back, folded her arms below her large breasts, and said, "We don't work for free around here, you know?"

"What? What's that supposed to mean?" Charlie said in a loud voice.

Ira grazed his hand across Charlie's arm. "She doesn't mean anything by it," he mumbled.

After a brief staring contest, the waitress balked and withdrew from the table. Charlie grumbled, "Bitch can't talk to you like that. Let's get the fuck out of here."

Charlie snatched her beer and the French bread off the table and rose so abruptly that her chair fell backward, slamming against the tiled floor. Ira took two hurried slurps of gumbo, wiped his face with the cloth napkin, stuffed the napkin into his pants pocket, and hobbled after her. She was halfway up the block before he caught up with her.

"I'm sorry, Charlie," Ira said. "Guess I have a bit of a reputation."

"Don't worry about it, so do I," she said. "Didn't want to be eating there anyway. Let's go on and get some ice cream."

6

It wasn't even dark yet and Charlie was already dressed for work. She had on a long white faux-leather coat over one of her skimpy outfits. Below the knee, she wore fishnet stockings and sandals. Her clear plastic pumps were most likely in the large knock-off Louis Vuitton handbag draped over her shoulder. It was an outfit Ira had seen on countless occasions, but each time she left in it, the knocks in his stomach grew louder. He wanted to stop her from walking out the door. He almost did, especially after the encounter with the man on his porch. But who was he to tell her what to do? He wasn't her father.

Instead he waved her goodbye and headed out for the evening. Lately he had avoided nights out; he'd been sitting at home waiting. Waiting in his rocking chair. Waiting for the breath of fresh air to walk through the door. Waiting for time. Waiting for the right time. But tonight, he needed to go out and hobnob with the falutins. That's what he called them. If he didn't start selling some ad space, there would no longer be *The New Orleans Jewish Monthly*.

JNOLA, an organization that brought together Jews from around the city for monthly get-togethers, was hosting a function at Pure on Freret Street. The night's event was called "Three Rabbis Walk into a Bar" and featured a set of stand-up comedy by Rabbi Maisel. Before Katrina, Ira used to organize Jewish socials, but as he grew older and less in-the-know, the numbers dwindled until it was just him and Nancy Edelman, the then-president of Temple Sinai. Now someone else was running JNOLA, and supposedly it was the place to be for Jewish networking. It had been years since Ira was comfortable in that kind of setting, but desperation was starting to creep up on him.

Three women of various ages congregated around a small high-top table near the entryway whispering to one another. When Ira walked in, the youngest, with long fake eyelashes, curly dark brown hair, and a thick layer of rouge asked his JNOLA name.

"What's a JNOLA name?" Ira asked.

"Either your Hebrew name or something clever," she said.

He raised his eyes in contemplation, puckered his lips, paused, and said, "Ira."

"That's kind of lame," she remarked.

"That's my name."

She scribbled his name on a nametag sticker, peeled it away from its backing, and handed it to Ira, who stuck it to the creased pocket of his striped collared shirt then looked back to see her giving a prissy smirk and rolling her eyes.

The center girl with the short blonde bob looked to be in her mid-thirties and either pregnant or obese. Hovering over a yellow legal pad, she said, "Twenty dollars, please," without looking up. The third woman—probably pushing fifty, but the most attractive of the three—opened a metal cash box and stuck out her hand.

"I should be on the guest list," he said, winking at the women.

The curly brown-haired girl looked up and said, "Name?"

He handed her a business card. She dropped it on the yellow pad and scanned the list with the end of a ballpoint pen.

She whispered something to the girl in the center and then said to Ira, "I don't see your name on the list."

"Are you sure? I'm with *The New Orleans Jewish Monthly*," he said, accentuating the word "the" so it sounded like "thee."

"Sorry, but you're not on the list."

"Is the director Susan Blumenthal here?" he asked.

"She's not," she said in a whiney voice reminiscent of all those Tulane girls that emigrated from Long Island every fall.

"She always lets me in these events. Trust me, I'm supposed to be here."

"Let me see if I can get her on the phone."

The girl in the middle looked around Ira and called to the group behind, "Next in line."

Ira stepped aside and watched a few dozen people grab their nametags, smiling at each person as they walked past. Surly Josh Goldstein, owner of the popular Goldstein's Deli, shook his hand and said, "Silver. Figures you'd be here."

"How's that ad working for you?"

"What ad?"

"The one you ran in the spring," Ira reminded him.

"What are you talking about? I was in your paper in the spring? Who gave you an ad?"

"Got it out of *The Gambit*."

"I didn't authorize that."

"You're in a contract," Ira said.

"Are you freaking serious? I told you I wasn't running with you anymore."

"But you're in a contract."

"Bullshit. I haven't signed a contract with you in years."

"Automatic renewals," Ira said. "I'll double-check my records."

"Yeah, you do that," Josh said, taking his nametag while grumbling under his breath.

"Mr. Silver," yelled the curly-haired girl. "Susan says it's okay, but you better do a write-up."

"Write-up, yes… sure… definitely. I'll send her a copy of the paper when it comes out."

The girl in the middle grimaced at him before thrusting her head to the right, pseudo-welcoming him into the bar.

Pure was full of pretty people in sport coats and miniskirts whose chatter morphed into one long incessant noise. Behind the bar, five rows of liquor spanned the entire back wall where three bartenders in aprons stood fixing drinks with squeeze droppers, muddlers, and tweezers. On the other side of the counter, thirsty patrons waved their hands at the insouciant bartenders, trying to get some attention. Pure had been the first high-end cocktail bar in the city, opened about five years prior in a renovated space on a dilapidated block in Uptown New Orleans. Freret Street was a shithole pre-Katrina, left to rot in the eighties and nineties after a series of high-profile crimes destroyed the neighborhood. But it was centrally located a mile from Tulane, presenting opportunity for anyone with balls enough to try to change it. Jeffrey Frankenberg was the man with the balls, balls so big he hadn't even put a sign over the front door. These days, he has three high-end bars in town, money growing out of his asshole, and women fawning over him. Thirty years ago, Ira and Jeff went to Tulane together. Jeff was a local success story. Jeff was a somebody. Everyone knew Jeff Frankenberg. Probably had five thousand Facebook friends. Does that make you somebody?

"Jeff," Ira shouted past the group.

He looked up and gave a half laugh. "Ira Silver. Girls, this is the infamous Ira Silver."

"That's *infamous*," he said, thrusting out his concave chest.

"What you drinking?"

"Whatever's fast."

"Is this your first time?" Jeff asked. "Nothing's fast around here. We serve craft cocktails. Want a beer?"

"I can't drink beer anymore on account of the gout," Ira said. "I'll take a Blanton's on the rocks."

"Nice try, dude. Call drinks only. Rain Vodka is the sponsor."

"Fine. Give me a vodka tonic."

Ira introduced himself to the girls. They were all from somewhere else; most of them had converged on the city post-Katrina. They all had rewarding jobs, or so it sounded: non-profit this, Teach for America that. One girl scouted locations for the burgeoning movie industry.

"What movie are you working on now?" Ira asked her.

"A TV show," she said. "*NCIS: New Orleans.*"

"I didn't know we had an *NCIS*," he said.

"Who doesn't know that?"

"Do you need any help?"

"You mean, like, staffing? Seriously?" she asked. "Ever since they pulled back the tax credits and all the other productions shut down, we've had more applications than we know what to do with. Why do you ask?"

"Thought maybe you could run an ad in my paper for staff."

She looked at him with her face scrunched up, her nostrils flared, and her eye twitching. "We don't advertise for stuff like that," she finally said before turning around and rejoining her crew.

Ira shrugged, still waiting for his drink with his hand tapping the edge of the bar, the chatter ebbing and flowing through his ears. He watched the bartenders with their squeeze bottles and tweezers, shaking this, stirring that, mixing drinks for the waiting patrons. It was an exercise in futility and patience. He cleared his throat and started whistling under his breath. Finally, Jeff gave a bartender a little wave of the hand and he hustled over like a butler answering the finger snap of a billionaire.

Jeff ordered the drink for Ira and said, "What brings you out tonight? Free booze?"

Ira felt momentarily shamed because Jeff hit the nail on the head. It was true, Ira never sold any ads at events like this because no one had heard of his magazine anymore. It was irrelevant, and so was he. "Thought I'd check in and see if you wanted to run something in the next issue."

"Seriously?" Jeff paused, staring at Ira like he was trying to figure out if he was joking. "We don't advertise."

Ira looked around at the packed bar. Everything was right about it. It didn't matter how long it took to get a drink because everyone was here just to see and be seen. That certainly wasn't Ira's scene.

The bartender handed Jeff a clear drink and he passed it over to Ira before he waved his employee away with the back of his hand. Jeff had given Ira more of his time than he had expected. Full of shame and dejection, he pushed through the double row of people standing in his way, drink in hand.

"Fuck! He gave me club soda." Ira winced. He hated club soda. "I ordered a vodka tonic and they couldn't make a simple fucking drink right." When he opened his eyes, he realized that the people on both sides of him were staring. "I guess I must have said that out loud," he mumbled. He made his way to the center of the bar by pushing back through the crowd, elbowing the girl next to him, and slamming the glass on the concrete bar top. All three bartenders stopped what they were doing, looked up, and shook their heads.

"Excuse me," Ira yelled.

They went back to fixing drinks and ignoring him.

"Excuse me! I ordered tonic and I got club soda."

Finally, one of the bartenders—a guy with a bald head and long scruffy beard wearing faux suspenders and a short-sleeved bowling shirt which exposed an armful of tattoos—stopped making his drink and walked his way. "Are you sure?" he said snidely. "We make our own tonic here."

"You make tonic?" Ira asked. "Isn't tonic just bubbled water?"

The bartender took a cocktail stirrer, held his thumb over one side, dipped it in Ira's drink, removed the straw, and sucked a few drops into his mouth. Shaking his head, he picked up the glass, emptied the liquid down the drain, and made another vodka on the rocks. This time he handed Ira a tiny bottle of tonic next to the rocks glass before returning to the drink he had been making pre-interruption.

Ira wrestled his way back through the crowd and found Rabbi Maisel walking out to the patio. Rabbi Maisel was another imported New Yorker. He had just replaced Rabbi Benjamin who'd been at Sinai for over thirty years. The board recruited him like a basketball player, offering him tons of money, a house, private school for the kids. It no longer meant something to be from New Orleans. These days, it meant something to be from somewhere else. The board of directors thought that was the way to recruit new members. Bring in the hotshot rabbi from up north.

Rabbi Maisel was dressed in dark blue jeans and a tan sport coat with the top two buttons of his dress shirt open to expose his curly chest hair. He didn't look like a rabbi. He looked like a single guy in his late thirties out on the town trying to get laid.

Rabbi Maisel saw him coming and started smiling. "Ira, so good of you to come."

He sounded so phony, kind of like a used car salesman. Ira really missed the old rabbi. Rabbi Benjamin was like part of the family. This guy was like part of someone else's family.

"I haven't been to one of these in years," Ira said.

"Pretty good turnout. Will you be at services on Friday night?" he asked.

"You bet."

"It starts at seven, you know?"

"Always has."

"I noticed you haven't been coming until the Oneg Shabbat at eight," he said. "It's hard not to notice when so few people show up."

"I'm sorry. I've been really busy," Ira said.

"You have a new issue coming out? Seems like it's been forever. Is it deadline time?" he asked.

"Summer issue's right around the corner. Are you running the same ad?"

Rabbi Maisel rubbed his chin with his right hand. Ira could tell something was on his mind. It was a look he was used to, the look of someone about to back out of an ad—so Ira quickly changed the subject. "Isn't that Candy Kramer from Muses?"

They both turned to watch Candy walking out to the patio. Everyone knew Candy. She was another one of those mid-eighties Tulane grads, another prominent New Orleanian: a mover, a shaker, a power player. After Tulane, she married into a prominent local family and started the biggest female parade in Mardi Gras. What's the difference? Ira thought. They'd both be six feet under one day. She gave him a sideways glance like she'd heard that, then snickered before brushing him off and shaking hands with the rabbi.

After she walked back to her table, Rabbi Maisel said, "Guess she didn't know you." He continued, "This week's sermon is going to be wonderful. It's the tov ayin, the story of Moshe Rabbeinu. The Torah was originally supposed to be given just to Moses and his descendants. However, Moses treated it with a generosity of spirit and gave the Torah to all of Israel."

"That's nice, Rabbi," Ira said, barely listening, still wondering if he was thinking out loud again.

"You might learn something from it," Rabbi said.

"What do you mean?"

"Generosity is not what you have. It's what you give."

"You mean like giving your time to see Mother?" Ira asked.

Ira saw the rabbi bite his lip. He'd been at Sinai for over a year and hadn't taken the time to stop by the Lambeth House.

"I'm sorry. You know how busy I am with the kids and all. That's really no excuse though. How's she doing?"

"Not so good."

Rabbi took Ira's hands and cocked his head to the side. "I should see her. I'm so sorry I haven't been over there yet. I will visit with her this week, I promise."

"I'm sure she'd appreciate it, if she could."

Rabbi nodded. "I'll see you Friday then."

"Right, Friday. Do you need any flowers for the bimah?"

"We don't have any donations lined up yet. Can you get us that same deal?"

"Of course. It's no trouble at all," Ira said. "We can settle up afterward."

"Wonderful. That's just great. We are so lucky to have you," Rabbi Maisel said in that same phony voice as he turned to talk to another group standing to his left.

Ira stepped back against a wall and scanned the crowd. He wished for a seat to ease the ever-present pain in his ankle, but none were open. Candy Kramer was still holding court at one of the tables; a small group had gathered around her. A young couple sat at another table leaning in toward one another, whispering and staring at the people around them. She giggled and thrust her head back, touching his forearm as he sucked on ice from his empty drink. Three guys in their early twenties stood to Ira's left wearing lightweight sport coats, passing around one of those electronic cigarettes, blowing little evaporating puffs of pungent smoke. No one approached; no one even looked his way. He used to be someone in this town. Ira Silver from the Silver furniture family; publisher of the first Jewish magazine in New Orleans; graduate of Tulane University with a bachelor's in liberal arts and a master's in journalism. His family's name adorned buildings at Tulane, a pavilion at Temple Sinai, an auditorium at the JCC, and even a little one-block-long street right off Audubon Park. All these ostentatious transplants had invaded his hometown, boldly oblivious of the old-timers who had held down the fort while everyone else fled, whether for white flight, an oil bust, or a hurricane. No one here knew when the Silver name had meant something. All they saw was a short, skinny, balding nebbish unworthy of a glance or a smile or the time it took to say hello.

The swollen crowd at the bar had thinned, so Ira made his way back over to grab another drink. Two of the bartenders were in the far corner talking with Jeff while the other wiped down the bar top and restocked the glassware. Minutes ticked off his imaginary watch as he stood there being ignored. He tapped the bar top, cleared his throat, made little sucking sounds between his lips, but to no avail. Finally he yelled, "Bartender," and they all looked up. The girl walked over nonchalantly and asked what he wanted.

"I'll take a vodka martini, dirty, up."

"Free drinks are over," she said.

"You've got to be kidding me? What time did it end?"

"Nine."

"Fuck me. It's not past nine," he said, tapping the watch on his wrist. "I've been standing here for five minutes trying to get your attention."

"Sorry. It's after nine."

"This is such bullshit. Where's Jeff?" he yelled.

Jeff had turned his back to Ira.

"You know what? Forget it. Forget about a good write-up. This place is bullshit. You people are a bunch of tools."

If no one noticed Ira before, they did now. It was like a needle sliding off an old forty-five: the reverberation of voices came to a screeching halt. Everyone stared at him as he pounded his fists on the countertop like a child in a highchair, pushed himself away from the bar, torpedoed past the girls at the check-in table, and hurled his body out the front door.

7

On the walk home, Ira pushed aside his rage and started thinking about Lin and the boys. He thought about calling off the trip, phoning Lin and telling her he had come down with a terrible virus. She would understand. She was a reasonable person.

"Reasonable person?" he repeated aloud with a chuckle.

In the mid-nineties, Mother and Father had thought it time for Ira to get married. He was twenty-eight years old and most of his high school friends were living on the North Shore, changing diapers and driving minivans. Since finishing college, he had been on a series of unfortunate dates that ended in embarrassing phone calls between his parents and the girls'. It became increasingly evident that there wasn't a Jewish female on Earth who could see the benefits of dating Ira Silver.

That summer—1994—catalogs started appearing in the mail. Mind you, this was before GlobalLadies.com and RoseBrides.com, and way before Tinder. About once a week, he opened his mailbox and found a catalog featuring beautiful women from exotic locales. First Russia, then the Philippines, China, South Korea, and Guam, to name a few. At first, he tossed them aside, embarrassed, as if they were *Playboy Magazine*, and his mom would find them hidden under his pillow. When he finally looked inside, he found the catalogs were filled with pictures of pretty faces accompanied only by names, ages, and locales: Nam, 21, from Guangzhou; Alix, 29, from Moscow; Xandra, 36, from Manila. After a few weeks, he started studying the faces while he sat on the toilet, scanning the eyes for a love connection. He remembered the smiles not matching the eyes, as if the girls had been forced in front of the camera and could only manage fake expressions. Or maybe they were just straining for a life outside the one they wanted to leave behind.

Ira was still living at home with his folks, itching to leave the house on St. Charles Avenue. He started noticing the catalogs appearing in different rooms around the house. In the Russian catalog, a few of the girls had been circled in black Sharpie. He found out later that it was Father who encouraged the whole mail-order bride idea. Mother was still holding out hope for a Jewish girl. Father was just holding out hope that he might finally move out of the house.

Ira started calling the women in Russia, a world away from where he was, but found it very difficult to connect, both literally and figuratively. Every phone call required a series of operator connections, clicks, and beeps. When a girl finally answered, it was like conversing through the cardboard tube inside of a paper towel roll. Sometimes her voice would be so loud he'd have to stand a foot away from the phone; other times, it sounded like she was talking in a whisper with her hand covering the receiver. He called a dozen of these women, some beautiful, some plain and ordinary, but every conversation quickly turned to money. They wanted to know what he did for a living; what kind of car he drove; how many bedrooms were in his house. When he told them that he had never owned a car and that he lived with his parents, an audible tone of defeat or frustration emanated from the reply on the other end of the line. None of those girls requested a second phone call.

Ira moved on to some of the other catalogs, and with each new country, he found it more and more difficult to understand the broken English. In Guam, he discovered Sirena, 34, from Dededo Village, who got his attention with her throaty voice and dark sense of humor. Their relationship lasted six phone calls, but she kept talking about bringing Nena with her to America. When her photograph arrived in the mail, he finally realized that Nena was Sirena's mother, and the sight of five children lined up next to her nearly made him give up.

The Chinese catalog became his last hope. Dozens of women with dark, almond-shaped eyes and high cheekbones filled the pages. They were from towns he couldn't say with names that reminded him of dishes at his favorite Chinese restaurant. The first one he called spoke decent English and they hit it off from the get-go. She worked as a hotel concierge in a city called Guilin, known for its picturesque landscapes and stalagmite caves.

Her name was Shyun and she was thirty-two years old, no kids, never been married. She had always dreamed of traveling to America and working in a hotel in Las Vegas. What attracted him most were her large, puffy lips and the slight lisp she had in her high-pitched voice. After a four-month courtship, they agreed that it was time to meet. There were very stringent laws against applying for a travel visa without following proper procedure. Most Asian countries required the prospective bachelor to be engaged in order to get a fiancé visa, so they agreed that it would be easier for Ira to visit Shyun in Guilin that summer rather than have her attempt a trip to America.

As the departure date neared, a nervous excitement grew in the pit of Ira's stomach. After thirty hours of flying halfway across the world, that nervous excitement turned into nervous excrement, and he spent his first day in China squatting over a hole in the floor at a two-star hotel in Shenzhen. When he finally made it outside, he was assaulted by a persistent smell of gasoline and a thick haze that dominated the industrial landscape. The first thing he encountered when he left the hotel was a little six-year-old girl begging for money. He couldn't stand beggars, but in America they were rarely so young. He watched two police officers grab the girl and drag her by her hair as she clutched a tiny doll in her little arms. One of the cops kept kicking her legs out as she tried to walk, suspending her in the air by her long black hair. A piercing cry wailed from her little mouth. She continued to cling to that doll until Ira finally noticed the doll was crying too. With steely resolve, those cops didn't care if the girl dropped the baby or if they ripped every shred of hair out of her little head. Begging was clearly not allowed in Shenzhen.

That was Ira's wake-up call to the fact that he wasn't in New Orleans anymore. After a night in Shenzhen, he flew to Guilin and was greeted by a jovial guide named Hai, who grabbed his bags and led him to a compact car. After thirty minutes of driving through a construction zone, he realized that Hai had no idea where he was going. Then he figured out that Hai wasn't his "assigned" tour guide. He was just the first person to walk up to him after he'd escaped the swarm of people crushed against one another on the outer side of the customs gate.

He tried to persuade Hai to drive him back to the airport, but to no avail. Instead Hai continued driving through the massive construction sites that dominated the city center. Ira was supposed to meet Shyun for dinner at the restaurant in the twenty-two-dollar-per-night Guilin Gudong Waterfall Resort Hotel, but as darkness approached, they seemed no closer to finding his destination than they had been two hours earlier. Finally, he convinced Hai to pull over and let him out. Hai kept bowing and apologizing as he stood by the trunk of the car. He waited for Ira to close the passenger-side door before jumping back into the driver's seat and speeding away, leaving Ira with nothing but his wallet and passport.

Ira was already dejected. He walked the streets of Guilin, stepping over huge craters in the sidewalks, passing orange rolls of plastic fencing on each and every block. All the stores looked the same, as did the signs and the young men walking the streets staring at the ground beneath their feet. No one made eye contact with him and not one person dared smile. He stopped at a currency exchange and asked the old woman if she knew the Guilin Gudong Waterfall Resort Hotel and she nodded and pointed down toward the river. He walked along the banks sniffing the back of his hand, trying to avoid the vicious odor wafting off the polluted currents.

After walking a mile or two, Ira found a cluster of high-rise hotels along the riverfront. All the neon marquees were emblazoned with giant Chinese lettering, making the hotels completely indistinguishable from one another. He must have walked into twenty different lobbies before he found the Guilin Gudong Waterfall Resort Hotel. It was three and a half hours past their meeting time when he finally made it to the restaurant in the hotel lobby. Shyun was nowhere to be found and none of the staff had any recollection of a beautiful girl waiting for her prince in shining armor.

Ira sat alone at a table set for four milking a lukewarm bottle of water. He was the only patron in a restaurant that could have seated a hundred fifty. The waitress, dressed in a colorful kimono, stopped at his table every ten minutes, smiling and nodding. The menu was in Chinese, no pictures, no translations. He played a game of charades with the waitress who eventually agreed to bring him fish and rice. Forty-five minutes later, she brought him a soup bowl of clear liquid and rice drifting about at the bottom. He swished his spoon around the bowl. As far as he could see, there was no fish, though it certainly smelled like fish and tasted like shrimp broth with a heaping spoonful of Chinese five-spice. Ira's eyes burned and his nose leaked all over the cloth napkin. The waitress kept bringing him another bottle of water, but he hated the idea of paying for water so instead he munched on some white swirly straw things that looked like dried worms and tasted like uncooked ramen noodles until the pain in his throat subsided.

Ira waited another hour, but Shyun had probably long since given up on meeting him that evening. So he made his way to his room on the fourteenth floor. He stood by the elevator for fifteen minutes, but it never arrived. Without a smile, the woman at the front desk pointed at the stairwell and he began the ascent, thankful that he didn't have any bags to drag up the fourteen flights. On his floor the carpeting had been ripped up, exposing old speckled white linoleum tiles screaming with asbestos. Three of the rooms which he passed had no door, just caution tape over the threshold. At room 1421, he entered to a rancid musty smell that years later he would liken to the stench of his refrigerator after their month-long Hurricane Katrina evacuation. He picked up the phone, but it was dead. He was too tired to walk back downstairs to complain. Instead, he kicked off his shoes and tried to sleep.

It was a long and restless night that ended with the sound of a jackhammer breaking through cinderblock in the room next door. With no clothes to change into, Ira decided to skip the shower, which reminded him of a high school shower stall with moldy green tiles and stained towels. He wearily made his way back to the restaurant and sat at a table in hopes that Shyun might come back to look for him. For breakfast he ordered egg and oatmeal, which came in its raw form and had the taste and texture of a bowl of snot.

Instead of subjecting himself to another miserable meal at lunch, Ira asked every person he saw to point to the nearest McDonald's. Thankfully the menu there was in Chinese and English, complete with pictures of the Big Mac, Filet-O-Fish, and Chicken Wing combination meals, all priced between seventeen and twenty yuan, which was roughly three dollars. He ordered the double cheeseburger meal, and it was without a doubt the best burger he had ever eaten, or so it seemed at that moment in time.

After lunch, Ira tried to call Shyun, but this was before most every human had a cell phone, and the number he had been using in the States was a nine-hundred number that kept feeding money to the catalog company. This whole trip must have been just a scam. Was Hai part of the scam too? Was it time to give up?

With nothing to do and the hope of meeting his future bride waning by the minute, Ira figured he might as well head over to a travel agency and secure an earlier flight home. The most convenient and least expensive flight change wasn't until the following evening, so the travel agent convinced him to take a tour of the famous Guilin peaks on the Li River with his leisure time. He had three cruises to choose from—twenty-five-, fifty-, and hundred-dollar options—and as far as he could tell, the only difference was the length of time on the boat. Of course, he settled on the twenty-five-dollar three-hour tour, which departed at two o'clock.

Ira had to run down to the dock and jump on the boat just before it left the tiny port. As it drifted away from land, he scanned the other faces and realized he was the only Caucasian. The twenty-five-dollar cruise was a guided tour in Chinese. For the following three hours, he tried to zone out the tour guide's monotone Mandarin while he watched happy couples taking pictures of grassy peaks jutting up from the ground, appearing from out of nowhere like magic. It was the first time that he was actually impressed by the natural beauty of this godforsaken shithole of a country. And it was the first time he saw Chinese people smiling.

And that is when he met Lin. They were floating down the river and every person on the boat was snapping pictures of this one cave as the sun began to set through the hole in its center, casting a shadow across the murky water. A tiny woman that he first thought was a teenage boy walked toward him, smiling and sticking her arm out from her nose. She made the sound of an elephant's trumpet and then giggled and stared at him, apparently waiting for some particular reaction. She grabbed his hand and pulled him out of his seat, pointing at the cave. Looking more closely, he discovered it had the shape of an elephant in the same way a cloud might have the shape of an ogre, but regardless, his acknowledgment made Lin smile and clap.

Ira checked out of the hotel but canceled the flight home. There was something about Lin that made him want to suffer China a bit longer. She brought him to her house to meet her parents. They lived in a modest two-bedroom apartment in a small village just outside the city. Her neighborhood reminded him of the projects that sprouted all over New Orleans in the 1940s and '50s. Tenement housing, brick, crumbling on the outside, cracked walls, old beaten-up appliances on the inside. Best he could tell, her father worked as a janitor at the local high school and her mother stayed at home and did needlepoints of the Li River which she gave to Lin to sell at the market right outside the river's port.

Lin had a tandem bike that they rode back and forth from her home to the river. They spent the next week walking along the riverbanks holding hands and trying to teach each other words from their native tongue. They learned words like love, river, sky, water, and boat. That week was the closest Ira ever felt to real love, and on the last night, he proposed to Lin as a full harvest moon reflected off the Li River.

Six months later, after working their way through the arduous task of securing Lin's visa, she made her way to New Orleans and moved into his house on St. Charles Avenue. Ira remembered her dropping to the floor, crying, and kissing his father's feet upon opening the door to her new home.

They were married at Temple Sinai three weeks later.

In New Orleans, Ira and Lin were never able to rekindle the fire they had in China. He thought it was because of the kids. She got pregnant within a month of arriving in the States, and their sex life from then on revolved around procreation. At first, he was surprised by the change in his wife. She barely talked to him. Her coldness manifested in a darkness that Lin attributed to her longing to be closer to her family. She spent much of her time at the JCC, immersing herself in classes ranging from parenting tools to introductory English, and she made friends with a Vietnamese woman who let her use her cell phone to communicate with her brother back in Guilin.

Sammy was born almost a year and a half after his brother. Lin spiraled into a deep postpartum depression after his birth that sent her to a psychiatric ward for nearly a month. After that, things were never the same. When they first came out with those little Bluetooth ear devices, she stole one from someone's locker at the JCC and wore it around everywhere. It didn't matter that she never owned a cell phone. She just liked to talk to herself in Chinese without anyone thinking she was a lunatic.

Nine months before Yang was born, Lin went to meet her brother in New York for a week while Ira stayed home and watched the kids with the help of his parents. Lin threatened not to come home, but when she did, her attitude was completely changed. Overnight she transformed into the mom that he always wanted her to be— rearing the children, teaching them about their Chinese heritage, and even walking over to the JCC every day to pick them up from summer camp.

For six months, Lin hid her baby bump until he saw her loading dishes in the cabinets one day and her belly popped out from underneath her blouse. The only time Lin had an outie bellybutton was when she was pregnant. Since he couldn't remember the last time they had sex he assumed it wasn't his, and, though Lin never confirmed his accusations, she picked the kids up from school one day and never returned home.

With the help of Mother and Father and their attorney, Shelly Rubenstein, they tried to get the children back, but the laws in New York really favored the mother. Even though Lin was clinically insane, he couldn't convince that woman judge that he was "more fit" to raise the kids than she was. Plus, there was the dubious relationship between Yang and Ira that forced the courts to side with Lin. The judge determined that the bond between the kids shouldn't be broken and they awarded her full custody. Ira still blames Shelly for her incompetence, even though she's known as one of the best divorce attorneys in all of New Orleans.

Lin ended up in Flushing, Queens with her new husband Chun, and they sent the boys to New Orleans for a visit once a year during spring break. The boys spent the week sulking and ignoring their father. Howie had just turned fifteen and was entering his puberty phase with zits dominating his wide forehead. Sammy was almost fourteen, ending the year of his official entry into manhood. Before they left for New York, Ira had them both enrolled in Sunday school classes at Temple Sinai. Rabbi Benjamin claimed they would have been the first Chinese bar mitzvahs in New Orleans history. But since Lin got remarried, the boys went to Catholic school and attended church every Sunday.

All three kids had straight black hair, dark eyes, and yellowish skin. The older two had round eyes and Ira's nose, but eight-year-old Yang looked one hundred percent Chinese. Mother didn't know that Yang wasn't Ira's, and he never told his parents otherwise, though he thought Father suspected the truth. It didn't matter that much to him. He tried to love them all the same, though they treated him with equal amounts of scorn and contempt. With each passing year, he wondered when they would stop visiting altogether.

Ira was ripped from his thoughts by the grind of broken glass beneath his feet. He was standing on his unlit porch with only the dim cast of a nearby streetlamp creating a shadow across the front door. He turned to his right and scanned the porch. It was empty. Behind him, the street was silent aside from a passing car. He took another crunchy step forward. His eyes wandered down the door until he reached the bottom right pane. Ira squatted down to peek through the emptied frame. The house was pitch black inside, but he could see the shimmering of glass in the foyer.

The door was locked. Ira opened it, took one step inside, and called for Charlie. There was no answer. He called again before stepping over the glass shards and turning the bathroom light on. The house looked undisturbed. He called out, "Hello?" and "Charlie?" into each room, but no one answered. He thought about calling the police, worried that the man had come back, but everything was exactly where he had left it hours earlier. He was pretty certain Charlie hadn't yet come home from work. It was too early, plus her blanket was still folded over the pillow on the couch and she almost always went to sleep the minute she got home.

The last time that window had been broken was when someone threw a football off a Mardi Gras float years ago. Father had called someone over the next day to patch it up. Ira couldn't afford that. The best he could do was sweep up the glass and tape the hole with yesterday's newspaper and some duct tape he found in an old toolbox in the shed out back.

With the mess cleaned up, Ira locked the door. He usually left it unlocked for Charlie, but under the circumstances, he thought it best to play it safe. He waited in the rocking chair dozing in and out of sleep, hoping she came home early, hoping she was okay.

8

Ira couldn't sleep in the rocking chair and, at some point in the night, retreated upstairs. Even in bed, he continued tossing and turning. Every sound made him jump and strain his ears. Three or four times, he went to stand atop the stairwell to listen more closely but heard nothing but the whistling of the wind. At sunrise, he finally went downstairs and unlocked the door. A few minutes later, he heard it slam shut. He got out of bed, put on his slippers, and shuffled down the stairs to find Charlie already asleep on the couch.

The boys were due to arrive at 11:30 on a Southwest flight from Newark. Ira tapped Charlie's arm, but she barely moved. He slapped harder until she opened one eye and grumbled a curse. He reminded her that it was Thursday morning and the kids were about to arrive.

"I forgot," she said groggily, rising to a seated position on the couch. Her matted hair stuck out in crazy positions like little Lisa on *The Simpsons*. She wore black leggings and a tight grey tank top with the faded logo of the South Carolina Gamecocks football team.

"You know what happened to the window pane?" Ira asked.

"Huh?" she answered.

"The window… by the front door."

"What happened to the window by the front door?" Charlie raised her head off the back of the couch and strained her neck toward the foyer. "When'd that happen?"

"Don't know. That's why I was asking you."

"No idea," she said, lowering her head back to the pillow.

"Maybe it was your friend?" Ira asked.

"What friend?"

"The one that came around yesterday."

"I told you he wasn't a friend."

"But now my window's broken."

"So?" she said, in a way as if the conversation was over.

"The boys are coming in a few hours," Ira said, changing the subject. "You need to go."

"Ugh. Come on. What's the big deal?"

Ira thought for a moment whether it was a big deal or not. Then he shook his head and said, "I love you sweetheart, but my kids would never understand."

"Who's gonna look after you then?"

"Me? I don't need looking after."

"Fine then. I'll be out of your way soon as I brush my teeth." Charlie stumbled into the kitchen.

He thought about Mother in the hospital. She was the one who needed looking after, not him. He wasn't that old. He got around just fine. He'd been thinking it was him looking after Charlie these past few months. Such a young girl turning tricks in the big city.

He called out to her, "You want to ride the streetcar with me downtown?"

"Why you riding downtown?" she yelled from the other room.

"To grab the free airport shuttle from the Marriott."

Ira heard Charlie cackling in the other room.

"What's so funny, Charlie?"

"Nothing. Never mind. You really gonna see your kids looking like that?"

Ira ambled over to the antique brass mirror hanging above the fireplace. The face in the mirror sprouted grey stubble on its cheeks and chin and was topped with hair like a modern-day Gollum's. Ira licked his palm and tried to stretch the weedy strands across his balding scalp, but to no avail. Sighing, he looked at Charlie and shrugged.

"Want a haircut?" she asked.

"You cut hair?"

"Mama wanted me over at Cloyd's."

"What's that?"

"Beauty school."

"That doesn't answer the question," Ira said.

"There ain't much to cut. Besides, ain't it time you got rid of that comb-over?"

"How long you think it'll take?"

"Fifteen minutes, tops," Charlie said. "Go on and get me a razor and some shaving cream."

"I don't have any shaving cream," Ira said.

"I got one of them little lotions from over at the Monteleone. We'll use that."

Charlie pushed Ira into his recliner and ran into the kitchen. She moved around the house at a frenetic pace chuckling to herself as she grabbed a Mardi Gras cup full of water, a white terry-cloth towel and disposable razor swiped from the JCC, and a plastic tray that looked like a holdover from one of Ira's kids' elementary school lunches.

Straddling Ira with her legs tucked inside the arms of the recliner, Charlie shoved his head back and started rubbing the tepid water across his cheeks. He closed his eyes as she used her soft fingertips to lather the lotion over his rough skin. He fought back lascivious thoughts of her warm body brushing against his thighs, her tight ass bouncing against his aging lap. Every so often, Charlie aroused him in a way that he knew wasn't right. A fifty-year-old and an eighteen-year-old were like a turtle and a frog to Ira. They just weren't meant to be together.

He kept his eyes shut as Charlie clasped long strands of loose hair and dragged the used disposable razor over the remainder of his follicularly-challenged head. Snickering and giggling, she ran into the bathroom a few times for toilet paper to blot the bloody nicks.

He opened his eyes after Charlie peeled the towel off his chest. She had the grin of a four-year-old that had just colored all over the living room walls. He instinctively raised his hand to touch his head, but Charlie lunged toward him, grabbed his wrist, and ordered, "Don't touch."

Ira dusted the loose hairs off his pants and looked in the mirror. His face still had the jagged lines of age crisscrossing his forehead, but without the grey stubble on his chin, he looked a few years younger. But his head. His head was covered in a dozen little white balls of toilet paper turning red. He winced and tried to smile.

"It ain't as bad as it looks," Charlie said.

"That's reassuring."

"I needed a better razor," she said, "and hot water."

"Don't worry about it," he said. "It'll stop bleeding. It's getting late, though. I got to run. Are you going to work or not?"

"Go on without me, I ain't feeling it today. I'll clean up before I go."

He smirked. "Great. That would be great, sweetie. And take care of yourself. I'll see you next week."

She came forward and gave him a soft peck on the cheek. It was the first time she had ever done that, and his cheeks immediately flushed and a warm sensation took over his belly.

Ira heard the whir of the streetcar chugging to a stop on the corner of his block. He took an empty row in the back, worried that his patchy, bloody head might scare the tourists. He lowered the window and let the spring breeze carry in the smell of fresh jasmine, hoping to cover the musty odor that usually followed in his wake.

Ira exited at the corner of St. Charles and Common Street. He snuck into the lobby of the Royal St. Charles Hotel, blended in with the tourists, and ate a complimentary breakfast of scrambled eggs, bacon, biscuits, and coffee. With his appetite satiated, Ira stepped out of the front door and came face to face with a man in a green army jacket leaning against a lamppost and holding out a tin cup with a sign strapped around his shoulders that read, *Homeless Vet. Will Work for Food.* Ira doubted the man was a vet, and he looked like he could have gotten a job if he just took a shower and bought some clean clothes at the nearest thrift store. Ira wondered why he even pretended he wanted to work. He probably made more standing out here begging than the women cleaning the floors of the hotel. Looking down at his feet, the dirty man held the cup up to Ira's face and shook it, only to receive a sneer and a purse of the lips as Ira tried to shoo him away. "Can you spare fifty cents?" the man asked, finally looking up at Ira with puppy dog eyes.

"No," Ira answered. "Can you?"

"If you need it," the man answered.

Ira was taken aback. He hated the homeless. Just a bunch of no-good losers loitering on every street corner, he thought. Gutter punks eviscerating the essential character of the French Quarter. They should all be rounded up and given a one-way ticket back to wherever they'd come from.

So Ira stuck out the palm of his hand and waited for two quarters. The man rummaged through his meager belongings and found one.

Ira grabbed the coin and hurried across the street, where passengers were boarding the nine-thirty shuttle in the Marriott's motor lobby. As the driver was stowing luggage beneath the bus, Ira snuck on and slouched down in the back row, hoping an extra person wouldn't be noticed.

On the ride to the airport, Ira lamented the fact that he hadn't picked up anything for the kids. In years past, he'd brought Mardi Gras beads, St. Patrick's Day T-shirts, stuffed animals, or whatever other things he caught at parades, but last year, they just discarded the stuff as soon as they arrived at the house. What they really wanted were video games for their iPads and Nintendo DSis, but Ira loathed those stupid little toys. He thought they were a huge waste of time and money.

Ira saw Howie first. He was dragging a giant red suitcase with one hand and talking on his cell phone with the other. Sammy was a few feet behind and to his left, walking with a backpack strapped to his shoulders and playing a game on his phone that required the use of both his hands. Ira couldn't see Yang at all until they were through the security gate and he realized that all four-foot-nothing of him was riding on the back of the suitcase.

They stopped in front of Ira and he pulled the two older boys in for a group hug, but they barely even raised their arms to return the show of affection. Yang looked around the suitcase, stood up, and gave Ira an odd little bow. Sammy went back to playing his game. Ira took the handle of the suitcase from Howie and rolled it toward the ground transportation area, where they waited for the Marriott shuttle to return.

"How's school going?" Ira asked.

"Fine," said Howie.

The other boys didn't answer. They were both focused on the DSi.

"How's your mom?"

"Fine."

"And Chun?"

"Good."

"Are you getting good grades?"

"Yes."

"What about your brothers?"

"Yes."

"Are you still playing soccer?"

"I haven't played soccer for two years," Howie said.

The shuttle arrived and a heavyset woman in tight nylon pants and a blue dress shirt and black cap got off the bus and started loading luggage into the back. The boys jumped on the bus first and Ira followed, cutting off the other passengers in line to board. Sammy and Yang were sitting in one seat and Howie was across from them on the aisle next to a guy wearing a ten-gallon cowboy hat. Ira found a seat two rows behind them and watched the boys whispering to each other the entire ride, barely taking their eyes off the video games.

At the Marriott, they entered the lobby and pretended to check in to the hotel. The boys were doing their best to ignore Ira as he walked over to the bellman, told him his name was Jones, and left the suitcases in his possession.

"Are you ready for some beignets, boys?"

All three looked up from their toys and shrugged.

They walked down Royal Street and stopped in front of a crowd of onlookers. A guy in a straightjacket with chains harnessed around his body was struggling ostentatiously and yelling at the crowd for encouragement. The crowd started clapping in unison.

"Howie, can you put your phone away?"

Howie looked up and feigned indifference before putting the phone in the pocket of his tan jacket.

"Guys, hey, over here. Are you catching this?"

Sammy and Yang looked up and stared at Ira for a second before returning to the DSi. The street performer popped his shoulder blade out of its socket and unbuckled the lock around his neck while the crowd cheered. Howie's emotionless eyes stared through the crowd. The clapping continued as the man contorted his body and loosened the lock around his waist.

"Come on, boys, let's go before he starts asking for tips."

They continued down Royal Street, passing disheveled street bands and other performers posing in costumes, a still-life picture in real-life colors. The boys hardly noticed, still ensconced in their stupid games.

The line at Café du Monde was close to a hundred deep. They waited for a few minutes at the end of the line behind a group of middle-aged women wearing oversized hats and fanning themselves in the spring heat. The women smiled at them and started talking amongst themselves, giggling and making snide comments about "Orientals" under their breath.

"Wait here, boys. I'll be back in a few minutes. Howie, watch your brothers."

There was a little trick Ira had learned from his father. People that waited in line at Café du Monde were suckers. The line was for seats. Regulars knew to head up to the shorter line by the take-out window and get beignets without much of a wait at all. But all those tourists ate with their eyes instead of their stomachs. How many powdered donuts did they think they could eat?

Even a fat person couldn't eat more than one or two orders. There were untouched orders of beignets sitting on half a dozen tables. All they needed was a little fresh powdered sugar and voila, perfect beignets.

Ira pulled three plates off the dirty tables and returned to the boys still standing near the end of the line. He handed each kid a small plate and some napkins and watched them as they started blowing the sugar at each other and laughing.

"Ugh," said Sammy once he bit into his. "These are cold."

"I'm sorry, boys. I hate when they serve cold ones."

All three boys stood there with long faces, holding the plates in their hands.

"You're not going to eat them?" Ira asked.

They didn't respond.

"Let me see if I can exchange them, get some fresh ones," Ira said, stacking the plates in his hand and walking back under the green and white striped awning.

Ira cut the line and told the waitress that the beignets were cold. She just looked at him with her head cocked to the side. Ira put the plates on the counter and demanded new ones until she finally relented and put three new orders up.

Ira finally got a modicum of contentment from Howie and Sammy when he returned with hot beignets. They sat against a railing taking huge bites of dough into their mouths, spraying sugar onto their pants and shoes. Yang just stood off to the side holding his plate away from his body.

"You don't want any beignets?" Ira asked.

"No thank you," he muttered.

"Suit yourself," Ira said, grabbing the plate and starting on its contents. "Time to go, boys. The Tulane shuttle leaves in fifteen minutes."

They scarfed down the rest of the beignets, tossed the plates on the nearest empty table and followed Ira as he walked briskly down Decatur Street toward Canal. Ira grabbed the bags from the valet at the Marriott and ran to the corner of Rampart Street, where the turquoise Tulane bus was idling on the corner.

"Students only," the driver objected.

"My son's a student," Ira said.

The driver looked down at them standing on the steps, rolled his eyes, and said, "Whatever."

9

Ira and the boys got dropped off on the Freret Street side of the Tulane campus and took a long stroll through the Quad, past the Silver School of Engineering where Ira remarked, "Yes, boys, this is an excellent institution of higher learning. When it's time for you to choose a college, Howie, I hope you decide to follow in the Silver footsteps and study at Tulane."

It was early afternoon when they landed on St. Charles Avenue and the boys were complaining about hunger pains. Yang was mired in a sneezing fit that he said was caused by an overabundance of pollen in the air. A couple of places on Carrollton Avenue took the trade card, so they walked single file on the neutral ground toward the Riverbend. Howie was having trouble rolling his luggage through the dirt so he crossed the street and walked alone on the sidewalk the final three blocks.

They filed into O'Henry's Food & Spirits and headed upstairs to the wrought-iron balcony overlooking the wide avenue below. Peanut shells littered the floor, half the tables were dirty, and the other half were filled with overweight people eating burgers and French fries.

They waited for a few minutes, Sammy and Howie still playing their handheld video games, before a middle-aged waitress finally brought them menus and took their drink order. Yang sat cross-legged in his chair with his arms folded against his chest and his eyes closed and cheeks puffed out like he was holding his breath.

"What's wrong with Yang?" Ira asked.

"He's allergic to peanuts," Howie said.

Yang opened one eye and let a slight wheeze blow through his nose.

"Since when?" Ira asked.

"Since always," said Howie.

"I had no idea. What else is he allergic to?"

"Pretty much everything," said Howie.

"What's that mean?"

"He's allergic to peanuts, all kinds of other nuts, beans, fish, shellfish, eggs, wheat, and soy," Sammy said.

"Holy cow. That's pretty much everything. What happens if he eats one of those things?"

"His throat swells up, then closes and he can't breathe, and then he dies," Howie said.

The waitress interrupted, "Are y'all ready to order or not?"

"What do you have without nuts, beans, fish, shellfish and soy?" Ira asked.

"And wheat," said Howie.

"And wheat what?" said the waitress.

"And without wheat," Ira said.

"I don't know. I'll have to ask the kitchen, I guess."

"Okay, you do that," Ira said.

"And it can't be made in the same pans or the same fryers," said Howie.

"Huh?" said the waitress.

"Yep, he can't eat anything that's been on the same cooking surface as any of those things."

"What things?" asked the waitress.

"Wheat, soy, fish…"

"You know what, boys?" Ira interrupted. "Why don't we go across the street to the Louisiana Pizza Kitchen."

"He can't eat pizza," said Howie.

"Why not?"

"There's flour in the dough."

The waitress started clearing dishes at the next table over.

"What does he eat at home?" Ira asked.

"Mom reads the ingredients on everything. It takes us four hours to go to the grocery store."

"What about school?"

"He eats in the teachers' lounge," Howie said. "He can't sit in the cafeteria with the rest of the kids."

Ira turned to Yang, who was scratching his arms.

"Let's get out of here," Ira said, picking Yang up in his arms and carrying his fifty-pound body over the loose peanut shells, down the stairs, and back out to Carrollton Avenue.

They scurried down St. Charles Avenue to Audubon Park where Sammy and Yang played on the jungle gym for a few minutes before getting bored. Howie left his suitcase next to Ira and walked down to the pond to look at the ducks. Huge oak trees dripping with moss formed a canopy above their heads as they walked the path around the park until they came out on the Magazine Street side.

Ira was limping noticeably when they finally arrived at the Whole Foods Market, which was housed in a once-abandoned bus barn converted to an upscale organic food market back in the mid-2000s in an attempt to revitalize a downtrodden part of the Magazine Street corridor. They entered through the huge glass doors that opened into the well-stocked produce department.

On that particular day, Whole Foods had grapefruit, red grapes, tomatoes, and melon to sample. Ira handed the boys a few toothpicks and they stood still for a moment watching Ira sample the produce before finally following his lead.

After cleaning out the grapefruit bowl, they headed to the seafood department, where a man in a green apron stood behind a glass counter displaying "responsibly" farm-raised and organic fish that cost triple what it cost in the freezer at the Save-A-Lot.

"Can I have some sample cups to try the soup?" Ira asked.

The man handed Ira a dozen one-ounce paper cups—the kind you rinse with at the dentist—and Ira took them to the self-serve soup station where everyone except Yang tried the five different seafood soups that were available.

Near the dairy department, a dreadlocked girl in a little green apron handed them samples of vitamin water.

"It tastes like water," Ira said.

"That's the point," the girl said.

"Why would anyone pay for water?" Ira asked while shaking his head.

"Because it has a lot of vitamins and nutrients in it."

"But it's still water."

"With hints of strawberry and rhubarb," she said with a cheesy smile across her freckled face.

"How much is it?"

"Four for six-fifty," she said.

"You've got to be kidding me," Ira said. "Four of those little twelve-ounce cans for seven bucks."

The boys left Ira's side and meandered over to the cheese department where they sampled little nuggets of cheddar and Gruyère and tried to pretend they didn't know the old white guy harassing the

Whole Foods employee. The girl opened another can of water and asked the man passing behind Ira if he'd like to try some.

"Eat as much as you like," Ira yelled over to the boys. The girl whipped her head back toward Ira and gave him a dirty look.

The boys froze and looked at Ira before sheepishly throwing their toothpicks in the nearby trashcan. At the bakery department, they sampled some focaccia bread and an olive oil pesto spread. Yang stood to the side with his hands clasped beneath his armpits and his feet crossed. Ira might have stopped with the samples at that point, but he felt really bad for Yang since he hadn't had much of anything to eat. He led him over to the prepared food station where an older guy with grey hair and glasses asked them what they wanted.

Looking at Yang, Ira suggested, "The green beans look good."

Howie nestled his way between the two of them, bent down to look at the glass case, and said, "Must have soy."

"How about the garlic rosemary potatoes?" Ira asked.

Yang shrugged. Howie asked the counter guy, "Do you use the same knives or cutting boards to cut the potatoes as the pecan-crusted chicken?"

The man asked, "Do you have allergies, young man?"

"He does," said Howie, pointing at Yang.

"We're very careful about cross-contamination," he answered.

"What's in the potatoes?" Howie asked.

"Olive oil, rosemary, garlic, salt and pepper."

They spent the next thirty minutes trying the seven items in the display case that passed Yang's dietary restrictions. When they turned to walk away, the man asked, "Did y'all want to order anything?"

"No thank you. I think he's full," Ira said, leading the boys to the water fountain near the checkout counter.

"Mom gave us money," Howie said, pulling a rolled-up twenty-dollar bill out of his pocket.

"I'll buy you anything you want," Ira said. "Are you still hungry?"

Howie's head was bowed downward in disgust, eyes fixed on the floor. He looked at his brothers, who were back to playing with their DSi. "No, we're fine," he said.

With lunch in the rearview mirror, they headed toward the house down Octavia Street, where Ira used to take Lin and the kids trick-or-treating on Halloween. He mentioned this fact to the boys, but there was no recollection on their part. It was just a faded memory of a time when Ira thought they were a happy family.

10

He should have known the moment he opened the door. Ira could usually smell her whenever she was around, but he thought maybe it was just her cheap perfume lingering in the air.

The three boys walked single file into the living room and stopped short, banging into each other like three of the seven dwarfs and knocking the rolling luggage out of Howie's hand and onto the hardwood floor. The slam startled Charlie awake, and she jumped up wearing nothing but thong underwear and a white wifebeater.

Charlie looked at the three boys who were now staring at her panties, grabbed the blanket off the couch, and wrapped it around her body. Ira seized Yang and laid his hand over his eyes, tugged on Sammy's shirtsleeve, and pulled them both back into the foyer.

"Who are you?" Howie asked accusingly.

"I'm Charlie."

"Are you my dad's girlfriend?"

"Of course I ain't, silly."

"Howie, get in here," Ira yelled.

Howie ignored Ira's demand and asked, "What are you doing here?"

"I'm Ira's roommate."

"No, you're not," Ira yelled. "No, she's not, Howie."

"What is she then?" he yelled back.

Charlie picked her clothes off the floor as Ira reentered the room. In her arms, she held a Catholic-school-girl dress, clear plastic pumps, white stockings, and a white lacy bra. They looked at each other for a moment and she winked. If Ira were her mother, he would have said, "Go to your room," but since he wasn't her mother and she didn't technically have a room in the house, Ira said the first thing that came to his mind: "Get out."

Charlie threw the rest of her clothes into a gym bag and ran out the front door without looking back.

Howie couldn't take his eyes off her, even stepping aside, following her into the foyer, and staring at her ass as she slammed the front door. Sammy and Yang both held their mouths agape, their eyes lit up like golf balls. A moment later, the boys began a synchronized chorus of loud hoots. Yang was bent over holding his stomach, laughing so hard he was crying.

"It's not what you think," Ira said.

"What do we think?" Howie asked.

"You think I'm hooking up with that little girl."

"Why would we think that?"

"Don't be a smart aleck," Ira said.

The boys didn't say anything. The chuckles subsided and the four of them stood in the living room wondering what to say next. Ira turned on the lamp by the couch and noticed all of Charlie's cheap jewelry in a little mason jar next to a dirty water glass.

He picked up the jar, hustled out to the front porch, and scanned the block, but didn't see any sign of Charlie. She must have run down St. Charles Avenue half-naked before turning up one of the side streets. Back in the house, Sammy and Yang were back to playing their video games while Howie had locked himself in the bathroom by the living room.

It seemed like Charlie actually had cleaned up a bit. Other than a wet towel strewn across the floor behind the sofa, the pine floors had been swept, the kitchen sink had been cleared, and even the trash had been taken out to the curb. It looked as if she had cleaned up, showered, and then fallen back asleep on the couch, most likely by accident.

Ira had no idea what to say to the boys, so he continued about the business of cleaning the house and not a word was uttered between them for the remainder of the afternoon.

11

Dressed in a beige sport coat, blue jeans, and the same white button-down he'd worn the night before, Ira found the boys congregated in Sammy's old bedroom, lying on the bed playing video games. With the last of the daylight flickering through the slats in the blinds, they ignored Ira as he entered the room.

"I have a work function," Ira announced. "I should be home in a few hours. I will bring you back something to eat."

"T a shige pianzi," Howie said to his brothers.

"You speak Mandarin?" Ira asked.

"Some."

"What'd you say?"

"Have a good night."

Ira backed out of the room to the sound of snickering laughs. He knew more about his late-night houseguest than he did about his own children. The barrier between them had grown exponentially over the past year. Lin asked nothing of Ira, financially, emotionally, or physically; and the children kept themselves so remote from Ira that he could no longer bring himself to feel love for them.

Love had always been a contrived emotion for Ira. If he had grown up in the twenty-first century, he probably would have been labeled on the autistic spectrum as a child. His mother's kiss or his father's embrace used to make him cringe or drop his arms and grind his teeth. As he grew older, he learned to fake it by pretending he was hugging a tree. Father saw through that deceit and did his best to profess his kinship by patting Ira on the head. Mother's distance grew exponentially over time, and Ira couldn't recollect the last time they touched each other affectionately. She was so cold to him as a child that one of Ira's most vivid memories was shivering when she entered the room, even on a swelteringly hot summer day.

When Howie and Sammy were growing up, Lin used to carry them in a sling and nurture them through endless attachment, rarely letting the boys out of her sight or even near the ground. Attachment parenting, it was called, and it left little room for Ira to show his own affection. That seemed alright to Ira at the time, but clearly it left a lasting disassociation between himself and his children.

Ira had a five-thirty appointment at Flesh with James Beard-winning chef Ori Kahn, just three days before the grand opening of his latest creation. Kahn, an Israeli-born Bostonian, had fallen in with the king of the New Orleans restaurant scene, Mark Tesh, and helped open a trendy Italian restaurant in a downtown hotel a few years post Katrina. Five years later, they opened a pizza joint on Magazine Street and then his eponymous Israeli restaurant, which quickly became the talk of the town. With their newest restaurant, they would attempt to conquer the butcher scene with an expensive renovation of an Uptown cottage into a sleek, hip, high-end sandwich shop.

Maybe calling it an appointment was a bit of an exaggeration. Ira had called an hour earlier and the girl that answered the phone told him that Ori was in the kitchen. Since Ira had been trying for over a month to meet with the top chef, he thought it best to just show up and try to snare a few minutes of his time.

"May I help you?" the pretty girl at the counter asked.

"I have an appointment with Ori," Ira announced.

"I'll let him know you are here. What's your name?"

"Ira."

The girl waited for a last name, but with none offered, she puckered her lips and said, "You can have a seat at the bar if you'd like."

Ira moved over to the bar, where two large flat-screen TVs were encased in a bevy of top-shelf liquors. A male bartender who was cutting lemons stopped what he was doing and asked, "Are you here for the friends and family night?"

Ira paused. "Yes. Yes, I am."

"You're a little early," he said. "What time does your card say?"

"Six," Ira guessed. "Is it too early to get a drink?"

He looked over his shoulder at the cooks bustling around the kitchen and shrugged. "What are you having?"

"Blanton's on the rocks and a glass of water, please."

The bartender looked toward the kitchen again for help or permission, but all the other employees seemed engrossed in some pre-opening activity. Servers rolled silverware, cooks prepped food, and managers congregated at a table tasting dishes.

The bartender slipped both drinks over to Ira, who took a large gulp of water and then poured the Blanton's into his water glass, which gave the water a slightly brown tinge that Ira hoped Ori wouldn't notice. He then pretended to watch ESPN as he waited for Ori to grace his presence. As the minutes ticked by and the evening got closer to the witching hour, Ira felt the opportunity squeezing through his fingers. With little to lose, Ira tried to get Ori's attention by walking past him toward the back bathrooms twice, but each time the chef was working the expo line barking orders to his eager cooks and barely gave Ira a passing nod.

The first guests were lining up near the front counter. With little hope of closing a deal, Ira hopped on the back of the line, grabbed a menu, and waited for his turn. The line moved at a turtle's pace as each group asked dozens of questions to a girl who had probably had her job no more than three days. Why anyone would think she was an expert on the Flesh menu, Ira had no idea, but what he did know was that he was darn hungry, knew what he wanted, and was ready to order.

"Excuse me, do you mind if I cut in front of you?" Ira asked the family of four next in line.

The man looked at his wife and then cocked his head at Ira.

"I'm by myself," Ira said, "and I'm in a bit of a hurry."

The family stepped aside and let Ira pass. He sidled up to the counter and smiled as he approached.

"Did you get to see Ori?" she asked.

"Oh yes, thank you."

"Do you have your invitation?"

"I left it at home, but Ori said it was okay."

She turned and looked at Ori firing away at the cooks. Helplessly, she said, "I guess it's okay then. What would you like?"

"I would like the salumi and formaggi, garlic knots, the burrata, the Brussels sprouts, and two sandwiches—the Peacemaker and the... oh, I can't decide. Which do you like better, the wild boar or the cold roast beef?"

"Is someone meeting you here?" she asked.

"My family will be here in a few minutes. Just go ahead and give me both of those."

"Both of what?"

"The wild boar and the cold roast beef."

"Instead of the salumi?"

"No, in addition to."

"Is that it?"

"Do you have anything that is gluten-free?"

The cashier again turned her back and searched the dining room for some help, but with no one within earshot, she said, "I think the rochetta cheese with figs and hazelnuts."

"Oh no, he has a nut allergy too. How about the roasted cauliflower and whipped goat cheese?"

"That'll work."

"How about drinks and dessert? Do we order that now or at the table?"

"At the table."

Ira scanned the dining room and chose a table closest to the window, furthest from the kitchen. The quiet dining room turned boisterous in just a few minutes, the tin ceiling pressing the volume back toward the floor. As he settled into his seat, a young waitress, probably still in college, appeared and asked if he wanted anything to drink.

"I would like a Blanton's on the rocks, and I think my friend would like one too."

"There's two of you, then?"

"No. Give us four waters."

"Oh, wait," she said, "I just remembered that we're only serving beer and wine tonight."

"But I can't drink beer or wine on account of the gout."

"Would you like a soda, then?"

"I really want a cocktail," Ira said. "The bartender made me a Blanton's earlier."

"I'll see if it's okay," she said.

"Thank you. Do you mind if I order dessert now? I'm in a bit of a hurry."

"I guess that's fine, but we don't have the crostata just yet."

"That's okay. My son's allergic to pistachio anyway. We'll try the other four."

"Ummm, okay. I'll be back in a minute with your drinks."

Ira scanned the dining room for familiar faces, but all he saw were a bunch of hip young white people, some with kids, some without, all snapping pictures or scrolling Facebook on their handheld devices. Ira never understood the fascination with Facebook. For a fleeting moment your friends think you're so cool, dining on the latest creations of an overrated chef. When the food comes out, you can snap a picture of the dish and everyone can hit "like" on their stupid phones. Ira could only imagine that those Facebook "friends" had problems of their own, problems that can't be seen in a photo. He had heard that the guy he grew up with who produced the Red Hot Chili Peppers had herpes. That girl from high school who became a famous romance novelist went through a horrible divorce. Ira couldn't imagine the allure of reading about their fake lives. No one's life was as good as it looked on Facebook, he was sure of that.

The waitress returned with two rocks glasses of Blanton's and four water glasses, spacing them neatly in front of each seat.

Ira returned to stealing glances at the families. What he felt for them wasn't jealousy, but a suspicion. He doubted that the bonds between mother and child, husband and wife, could defeat the human instinct to love oneself. Ira knew better. He knew that to survive, he had to put himself ahead of anyone else.

"Excuse me, miss," Ira barked at his waitress, who was taking drink orders at the table next to him.

"I'll be right with you," she said.

Ira twiddled his thumbs and slumped in his chair until the waitress said, "Can I help you?"

"I have an emergency I have to deal with. Can you make my order to go?"

She let out a breath of tense air and said, "I'll find out."

Ira followed her with his eyes until she landed next to Ori. They went back and forth for a minute until Ori finally started shaking his head and pulling to-go boxes off the shelf. She returned a few minutes later with five large plastic bags filled with black boxes.

"Do you have a go-cup for my drink?"

"You can get one at the bar," she said.

Ira mixed his two drinks into one glass, rose from his chair, and eyed the other patrons, many of whom were staring at the little man with arms full of food. He stopped at the bar to grab a go-cup for his drink and then, balancing the five bags and his cane in his short arms, waddled out the front door.

12

"Who wants sandwiches?" Ira yelled as he entered his front door.

The darkness of the main floor broke when Ira turned on the lamp near the kitchen. Opening the bags and placing the boxes on the countertop, Ira called again for the boys but heard only the echo of his own voice. A slight panic crept into his chest as he dropped the last box and hurried into the living room.

At the bottom of the stairwell, Ira heard a noise that sounded like static from an old transistor radio tuned to an AM station hundreds of miles away. "Howie, is that you?" he yelled.

This time he heard what sounded like little feet pattering over the floor, yet his calls remained unanswered. He made his way up the stairs, the static growing in volume, his mind edging with concern. The bedroom doors were all closed. Ira tapped lightly on Sammy's door, squeezed the knob, and leaned into the room, but it was dark and empty. He tried the light, but the bulb had long since died. At the end of the hallway, a dim light flickered beneath the edge of the door in Howie's old room. Ira turned the handle and pushed into the bedroom, where startled children halted their dance moves mid-step.

Yang was in his tighty-whities, shirtless with one of Ira's ties strapped around his head like Tom Cruise in *Risky Business*. Sammy's feet were bare and his T-shirt soaked with sweat. Howie and Charlie wore matching wifebeaters and were caught embraced in a dance move straight out of *Dirty Dancing*. The music coming from Howie's iPhone was the only sound in the room besides the panting of the kids who had frozen at Ira's appearance.

"What's going on in here?" Ira demanded.

"I'm teaching them the electric slide," Charlie answered.

"I thought I told you to leave."

"Sorry, Ira. I came back to get my jewelry, and your boys looked so…"

"Pitiful?" Ira asked.

"I was gonna say bored, but…"

All three of the boys were staring at the floor. Howie reached for his phone and lowered the volume.

"I think it's time for you to go," Ira said to Charlie.

A chorus of "Come on, Dad!" came raining down on Ira.

"Can't she stay?" Howie asked.

"This is exactly what I didn't want to happen," Ira said, exasperated.

"It's alright, boys. I'm thinking it's time for me to go."

"Where will you go?" Sammy asked.

"I'll find a place," Charlie said. "I always do."

Charlie led the crew out of the bedroom, down the long dark hallway, and onto the stairs. She stopped for a second, said, "I forgot my shoes," and ran back to the room to grab her sandals. When she rejoined them, Yang smiled and said, "Can't she stay for dinner?"

"How'd you know I had dinner?" Ira asked.

"I smell it. I smell meat," Yang said.

"I brought you some cauliflower."

"I'll eat it if you let her stay."

"Fine, she can stay for dinner, but she can't sleep here," Ira said.

13

Madagascar was left completely unprotected. It was an easy attack for Howie, but instead his attention was drawn to the heavily fortified African border where Ira had been strengthening his troops. Howie's eyes shifted to his brothers' and then to Charlie's, before a slight nod of the chin signaled his counterattack. Cupping the dice in his right hand, he blew a kiss on his fist and thrust them into the box at the same time as Ira released his dice.

High-pitched screams followed by huge guffaws broke out as Ira replaced his cannon with three soldiers. "Again, again," the kids yelled. And they rolled again and again until Ira lost his stranglehold on Africa. By the time it was Ira's turn to roll, the kids had pushed him all the way back to South Africa, and he was unable to strike and earn the next card.

A game of Risk can go on for hours, so once Ira had lost all his troops, he let the kids finish up and began his Friday like he would any other. With his gym bag packed, he walked to the JCC, grabbed a quick shower, and changed into Dockers, a button-down shirt, blue blazer, black shoes, and brown socks. On a table by the exit, candles and a breadbasket signaled the coming Shabbat. Ira scooped six pieces of challah bread out of the basket, ate one, wrapped the other five in a clean white gym towel, and hid it in the bottom of his bag.

The staff at Mitch's Flowers on Magazine Street greeted Ira warmly. They had come to expect his Friday visits, where he carefully curated the flowers for the altar at Temple Sinai: six roses, three hydrangea, four tiger lilies, three birds of paradise, and a random assortment of carnations and snapdragons for a total of one hundred dollars on his Crescent City Trade card. The owner always took the arrangement to the temple herself because she was the only one who would deliver without a tip. For Ira, it meant a hundred dollars in cash would be waiting for him in an envelope at the temple business office. Ira loved swapping trade for cash any chance he got, and whenever the temple needed flowers, Ira jumped at the opportunity.

With his head beginning to pound, Ira hurried along to the Best Western, grabbed the *Times-Picayune* off the counter, poured himself a cup of coffee, sat on the couch, and perused the obituaries. Shirley Jones departed this life last Monday and her visitation was at the Schoen Funeral Home on Canal Street at noon. Ira asked the desk clerk what time it was. It was nearly eleven. He assumed the kids were probably fine. He might even be able to grab some food for them at the funeral. In the Living section, Ira checked the weekend events for the conventions in town. The National Association of Nurses brought five thousand people to the Convention Center. The Hotel Monteleone had two thousand romance novelists lined up for the RT Book Lovers Convention. Over at the Hyatt, there was a small conference of three hundred people gathering for the Association of Occupational Health Professionals.

Ira always wore his blue blazer on Fridays, even in the summer when the weather became unbearably hot. It enabled him to show up at funerals for people he didn't know, stop in at bars for free happy hour food, crash weddings in hotel ballrooms, or blend in with a bunch of haughty conventioneers. Selecting events had become somewhat of an art form for Ira, who on particularly successful Fridays could stock his fridge for an entire weekend or get loaded on complimentary cocktails into the wee hours of the evening.

Funerals before eleven were a dicey prospect. Sometimes mourners were too cheap to pay for two meals, so they skimped on the viewing hour and spent their money on food for the after-party. Ira wasn't overly fond of the viewing hour anyway. Open caskets weren't part of Jewish tradition, so Ira hadn't ever seen a dead body until he started going to random funerals. At first it wasn't too bad—he was able to sit in the back and avert his eyes. But New Orleanians had become more and more brazen with their rituals, going so far as to prop the body outside the casket as if they were still alive. Ira was aghast the first time he saw a dead person holding a Budweiser in one hand and an unlit cigarette between his macabre lips.

Funerals for people that died in their eighties and nineties often presented only a handful of mourners, which resulted in awkward conversations with strangers trying to determine Ira's relation to the deceased. On the other hand, funerals for youngsters, especially teenagers, left Ira with an empty feeling in the pit of his stomach. Lives lost to gun violence, drunk driving, overdose, or suicide took most of the fun out of crashing funerals.

Shirley Jones's funeral looked perfect. She died in her seventies after a long battle with cancer surrounded by family and friends. She was white and the obituary announced that lunch would be served immediately following the service. Ira had stopped going to the black funerals because, more often than not, he was the only white face in a sea of darkness. Most of the time, the mourners ignored Ira, but there were a few instances where his presence had become a distraction and he could hear the murmurs of some growing upset by the unwanted stranger.

Ira made his way over to the Schoen Funeral Home by streetcar at half past eleven. Thirty or forty people mulled around the waiting area, signing the logbook, chatting, and watching the video monitor shuffle photos of Shirley's life from childhood to convalescence. Those videos always reminded Ira of how minuscule and unimportant lives can be. After a year passed, how many people would still remember Shirley Jones? Some. How about ten years? A few. A hundred years? Doubtful that any would. Maybe one or two would have heard a tale about her. But after a thousand years, Shirley's life would be just a speck of sand in a barren desert. It always reminded Ira of his own mortality and how he would be remembered on this planet. Ira had long ago established the reality that his life would be remembered for nothing. Maybe his family name would survive the test of time, but Ira Silver? Ira Silver would be forgotten the moment his children shoveled dirt onto his pine casket. He doubted that even a tear would be shed or that anyone but a few lost souls would attend the last rites of Ira Silver.

Those thoughts didn't dissuade Ira from enjoying a barbecue pork slider, potato salad, collard greens, red beans, and three beers. He had a long conversation with Shirley's sister-in-law who, he learned, didn't particularly care for her brother's wife. Apparently, a big lawsuit was brewing over Shirley's mother's estate. Shirley's mother—who was ninety-six and living at the Poydras Home—couldn't make it to the funeral, but this woman was certain that with Shirley out of the picture, the inheritance would be all hers. Just as Ira was certain that once his mother took her final breath, he would finally be able to enjoy the fruits of the Silver estate.

As the mourners shuffled into the chapel, Ira stuffed rolls and sugar cookies into the gym bag he had left near the coat stand before sneaking out the front door. Above Ira's head, the skies had darkened and streaks of rain crisscrossed the horizon. The first sprinkles pitter-pattered on his bald head as he waited with arms crossed at the streetcar stop.

The doorman at the entrance to the palatial Hotel Monteleone held the door open and nodded at Ira as he walked in. Checking the sign for the day's events, which included two weddings, two conferences, tea at high noon and three different bands in the Carousel Bar, Ira zeroed in on one of the second-floor ballrooms.

A few dozen stragglers sipped sodas in the hallway making small talk. Ira usually does one pass through, meandering the hall, glancing at the faces, smiling at strangers before heading to the restroom. Often there would be a nametag on the floor or at the top of a trashcan. Ira had assumed the names of everyone from Joy to Jeff,

Manny to Miranda, and only a handful of times been called out for not looking like the name on the tag. In all the years Ira had been mooching meals from unsuspecting event organizers, he had never once gotten tossed to the curb.

The women at RT Book Lovers Convention outnumbered the men ten to one. Since this event did actually have some semblance of an association to Ira's real profession, he bee-lined it to the huge foldout tables cluttered with hardcover books in front of the ball-room entrance. A half a dozen middle-aged women were all engrossed in conversations with a group of seniors trying to procure their nametags. Fidgeting with his thumbs, Ira locked eyes with a lithe young lady wearing a floral sundress.

"Excuse me, miss," Ira yelled over the shoulders of the blue-hairs in front of him. They turned in unison and shot Ira a look of scorn.

"Can I help you?" the woman asked as Ira nestled his way to the front of the table.

"I should be on the guest list," he declared comfortably, handing the woman his business card.

"We don't really have a guest list," she said. "Do you mean will-call?"

"Maybe I'm on the press list."

"Oh, that would be Janice. Let me check with her."

The young woman sauntered over to the other end of the table. She whispered into the ear of an obese redhead sitting down with a note pad. She scanned the list, shaking her head at the same time, as if she had memorized every name that appeared on it. The younger girl handed her Ira's card and she looked again.

The sitting woman looked back up and said something to the young girl, who eagerly stepped out of her way. Pushing both hands down flat on the table, the big woman attempted to rise from the chair, knocking a few of the books off their display stand in the process. Barely squeezing her way between the row of chairs and the wall, she stomped toward Ira with arms flailing at her sides. As she neared, Ira noticed huge craters below her chin that looked like rolling hills that stopped at the top of her humongous breasts. She was wearing what looked to Ira like a tablecloth or light bed cover with ruffled short sleeves. Handing Ira back his card, she grumbled, "You're not on the list."

"My editor confirmed it last week," Ira said.

"What's your editor's name?"

"Marc Cohen."

"I don't recall a Marc Cohen calling the office," she said.

"I assure you that I am supposed to be covering this event," Ira said.

"What exactly does your magazine cover?" she asked.

"Jewish events, Jewish books, Jewish celebrities. Really, anything that involves Jews in New Orleans."

"Do you have a copy of your magazine?" she asked.

"Not on me. But I can bring one tomorrow. This event is all weekend, isn't it?"

"Of course it is. Can you get your editor to send me a proposal on company letterhead?"

"Yes, sure. He can send it over first thing in the morning," Ira said.

"I really need something now so I can let you in."

"That's simply not possible," Ira said. "Marc is covering the Purim Festival at Gates of Prayer. He won't be back in the office till tomorrow."

"Look, Mr...."

"Silver."

"I am going to let you in, but I am going to need a letter first thing tomorrow if you want to come back."

"Sure, sure. Of course."

"And I will need you to mail me a copy of the article when it comes out."

"Absolutely," Ira said, as the young girl standing behind Ms. Ratchet handed Ira a blue and white nametag.

Ira spent the next few hours sipping cocktails, eating petit fours, and watching ostentatious women from across the globe mingling with one another. There was one man in the room that seemed to get all the attention, and of course, it wasn't Ira. This man wore a yellow suit, matching fedora, and white bucks and had a grey beard trimmed neatly just below his jawline. All the women found him charming, listening to his tales of New Orleans debauchery while laughing and touching his forearm. Jealousy tormented Ira in times like this, so he kept on drinking, slurping down Crown and Cokes every fifteen minutes. He became more and more inebriated, swinging his body back and forth against the wall until he became the albatross in the room, spouting off to himself about nonsense that no one could understand. There was an open door next to him out of which flowed the voices of authors reading passages from their novels, sounding like the backdrop to a porn movie. But no one was listening to the panelists anymore; they were all facing the back of the ballroom where Ira was making a scene. Ira shook his head and screamed the word "breathlessly" a couple dozen times until he couldn't take it anymore and stormed out of the room.

Back out on Royal Street, the clouds had dissipated and the sun was heading toward the west. The buskers and magicians, statues and street performers, miscreants and delinquents had taken their rightful places along the street. Ira closed his eyes and inhaled the sounds and smells of the French Quarter. As always, it brought him back in time as if he could hear and smell the same things his father and his father's father had heard and smelled.

Ira knew it was time to head back home. Many times, he stood in this same spot in the same condition and the night was just beginning. If he turned away from Canal Street, trouble would find him, whether in the back room of a club on St. Ann or on a stool at the top of the Dungeon. Ira took one more deep breath, spit a glob of mucus onto the curb, and stumbled toward the streetcar.

14

Back at the house on St. Charles, Ira sobered up on three cups of coffee before finding the boys lying on Howie's bed, huddled around their electronic toys. "Time for services, boys."

In unison, "Aw, come on."

"Howie, this is the only thing I am asking of you. Get your brothers ready for temple."

"We're not even Jewish," Sammy mumbled.

Ira sat at the end of the bed and tried to put his hand on Sammy's leg, but it was quickly rebuked. He sighed. "Whether you like it or not, you will always have Jewish blood in you."

A long silence hovered in the air. Part of it was the elephant in the room; part of it was a test of willpower. Finally, the boys put down their games and Ira stepped out. Charlie wasn't around. She had likely left hours ago, as Friday was her money night, and she was usually at work by the middle of the afternoon.

Ira entered his bedroom and slid a box out from underneath his bed. Removing the lid, Ira stared at the handful of yarmulkes passed down through the generations of Silvers. He placed an ornate gold and white yarmulke on his bald head and three others in the inside pocket of his jacket.

The boys came downstairs in gym shorts, T-shirts, and flip-flops. Before they even reached the landing, Ira pointed them back upstairs to change into the nicest clothes they had brought with them. When they reappeared, they were wearing matching blue jeans and black turtlenecks, looking completely out of place for a spring evening in New Orleans and kind of like Steve Jobs' Asian offspring.

Ira forced the kids to leave their handheld devices on the table in the front foyer, which predictably caused a verbal altercation that lasted pretty much the entire walk to Sinai. Holding the door open, the kids filed in like mute mummies with looks of utter disgust for their predicament. Ira, of course, knew little about the surly attitudes of teenagers. Sammy and Howie were just acting like any other kids would in this situation, but Ira was mortified by their inability to make small talk with the handful of senior citizens mulling about the lobby. Instead, the boys stood near the corkboard calendar with their backs to everyone, pretending to be interested in a flyer for the following night's sock hop at the JCC.

At precisely six fifteen, the sanctuary doors popped open, the organ pipes chimed, and Rabbi Maisel and Cantor Cohen led the worshipers inside the intimate room. With the big sanctuary used only for the high holy days and well-attended bar mitzvahs, Ira pushed the boys into the little room containing eight rows of wooden benches under a vaulted ceiling with stained glass windows. The cantor and the rabbi took their places on the small stage as twelve more people filed in. A large bouquet of flowers resting in front of the altar gave Ira a double-take because they looked different from the ones he had picked out earlier in the day.

The crowd was typically sparse for Friday night services. Reformed Judaism had suffered a crisis over the past few decades, as all across the country it had become more and more difficult to find congregants willing to give up a Friday night for an hour of prayer and an Oneg Shabbat. Tonight's crowd was atypical. Three elderly women occupied the front row with one of their caretakers. In the middle rows, a young couple probably new to town, a middle-aged gay couple with their toddler son, and two college-aged girls, most likely from Loyola and only attending for the credit requirement for their theology class. In the back row sat the one regular attendee who wore a white tallit draped over his grey suit and Carol-Ann Goldberg, the raspy-voiced red-headed executive director.

Before sitting down, Ira handed each boy a yarmulke and they disdainfully covered the crowns of their heads. As they nestled into a row toward the front, the yarmulkes slid off their silken black hair as soon as they sat down. The large jovial Cantor Cohen motioned the audience to rise and led them in the opening hymns with his deep baritone booming throughout the room. The cantor kept looking toward the boys with a warm-hearted grin, genuinely happy to see them for the first time in years.

Ira hoped the boys would be captivated by the sermon, but all three slouched in their chairs with their arms folded, staring at the ceiling. When they stood up for the prayers, their yarmulkes slipped off their heads and each tried to grab the others' out of the air. They looked like Larry, Curly, and Moe swatting at falling plates as they crashed on the floor. Eventually, they gave up on the balancing game and held one hand atop their heads, barely standing when the rabbi motioned for the audience to rise for the opening of the arc. The boys whispered to each other, ignoring the rabbi and cantor while they strolled down the aisle holding the Torah. Ira wanted to smack them upside the head but was afraid the noise would exacerbate the situation, so he bated breath until the final hymn.

After the rabbi blessed the congregation, everyone filed into the ballroom for a light dinner. In brighter times, chaffing dishes took up the entire eight-foot table loaded with Jewish delicacies like salted fish and kugel, but that night, there was just a Caesar salad, challah bread, and one chaffing dish containing some kind of creamy chicken pasta.

Ira looked at the boys, who had strayed over to the drink station and grabbed themselves a couple of Sprites. He loaded a Styrofoam plate with pasta and salad and motioned for Howie to join him.

"Aren't you guys going to eat?" Ira asked.

"I'm not hungry," Howie said.

"What do you mean, you're not hungry? What did you have for lunch?"

"Mexican food."

"Mexican food? Where'd you get Mexican food?"

"I don't know," Howie said. "Charlie picked it up for us."

"Charlie bought you guys lunch?" Ira asked, while shoving a forkful of creamy pasta into his eager lips.

"Yeah."

"So you're not going to eat?"

"Yang can't eat any of this stuff anyway," Howie said, pointing toward the table.

Ira shook his head as the two of them walked toward one of the round cloth-covered tables. Before Ira could sit, Cantor Cohen came over and gave Howie an awkward hug, enveloping the small boy with his huge belly.

"How've you been, Howie? How's New York treating you?" Cantor Cohen asked.

"Fine," he said.

"Is your mom doing okay?"

"Yes," Howie said, lowering his gaze toward the cantor's shoes.

"Well, tell her I send my best. It's so nice to see you."

Howie shrugged his shoulders and took the seat next to Ira. Ira was scarfing down the rest of his food while Sammy and Yang climbed into the seats next to him.

Ira went for a second plate, while the boys laid their heads down on folded arms. They looked like tortoises hiding under their shells, biding time until their prey gave up and moved on to its next victim. When he was finished eating, Ira grabbed a few rugalach off the table, scooped up the boys, and headed for the exit.

As the boys stood outside, Ira ran back inside to grab his cash for the flowers. Carol-Ann was standing by the office door, nodding her head as Ira approached.

"What?" Ira asked.

"Mitch's never brought the flowers," Carol-Ann said, scrunching her nose and still slightly nodding.

"What? That's impossible. I set it up this morning."

"It never came. I ran over to Whole Foods right before services."

Ira's face was flushed red, furious that he wasn't going to get that crisp hundred-dollar bill in a long white envelope. "That's preposterous. They wouldn't not come."

"Did you pay them?" Carol-Ann asked with bulging, accusatory eyes.

"Of course I paid them. That's the last time I trust those motherfu—" Ira caught himself before completing the sentence.

"It's fine, it's fine. Don't worry about it. We got a nice arrangement."

"But I was counting on that hundred dollars," Ira huffed.

"Sorry, Ira," Carol-Ann said, walking to the door and holding it open. "The boys are waiting for you."

Ira met the boys at the curb. Darkness had descended over the avenue; a bicyclist zoomed by, three college girls walked the streetcar tracks on the neutral ground, Friday night traffic cluttered St. Charles Avenue. The boys huddled next to each other whispering insults. "Time to call it a night," he shouted, and they followed their father for a walk toward their last vestige of life in New Orleans.

15

The sun spilled over the horizon at just past six, adding a soft glow to the ever-present darkness. Everyone was up early, Yang already on the couch staring at the broken TV screen. Ira poked his head in Sammy's room while the boy was getting dressed. He had a soft, doughy body just like his dad did at that age. In the next room, Ira poked his eldest son a few times, trying to rouse him from his teenage slumber.

In the kitchen, Ira slathered little packets of butter on toasted French bread. Yang finished the job by scooping jelly out of six little packets with his pointer finger. They drank lukewarm water out of plastic parade cups and sat in uncomfortable silence. Just before seven, they made their way to the Lambeth House.

Father had passed away two years prior, and Mother's health had been in serious decline ever since. It seemed like so long ago, but it really wasn't. They'd both been in good health before the Madoff thing. The stress of losing all the family money sent Father to his grave. Mother's problems began with little lapses in memory: a forgotten cousin, a missed birthday. When Father got diagnosed with the prostate cancer, Mother's dementia got progressively worse. She was like a teenager aging backward, remembering less each day until her only son became barely recognizable.

The Shiva and the week of mourning for Father were bizarre. A horde of guests, many of them old employees or former classmates, came to acknowledge this once-great man who made a profound impact on their lives. They tried to convey their sympathy to Mother, who stared at their chests and spat out random epithets. It was left to Ira to comfort these strangers, and comforting strangers was not one of Ira's fortes. His sister Sarah managed to turn up at the funeral, but she was long gone by the time the Shiva began, back to her high-falutin life in San Francisco. She didn't even bring her daughter or husband along; just herself, for less than forty-eight hours.

By the time the week was over, Ira had helped move Mother's belongings to the Lambeth House, into the same apartment that her own mother had once occupied. Though the musty smell that Ira remembered emanating from Grandmother had not yet taken hold over Mother's body, it gave Ira the chills to think about her withering away in that depressing state of mind.

For the past one hundred Saturdays, Ira had showed up in the morning and spent a few hours in the company of the woman who gave him life. The first six months, they walked around the grounds together, mostly in silence. The next six months, Mother seemed more agitated and even scared. She would let out a small scream when Ira popped his head in the door, and she was lucky to get out of bed for a walk to the bathroom. She barely talked, and when she did, it would either be a sing-songy version of a nursery rhyme or some other memory of a childhood long ago.

Ira kept reminding the boys that this might be the last time they saw her. Howie had spent a good eight years living under the same roof as Mother, yet it was difficult for him to utter a kind word about the woman. Sammy was a little more generous, offering thanks for the time she bought him an old Lionel train set for Hanukah. It was the same train set that was given to Ira every two years when he was a boy. Little did Sammy know that it was actually brought down from the attic and re-gifted on the eve of that holiday. Ira remembered the heat flash that seared through his cheeks when he saw that train set for the umpteenth time. He wanted to break it and smash the conductor's car into tiny pieces so no other child would have to endure the humiliation of opening that stupid gift again. But he didn't. Instead he suffered his indignity in silence, resigned once again to the shame that came with being a Silver.

Though the circumstances may have been depressing, the Lambeth House is not. Mother had a nice apartment with palatial views of the Mississippi, stainless steel appliances, good food, and twenty-four-hour supervision. But lately the director had been advising Ira to send Mother over to hospice care. Her bedsores were becoming more and more difficult to care for, her eating regimen less and less regular. The money set aside years ago for her geriatric care was dwindling faster than the polar ice caps.

On that morning, Mother lay in bed with her hands clasped together on her stomach. If her chest weren't moving ever so slightly up and down, you would have thought she was already dead. The boys stood by the door afraid to venture too deep inside the room. Ira glanced back at them with a scowl while he nestled his way up to his mother's side.

Her high cheekbones had withered away, and the usual rose color had darkened toward slate grey. Large lines ran from the side of her nose to the corner of her chin. Her cracked lips looked as dry as hot asphalt on a summer day. Even in her diminished mental capacity, Ira was used to seeing his mother's face caked in makeup, but today it was the bare, weathered face of a woman near the end of her existence. It looked as if it had been months since she had had a haircut. Wisps of grey hair matted to her forehead with a thin film of greasy sweat. As Ira gently moved a strand from her cheek, she opened her left eye and scanned the room.

"What do you want?" she yelled. "Who are you?"

"Mother, it's me. Please. Calm down."

"How do you know me?"

"I am your son," Ira said, again glancing back at the boys who were standing so close to each other that they looked as if they had only three legs between them.

Mother turned her head toward the bedside table and then gazed at the boys in the corner of the room. She said nothing.

"Hi Grandma," Howie said meekly.

"She can't hear you," Ira said. "You know that. Why don't you come a little closer? She isn't going to bite."

The boys shook their heads furiously, holding each other back as if they were facing the entrance of a haunted house. Ira stood up and walked toward them, but they pushed their backs against the wall to make themselves as inaccessible as they possibly could.

"Look, kids. Just suck it up. What's the worst that could happen?"

"She could throw up on us," said Yang.

"Yeah, her head could start spinning around like that little girl in *Psycho*," Sammy said.

"That was *The Exorcist*," Ira said.

"See?" they said in unison.

Ira sidled back over to his mother's side. She now had both of her cloudy grey eyes wide open, staring at the boys on the other side of the room. Her lips were in a frown and her eyebrows arched to the top of her forehead. Ira couldn't tell if she was scared, angry, or upset. She looked confused, more than anything. "Do you remember your grandchildren?" Ira asked.

Mother's eyes narrowed, trying to make out the figures across the room. Ira waved the boys closer, and they inched in. "Oh, yes," she squealed. "Of course I remember Eden."

"No, Mother. Eden is Sarah's kid."

"It is so good to see you, Eden," Mother said, slowly reaching out her hand as if to hail a passing cab.

"That's Howie," Ira barked. "Eden hasn't been to New Orleans in ten years."

"You were always such a good girl," she said, pausing for a moment before adding, "A good girl, you were."

"Mother, please," Ira yelled. "Eden hasn't been back here since she was four. And don't get me started on Sarah."

"Your sister was always so beautiful. Beautiful girl. Those braids. The freckles."

"Sarah's a bitch, Mother." Ira glanced back at the boys. Their eyes were popping so far out of their heads they looked like Buckwheat's Asian offspring.

Ah yes, Sarah: the darling of the family. The one who got. The one who took. The one who was doted on and given the world. And yet, the minute she was old enough to be on her own, she left. Left Ira to care for Mother and Father as they aged and became incontinent. Left him to look after the house and pay the bills and make sure that Mother didn't wilt away in solitary confinement for the past two years.

When Ira turned back to look at his mother, she was trying to catch her breath, sort of wheezing and gasping for air. He held her hand while she coughed up some phlegm, which drizzled out of her mouth and hung awkwardly on the side of her chin. Ira waved at Howie to bring him a tissue from the tissue box, and the boy hesitantly obliged.

Howie leaned in to hand his father the tissue at the same time that Mother opened her eyes again. She looked straight at the boy with shock in her eyes. Then her eyes went from bulging out of her head to narrow little squints. Ira sensed her recognition. While wiping the spittle from her chin, he said, "I knew you'd remember him. It's only been a year."

"Well, isn't that something," Mother said. "You're the little boy from the Golden Dragon."

"No, Mother!" Ira screamed. "This is your goddamn grandson, for Christ's sake."

"Well you don't have to scream at me, son," Mother spat. "Get me some General Tso's chicken, would you?"

Ira turned to see Howie ushering his brothers out of the room. His face and neck had reddened something fierce. Ira felt the sudden urge to pick up a pillow, cover his mother's face, and smother her until she took her final choking breath. Instead, he took a long, deep, guttural breath of his own, let the air out from his chest, and choked down a sob.

16

After the debacle at the Lambeth House, Ira tried his hardest to relieve the tension in the air. The walk home was brutal, though, as the boys refused to communicate with Ira. They talked amongst themselves in Chinese, likely plotting an early return to New York.

But Ira pushed on. He was determined to turn the week around, and he figured the Irish Channel St. Patrick's Day parade would be just the thing to turn the tide. He dug through the back of his attic and found a bag full of St. Patrick's Day beads, hats, and decorations and spread them over the dining room table. The boys sifted through the old beads looking disinterested while Ira pleaded with them to try things on.

Howie spent the entire time staring at the front door, most likely hoping Charlie would pop in at any moment. It was nearing noon and she hadn't yet returned from her night's debauchery. That's the term Ira always used for Charlie's nights out. It wasn't "work" or "prostitution" or "pole dancing," it was excessive indulgence of sensual pleasures. Truth be told, Ira too hoped for Charlie's return. He wanted nothing more than the thick ice between them to break, and she seemed to be the only thing that made the kids happy.

It was unusual for the St. Patrick's Day parade to be so close to Mardi Gras, but this was the latest Fat Tuesday on record. Ira figured a parade would be just the thing to turn the mood around, and he was certain that Charlie would garner plenty of attention from the benignly belligerent marchers that roll through the Garden District.

The boys were less enthused about the plan. They made it quite clear to Ira that they would have preferred to sit around and watch TV, had Ira owned a working TV. Through their petulant whining, Ira could sense their indifference to the things he cherished, any fleeting appendage to his hometown nearly obsolete.

With the four of them now accessorized in green, they opened the front door to depart and saw a disheveled devil sitting with her back to them, shoulders pulsing up and down, as if she were weeping.

"Charlie," the boys called out.

She half turned to look over her right shoulder, black eye make-up smeared down the sides of her cheek. The boys huddled next to her, putting their arms around her back, trying their best to comfort the wayward soul.

Ira asked, "Are you okay?"

Charlie glanced back at Ira ready to make a snarky comment, but instead straightened her shoulders, wiped her eyes with the back of her hand, and said, "I'm fine."

"Was it the big man with the aviator glasses?" Ira asked.

"No. It's not important," Charlie answered while shaking her head.

"Should we call the police?" he pressed.

"No," Charlie answered, "definitely do not do that."

"Do you want us to stay with you?" Ira asked, and the boys all nodded in agreement.

Ira saw Charlie grimace as she rubbed her swollen cheek.

"Want to come with us to the parade?" followed after a short pause.

Charlie sighed. She stood up and turned toward Ira. It was his first glimpse of her fat lip and torn shirt. The latter was barely synched together just below her armpit so that her sequined bra was visible almost all the way to her nipple. "Not today," she said. "I need some sleep."

"Are you sure?" Ira asked again.

"Yes, please go. I want to be alone."

"Well, alrighty then. We shall bring you back some cabbage and potatoes for dinner," he said, smiling and laughing, trying his best to lighten the mood.

Charlie half-heartedly waved at the boys before disappearing into the confines of the house. They started in after her, but Ira barked out, "No."

They stopped in their tracks.

"She doesn't want to be bothered, boys. We'll see her when we get back."

"Here they come, here they come," Ira jumped up and down as the first police car flashed its lights, signaling the oncoming onslaught of marchers and floats barreling down the commercial district at the edge of the Irish Channel, just before Louisiana Avenue.

First came the Shriner's dune buggies and the dikes on bikes. Then the walking clubs: hundreds of old drunk men dressed like leprechauns holding sticks full of green and white plastic carnations, spying susceptible women willing to trade a kiss for a keepsake, wobbling back and forth down the street, jostling with the crowd for the adulation of the prettiest victim they could find.

The crowd swelled to five rows deep and Ira sensed the boys' claustrophobia as they spun in circles and realized they were trapped between a police barricade and a throng of drunk revelers. The young girls directly to their left, maybe college-aged, were attracting the most attention from the costume-clad men walking the street. Wearing green knickers or plaid kilts with white knee-high socks, the mostly overweight and sweaty old men with glazed eyes and hands full of beer made eye contact with the group and slithered their way toward them, trying desperately to remove a cheap flower to offer before slobbering their wet lips as close to the girls' as they could. Occasionally, the men glanced toward the boys, and out of pity or pride, beckoned one of the kids to pluck a carnation from the foam bouquet of plastic flowers. The boys, in turn, half-heartedly took the useless trinket and tossed it into a plastic bead bag that Ira had brought from home.

After the walkers came the floats. First the small ones, some decorated in St. Patrick's theme, others left over from the previous week's Mardi Gras parades. Women and children showered the crowd with beads, MoonPies, oversized sunglasses, miniature boxes of Lucky Charms, and bars of Irish Spring soap.

"Get the soap, get the soap," Ira yelled to the boys, who were barely visible behind the barricade.

The noise of the parade drenched the crowd in whistles and screams, shouts and blasts. Dance music pumped out of the Bulldog Pub, mixing with the Celtic sounds of bagpipes and bullhorns amplified from the back of the floats. Men and women called for more—"Throw me somethin', mister," was the phrase of the day. Occasionally, people would call out the names of the riders they knew, and the crowd would be showered with dozens of beads while Ira and the boys raised their arms in a desperate attempt to avoid getting smacked in the face.

As the floats grew in size and the number of riders swelled, the ammunition changed from harmless little trinkets and soft furry animals to edibles like red potatoes, giant heads of cabbage, and random other vegetables. Thrown high above the crowd from the twenty- or thirty-foot-long floats, the veggies projected like missiles dropping into war zones. Sometimes the crowd parted and the object smashed to the ground or busted a nearby window; other times brave parade-goers stretched out their arms and attempted to catch a flying cabbage, resulting in plenty of bruised and battered appendages.

Ira and the boys were up front, so the cabbages tossed from the bottom row fell harmlessly to the ground. Their bag filled up quickly and Ira was ready to leave, if not for the depth of the mob standing behind them. The boys seemed eager to leave as well, squished behind the barricade while trying to read the ingredients of the Moon-Pie, presumably to find out whether Yang might be able to eat one.

Ira was bending over, trying to squeeze a few final potatoes into the full grocery bag when, out of the corner of his eye, he saw a cabbage drifting toward them. He stuck out his hand, feebly attempting to block the incoming projectile, before a loud thump signaled someone or something had made contact. At first, Ira thought maybe they had escaped injury, but then the crowd momentarily silenced and a gasp took over, followed by a high-pitched wail.

Two or three women to their right grabbed Yang's hand and pushed the boys through the crowd away from the floats, Ira following with his plastic bag full of vegetables. They were ushered onto a side street behind the Bulldog where the women huddled around the young boy, poking and prodding to determine the extent of his injuries. For a minute, Yang was crying and refused to move his little hand away from his eye, but it was determined by the lack of blood that he had eluded serious injury. When Yang was finally coaxed into moving his hand, his right eye had already begun to swell. One of the women returned with a plastic grocery bag full of ice, and after much cajoling, Yang held the bag to his face, whimpering, as Ira, Howie, and Sammy thanked the women for their concern.

Then they headed home.

17

With floats still rolling and crowds still screaming, Ira led the boys up Magazine Street. Young girls held each other up by their waists, grasping plastic cups full of copious amounts of green beer. Desperate young men followed, slurring profanities, zigzagging the sidewalk, cradling cabbages and armfuls of strung beads.

Ira heard Yang sniffling beneath his ice pack as his brothers consoled him with their arms draped over his little shoulders. Sammy finally spoke up with a whine. "We're hungry."

Ira stopped short and pointed out with a half-hearted grin, "Look at all this food we caught."

The boys' shoulders dropped so low, they reminded Ira of hunchback leprechauns. Howie crossed his arms as if refusing to take another step. "I hate cabbage."

"Since when?" Ira asked.

"Since I don't know when," Howie said. "Can't we have some fried chicken or jambalaya or something?"

Ira sucked his lips into his mouth and whistled. "Okay, let's take this stuff home and I'll run out for some food."

"Isn't Popeye's on the way?" Howie put in.

"Popeye's? No, they closed down last year. Rent's getting too high on Magazine, even for Popeye's."

Ira left the kids alone in the house, back to the comforts of their video games. Charlie was passed out on the living room couch smelling like an empty bar after lights out. She didn't move despite the babble of the boys dropping Chinese curses at their miniature screens. Yang had already forgotten about his swollen eye.

Doubling back, Ira retraced his steps in search of a party or two he could crash. With the parade long since passed, people flocked to parties throughout the neighborhood; revelers were congregating on porches, barbecuing on lawns, and firing up their boilers. Most Saturday nights, Ira found a gallery opening on Magazine Street where he might sip free wine and eat cheese and crackers, but on the Saturday before St. Patrick's Day, he had a plethora of options and desired to bring something special home for the kids.

On the corner of Soniat and Magazine, a two-story double with tattered paint had a group of people on one side of the wrap-around porch huddled around a keg and another group on the other side surrounding a long table on the front lawn peeling crawfish. Ira figured it would be a good place to stop because he could always pretend that he knew the people from the other half of the double.

But locals hardly ever gave Ira trouble, and certainly not tonight since he was still wearing a green felt bowler hat and dozens of beads around his neck. He blended in at the crawfish table, smiled at the people on both sides, and introduced himself as John Sullivan. The trick to crashing parties was to never outstay your welcome, so Ira spent about thirty minutes drinking green Miller Lite and eating crawfish. He felt the inflammation in his ankle warm with every bite, but he just slipped off his shoe and flexed his foot for temporary relief. Before heading out, Ira snuck a plastic Thank You bag out of his pocket and scooped some potatoes, corn, mushrooms, and crawfish into it before quietly walking out of the cast iron gate.

Ira hit a few more parties, nodding to strangers like he belonged there, drinking beer, mooching free food and drinks. He realized he'd been out far longer than he had planned to be and thought it best to head toward home, but he still only had a few pounds of crawfish. As the glimmer of the sun set and the sky turned charcoal, Ira heard a brass band blasting on a nearby porch. It was a stately Victorian with immaculate landscaping and colored lights streaming up thick white columns. Dozens gathered on the lawn in front of the band shaking their booties and doing the funky butt. The front door was wide open, and people of all ages streamed in and out. Ira dropped his bag of crawfish on a little patch of grass next to the front gate and let himself in. One or two people looked up as he entered, but no one really paid him much attention.

Ira watched the band and blended in with the dancers with his own white boy shuffle, stiffly swinging his body to the harsh blasts from the horns. As throngs of partiers emerged from the house with hands full of barbecue, Ira drifted toward the front door and made his move. Smiling at the first person he saw, Ira asked, "Do you know where the bathroom is?"

The woman was tiny, maybe four foot nine with silver hair and green eyes, and she walked Ira down the center hall toward a closed door. "I think someone's in there," she said, knocking lightly on the white door.

Someone yelled from inside and the woman started to walk off. Looking back, she said, "You must be a friend of Brian's."

"I am. Where is Brian?"

"Must be out back. He's been smoking meats all day."

"He's so good at that," Ira said.

The woman smiled and said, "He sure is. Did you get some of that brisket?"

"I haven't yet. I just got here. Where's the food?"

"Oh dear Lord, you haven't been in the kitchen yet?" she asked, taking Ira by the elbow and leading him into a huge marble kitchen with a bay window overlooking a backyard pool and lush tropical fauna.

A dark-haired woman was washing dishes and others were standing behind the huge island in the center of the room, making sandwiches and drinking cans of NOLA beer. Ira introduced himself as Ken Toole and started building a plate full of sliders. The little woman bid him farewell as he slathered coleslaw on his bun. A big fat guy lumbered in from the yard and everyone in the kitchen cheered. He dropped another aluminum half pan of pork on the counter, glanced at Ira, and said, "Who are you?"

"Kenny Toole. Brian, you don't remember me?"

Brian scrunched his fat face, wiped sweat from his forehead with the back of his dirty hand, and tilted his head toward his shoulder. "Toole…Toole… I know the name from somewhere. You from Brother Martin?"

"Yeah, yeah, yeah, yeah. Brother Martin."

"Oh right, sorry dude," Brian said. "You enjoying the barbecue?"

"Yeah, man. It's great. But I gotta run and pick up something for the kids."

Brian thought for a moment and said, "Julietta, why don't you wrap some sliders up for Kenny's kids?"

Julietta smiled from the sink and looked at Ira with a, "Sí, sí," before wiping her hands with a dish towel and taking a box of aluminum foil out from the bottom of the pantry. She wrapped two plates of sliders and some ribs, slid them into a plastic bag, and handed them to Ira. He grabbed the offering, hobbled out of the house, found the other bag full of crawfish, and smiled to himself the entire way home.

18

The front gate hung ajar, the house cloaked in a dull light reflecting off the full moon. At the front door, only the sounds of crickets chirping and cars rolling down the avenue broke the silence. Ira fumbled for his key while juggling the bags of plates filled with leftover food. He elbowed the door a few times before he finally tucked his cane under his armpit, lowered the bags to the ground, and squeezed the key out of his pocket.

The foyer was dark. Silence draped the house in a veil of emptiness, torn asunder by the shuffling of his feet. "Hello," Ira called. "I've got dinner." His voice echoed off the walls like a PA announcer at an empty stadium.

Ira tottered into the kitchen, felt his way to the sink, and hoisted the bags onto the Formica countertop. He fumbled with the string, nearly knocking over the lamp. When the light came on, he noticed a partially eaten French bread and jelly sandwich sitting on the table and crumbs strewn across the chair. It looked as if someone had left in a hurry.

"Where are you?" Ira yelled as he crossed the threshold from the kitchen into the living room. "Are y'all upstairs?"

He turned on the lamp by the stairwell and observed darkness emanating from the floor above. He hurried up the stairs with his heart racing, accelerating in speed with each bedroom he entered. Finally, he paused at his own door before pushing in and letting out a breath of stale air.

When he was sure the house was empty, Ira did a quick walk around the confines of his property. The front porch was clear and both sides of the house were made impassable by overgrown weeds stretching high above his head. The back door looked as if it hadn't been opened in years, but Ira unlatched the deadbolt and walked into the darkness anyway. He saw nothing but dead plants and the outline of the shed. His muted calls for the boys went unanswered.

Ira returned to the house, where he spent the next hour pacing back and forth, glancing out the window behind the velvet curtains every few minutes, and chewing on his fingernails. He had never felt so alone. There was no one to call, no one to talk him down from the bottomless feeling he had in the pit of his stomach. It was now past ten and Ira looked at the cordless phone a few times, begging it to ring. Once, he even picked it up readying his finger to dial Lin's number; but there was nothing she could do from a thousand miles away. This was his problem and he had to solve it on his own. He feared his worst nightmare: that the man had come back for Charlie and taken all the kids with him.

At eleven, Ira picked up the phone again and dialed 911, but hung up before the first ring. Instead, he put on his coat, stood on the patio, and loudly called the names of the kids. The streetcar rumbled past and Ira limped toward it, hoping, praying that the kids might disembark at the next stop, but only a single man stepped off.

Interminable thoughts of disaster continued to pulse through Ira's brain. His stomach churned and his face flushed with grief, anxiety, and aggravation. He ran as fast as his creaky body could run up and down the side streets calling after the kids like an old woman chasing after a lost dog. It seemed like hours since he had left the house, but the grandfather clock just ticked past eleven thirty when he reentered the foyer.

Finally, Ira sat at his desk and dialed 911, feeling his head pounding as blood pulsed through his veins and the phone continued to ring. Minutes later, Ira jumped at the sound of the female operator's voice. "Orleans 911. What is your emergency?"

Ira fumbled for his voice before saying, "My kids."

"What is your location?"

"St. Charles. St. Charles Avenue."

"Do you have a number?"

"4238."

"What is your emergency?"

Ira choked on his voice again, this time taking a long, deep breath before saying, "My kids are gone."

"When did you last see them?"

"This afternoon."

"How old are these kids?"

"Fifteen, thirteen, and eight."

"Male or female?"

"All boys."

"Were they in the company of an adult?"

Ira paused. It wasn't that the question was unexpected; he just wasn't sure how to answer it. He took the phone receiver away from his mouth, wiped the sweat off his brow with the back of his hand, and said, "No. They were alone."

"I have an officer in route, Mr... what is your name?"

"Ira Silver."

"Mr. Silver."

"Thank you."

"Please stay on site, Mr. Silver, and an officer will be able to assist you."

Ira was startled by a loud knock on his front door minutes after he hung up the phone. He had recently read in the *Times-Picayune* about the pathetic response times from the NOPD, but they had arrived in less than five minutes. He couldn't stand up, too stunned to move, with crazy thoughts racing through his head. For a second he hoped it was the kids but, fully aware of Charlie's custom of barreling through the door, he knew it wasn't them.

Two uniformed NOPD officers stood on the dark porch. One was tall, lean, and in his mid- to late thirties with short blonde hair. The other was of medium height, with dark chocolate skin, large eyes, and a thick mustache. As Ira held the door open, the blonde-haired cop asked, "Did you call for an emergency?"

Ira motioned for them to come inside and led them to the light in the kitchen. "It's the kids. They're gone."

The blonde-haired cop, whose nametag Ira could now read—*H. Hanson*—said, "When did you last see them?"

"This afternoon."

"What time was that?"

"Four, I guess."

The other cop with the nametag *R. Miles* slowly made his way around the living room, looking disinterested.

"These are your kids, correct?"

"Yes."

"How old are these kids?"

"I already told the lady on the phone," Ira said with a hint of exasperation.

"What's your name?"

"Ira Silver. I told her that too."

"Sir, we are trying to help you. What's their ages?" he said, with his voice lifting slightly in volume.

"Fifteen, thirteen, and eight."

"Can you give me a physical description of these boys?"

"They're Asian. Chinese. Howie's about five foot four, a hundred and thirty…"

"Did you say they're Chinese?" R. Miles interrupted.

"Yes, my wife is Chinese."

"Where is your wife?" H. Hanson asked.

"She's in New York. We're divorced."

"Does she know these kids are with you?" H. Hanson asked.

"Of course she does," Ira said. "What kind of question is that?"

"Why's it so dark in here?" asked R. Miles. "Can you turn on the lights?"

"The overheads don't work," Ira said, shuffling over to the bathroom, opening the door, and flicking the light on.

"So you have three Chinese boys staying with you. How long have they been here?"

"Two days."

"Do they have a habit of staying out late?" asked H. Hanson.

"No. They're good kids. Yang's bedtime is eight o'clock."

"Yang?"

"The eight-year-old."

"Continue."

"They come to visit me every year on spring break."

A chirping sound that started far off in the distance grew louder as the men talked. Ira heard it first and squinted, and then all three men turned their heads and watched the front door. A few seconds later, the gate creaked and feet stammered off the rotting wood on the porch stairs. Ira raised his head, let out a huge thrust of air, and stared at the ceiling as Charlie bounced through the front door, followed by three giggling boys. They all stopped in their tracks when they saw the feral look of the two officers standing in front of them.

No one said a word. Everyone stood completely still for what seemed like an eternity. Finally, Ira shot like a scolding mother, "Where have you been?"

"The sock hop over at the JCC," Charlie answered.

"The sock hop at the JCC," Ira repeated with a grunt at the end.

"What are the cops doing here?" Howie asked.

"I thought you were missing," Ira said.

"Who are you?" R. Miles asked.

Charlie looked at Ira, then at Howie, before looking back at R. Miles. She was dressed in cut-off Daisy Dukes, a pink tank top, and flip-flops.

"That's Charlie," Ira answered.

"You told the dispatcher the kids were alone," R. Miles said to Ira.

"I said they were not in the company of an adult."

"How old are you, young lady?"

Ira answered, "Eighteen."

"I didn't ask you, Mr. Silver."

R. Miles walked over to Charlie, leaned down a little to stare directly into her eyes, and said, "Are you the babysitter or something?"

"Yes," Charlie answered.

"Where do you live?" R. Miles asked.

Now H. Hanson was walking around the room, more intently than his predecessor.

"Third Street," Charlie answered.

"Third and what?"

Charlie stammered.

Both cops looked at Charlie, who was hyperventilating a bit. "Third and what?" R. Miles asked again.

"Constance," Charlie finally answered meekly.

"That's over by…" R. Miles looked at H. Hanson. "What's that bar?"

No one answered.

"I just moved there," Charlie said. "Don't know the area too well."

"Ain't that across the street from Parasol's?" H. Hanson said, as he lifted a half-open gym bag from the floor next to the couch, a sequined bra draped over the top.

"This your stuff? Miss… What's your name?" asked H. Hanson.

Charlie again looked at Ira for help, but since she had never offered him her last name, this was a question he couldn't answer.

"It's her stuff," Howie finally affirmed, breaking the awkward silence.

R. Miles walked over to Howie, put his hands on his hips, bent down a bit, and said, "What's her stuff doing here?"

Howie, unaccustomed to lying to a police officer, blurted out, "She lives here."

The slightest of groans could be heard coming from both Charlie and Ira.

R. Miles, still bent down with his face just inches from Howie, said, "Why'd she tell us she lives on Third Street?"

Ira saw Howie's eyes starting to tear up and a little quiver shook through his hunched shoulders.

"What is the problem here, officer?" Ira said, moving in the direction of R. Miles's back.

"Sir, don't move," H. Hanson said.

Ira put both his hands out, palms facing forward in front of his chest in a "Who, me?" gesture.

R. Miles stood up straight while the rest of the room remained frozen. "The problem here, Mr. Silver," R. Miles said with his back turned, "is that you called the police."

"Because my kids were missing," Ira said.

"But they were in the company of the babysitter," R. Miles reminded him.

"That's right."

"But you neglected to tell us that. Why?"

Ira didn't answer. He looked at each of the kids. The three boys were all dressed up—as dressed up as three young boys could make themselves. Ira wondered for a second how they'd gotten an eight-year-old into a sock hop and the thought made him smirk. "I don't know why."

"This is nothing to smirk about, Mr. Silver." R. Miles moved over to Charlie, who had somehow managed to inch herself closer to the front door as if she was ready to make a break for it. "Where are you from, young lady?"

Again, Charlie was unable to speak. Ira answered for her, "Gulf-port."

"Mr. Silver," R. Miles said in a voice that sounded a little like Samuel Jackson. It was so deep and loud that Yang jumped. "I was not talking to you, now was I? Please do not speak unless spoken to. Do you understand me?"

"Yes," Ira said meekly.

"Now, Ms. Charlie. I am going to need to see some identification."

Charlie shrugged her shoulders and puckered her fat lip. "Don't got none," she said.

"Do you have a last name?" R. Miles asked.

"Jones," Charlie said.

"Charlie Jones?" R. Miles said as he bit his bottom lip and quivered his eye.

"Charlene," she said.

H. Hanson was busy pulling clothing items from the gym bag, picking them up, looking at each item and placing them on the back of the sofa. R. Miles walked over to him and they spoke to each other in hushed voices with their backs to the rest of the room.

Turning in unison, H. Hanson took over the questioning. "Ms. Jones, you say you are from Gulfport?"

"*I* said she was from Gulfport," Ira reminded him.

H. Hanson put his hands on his hips and looked at Ira like he was about to pounce on him in the UFC ring, silently reminding him to shut up.

"What are you doing in New Orleans, Ms. Jones?"

"Working," she said.

"Working where?"

"I bartend."

"Bartend where?"

"Tricky Dicks," she said.

H. Hanson chuckled. "Nice place."

"How do you bartend without any identification?" R. Miles asked.

"Lost my ID over Mardi Gras," she said.

"What is the address on your ID?" R. Miles asked.

Charlie looked like a mouse caught on a sticky trap squirming to get away. Static and cackling started coming from the walkie-talkie on H. Hanson's waist. He dropped Charlie's bag on the floor and turned the volume down. Then he came and put his hand on Charlie's shoulder—taking the "good cop" approach, Ira noticed—lowered his voice to almost a whisper, and said, "Ms. Jones, as soon as we get some identification from you, we are out of here. Can you give us your ID?"

Charlie slinked over to the couch and thumbed through her bag, finally pulling out a small powder tin. She pulled a thin plastic card from underneath the powder puff and handed it to H. Hanson.

H. Hanson inspected the card, turning it from front to back several times before looking back up. "This is a Maryland identification card," he said, "and it don't look anything like you."

"Changed my hair color," Charlie said with a fake laugh.

H. Hanson picked the card up, held it at arm's length in Charlie's direction, squinted his eyes, and shook his head. He turned the card over to R. Miles, who looked at it much more quickly and shook his head saying, "This ain't you."

Charlie reached for the card, but R. Miles brought his hand behind his back and said, "Uh-uh."

"How did you get that fat lip?" H. Hanson asked.

Charlie touched her lip, seemingly forgetting that she looked like an abuse victim. She stuttered, "I, I, I fell."

R. Miles had moved over to the boys and bent down next to Yang to inspect his eye. "Humph."

H. Hanson said, "Mr. Silver, why don't you put your boys to bed while we talk to Ms. Jones out here on the porch?"

Ira glanced at Charlie, who in her sheepish state looked much more like a child than he had ever noticed before. There didn't seem to be anything he could do, so he grabbed Yang and Sammy by the shoulders and led the three boys in a hushed march up the staircase.

19

"What are they going to do to her?" were the first words out of Yang's mouth as Ira tucked him into bed.

"Nothing, Yang," Ira answered. She's going to be fine."

"Why does she have someone else's ID?"

"I don't know."

"Where are they taking her?"

"Yang, I don't know. I'm in here with you. I know as much as you do."

Yang rolled over in the fetal position with his back to Ira, who patted his head a few times before standing up to leave. He heard a few sniffles as he closed the door and headed to his own room. Straining at the windowpane, he heard muffled voices from the front porch, but he could not make out the words. So he went to Sammy's room to tuck him in. The room was empty.

Howie and Sammy were on Howie's bed with their legs crossed, facing each other. That pose, combined with the fact that their feet were touching, made Ira realize how close the two were. They were obviously in the middle of a heated discussion because as soon as Ira entered the room, their voices went mute.

"Are you boys okay?" Ira asked.

"We're fine," Howie said. "What are they going to do to Charlie?"

"I have no idea."

"Can we help her?"

"I'm not sure."

"But you'll try," Howie pleaded with a long face. "Promise us you'll try."

"I'll try," Ira said. "Now go back to your room, Sammy, it's past midnight. You boys need to get some sleep. This will all blow over. You'll see."

Sammy brushed past Ira, who had his arm outstretched to give his son a hug. Ira looked at Howie and gave him a weak smile. "Goodnight, son."

As Ira shut off the light and returned to the dark hallway, one of the police officer's thunderous knocks slammed against the front door. The boys all peeked out of their rooms, but Ira put his hands up, beckoning them to stay. After they closed their doors, he took a deep breath and hobbled down the stairs.

R. Miles stood on the porch with his right hand resting on the handle of his gun. He had a different look in his eyes than when Ira saw him last, more squinted, more menacing. "May I come in?" he asked.

Ira held the door open and R. Miles walked to the desk in the living room before turning and facing Ira, who was looking out the front door wondering where H. Hanson and Charlie had gone.

"Mr. Silver, are you aware that you are harboring a minor?"

"Charlie's a minor?"

"She's sixteen. Are you having a sexual relationship with a minor?"

"Did she say that?" Ira asked.

"Mr. Silver, I asked you a question."

"I would never have inappropriate relations with a minor."

"What kind of relations were you having with Ms. Jones?"

"I wasn't," Ira said. "What? I don't understand the question. You're trying to put words in my mouth."

"You've got a sixteen-year-old minor from another state living with you that may be involved in illegal activities. She also has bruises all over her face. Can you explain why you are involved with this young lady?"

"What kind of illegal activities?"

"Mr. Silver, I am the one asking the questions here."

"Should I be speaking with a lawyer?" Ira asked.

"You are not under arrest, but if you feel like speaking with a lawyer, we can bring you down to the station for questioning."

Ira sat down on the couch, then stood back up. He didn't have a lawyer, nor could he afford one. And he had done nothing wrong, or at least nothing inappropriate, with Charlie. He wondered if it was illegal to have a sixteen-year-old in his house.

"Is this your computer?" R. Miles asked.

"Of course it is."

"Do you mind if I look on your computer?"

"Don't you need some kind of warrant to look on someone's computer?"

R. Miles ambled over to Ira, bent down, and stood with his face approximately three inches from Ira's large nose. The proximity made Ira's knees quiver. "We can do this the easy way or the hard way. The easy way is, you turn on your computer and let me look through it. The hard way is making me go get a warrant, ripping every piece of electronic equipment out of this house, dragging it downtown, and downloading every file you ever created while you sit here and hope there's nothing incriminating on it. The choice is yours."

Ira paced the living room with his arms clasped behind his back before conceding, "Fine... go ahead... look. There's nothing on there."

R. Miles returned to the desk, fiddled with the mouse, and said, "Come here and start this thing up."

Ira sat in the chair with R. Miles hovering over his right shoulder. He turned on the computer and waited, breathing quietly, until the home screen appeared. He waited for R. Miles's next command.

"Which browser do you use?" R. Miles asked.

"Microsoft Explorer. That's all I have on here."

"Good. Fire it up."

Ira hadn't been online in weeks. He'd been using the computer at the Latter Library lately, frustrated with the spotty service of his neighbor's Internet provider. What popped up when the browser finally opened surprised Ira as much as anyone. It was a website he had never seen or heard of—Backpage.com—featuring a profile of a girl named "Rose," complete with pictures of a spiky-haired blonde lying on a mattress in white lace bra and panties, hands cupped below her breasts. The image made Ira's face turn as pale as the panties. A random quote from Shakespeare popped into his mind: "a rose by any other name is still a rose." He lowered his head as R. Miles seized control of the mouse and scanned the other profiles.

With Ira still seated and his shoulders slumped, one hand covering his eyes, R. Miles asked, "Where are the other kids?"

"They're upstairs, why?"

"You have any identification on them?"

"What do you mean? Why?"

"Can you reach their mother and have her pick them up?" R. Miles asked.

"She's in New York. What's all this business about? Where's Charlie? She can explain everything."

"She's on her way to Child Services. If you can't find the mother of these kids, they're going to be following right after her."

"What? That's insane. I didn't do anything wrong."

"Solicitation of a minor is a sex crime." R. Miles said. "It's a felony."

"I didn't solicit anyone."

"Mis-ter Sil-ver," R. Miles said in four very long syllables, "you have an advertisement for a prostitute on your computer who happens to be a sixteen-year-old minor. You just admitted that she is living with you. And you have three Chinese kids here with no proof they are even your children."

"Wait," Ira cut R. Miles off, "are you insinuating that those are not my kids upstairs?"

"They certainly don't look nothing like you."

Ira rifled through his desk, mumbling something like, "I must have some pictures from when they were kids."

"Look, Mr. Silver. You're going to have to come downtown for more questioning. I'll have Child Services come pick up the kids. You can sort this all out with your attorney."

"I don't have an attorney," Ira snapped.

"Then one will be appointed to you. Now stand up, turn around, and put your hands behind your back."

"I didn't do anything wrong," Ira insisted, leaning toward R. Miles, who was now in the middle of the living room.

"That's not for me to determine. You can explain everything to the judge," R. Miles said as he grabbed Ira by his shoulder and the back of his hand, spinning him around. Before Ira could react, handcuffs were slapped around his wrists. The words that followed barely registered, as if this wasn't real life and he was watching himself on TV. "You have the right to remain silent. If you give up that right, anything you say can and will be used against you. You have the right to an attorney. If you cannot afford an attorney, one will be appointed for you. Do you understand those rights as I have read them to you?"

Ira had the stunned look of a bird that had just been shot. He nodded to R. Miles, who led him out the door and into the back of a waiting squad car.

20

Ira had never seen the back of a police cruiser, let alone a jail. For thirty minutes, he sat uncomfortably in the back of R. Miles's car as the officer made several trips to and from the house. The lights went on upstairs and shadows wandered through the small windowpanes next to his front door. Three more men and a woman arrived, dressed in civilian clothes. Ira surmised they were detectives or people from Child Services. The woman escorted his three children, still in their pajamas, out of the house and into the back of an unmarked car. The sight of his scared boys made Ira's eyes fill with tears.

With the children secure, R. Miles finally returned to his car, buckled himself in, and without a word to Ira, began the journey to Orleans Parish Prison. Ira was already in pain. His wrists hurt, his back ached, and his ankle throbbed. His hands were shackled behind his back so he couldn't even rub his flaring ankle. A short time later, they arrived at the dilapidated prison entrance on the corner of Tulane and Broad.

Officer R. Miles escorted Ira through a succession of metal doors into a cold cinderblock room with a Plexiglas partition separating the criminals from an aging sleepy-eyed woman who sat at a counter scrolling through her cell phone. A Styrofoam takeout container holding the remnants of cheap Chinese food splayed out in front of her while grease smears and grains of fried rice littered her computer keyboard. She started typing when Ira and R. Miles approached. Barely glancing at the two figures in front of her, she bellowed flatly, "Name."

"Ira Silver," R. Miles responded.

"Identification," the woman droned.

R. Miles patted down Ira's pockets, producing a thick black wallet stuffed with business cards, loose papers, his identification card, and a single dollar bill. R. Miles handed the woman the ID separately from the wallet.

"Is the information on your ID correct?" she asked.

Ira nodded, but she wasn't looking at him. "Yes," he repeated aloud.

She punched information into the computer and then produced a gallon-sized Ziploc bag that she dropped the wallet and ID into. The printer punched out a small ticket that she affixed to the front of the Ziploc. "Go ahead," she prompted less than invitingly.

A buzzer sounded and a metal door clicked open. Ira entered a room with a dozen desks, each hosting a computer. Six officers punched away on the keyboards. In front of the desks, two seats were occupied with what looked to be criminals. One was a woman dressed in a sequined halter top, black leather miniskirt, and four-inch pumps. She had been crying, as evidenced by the mascara smudged under her eyes. The other was a short guy with cornrows and baggy pants, slouching in his seat, grabbing his crotch. He glared at Ira once as if to threaten, "What the fuck you looking at?"

R. Miles led Ira to a seat at an empty desk where he unlatched his handcuffs. Ira rubbed his sore wrists for a second before R. Miles refastened them with a plastic zip tie, this time in front of Ira rather than behind his back. He then pushed Ira forcefully into the empty seat and commanded, "Sit here."

Ira nearly dozed off in the hard plastic seat, but as his eyes narrowed into little slits, another officer kicked the seat, startling him awake. This man was older, around sixty, and dressed well in a dark blazer and grey slacks with recently polished wingtip loafers. He didn't have a nametag but instead a plastic identification holder hanging around his neck. Nestled in clear plastic was an ID displaying his picture and the name Jessie Clark. He opened the top drawer of the desk and produced a small black plastic box. "Mr. Silver," he began, "do you know why you are here?"

"Not really," Ira said.

"The arrest report says: carnal knowledge of a juvenile, indecent behavior with a juvenile, contributing to the delinquency of a juvenile, possession of child pornography, and promoting prostitution. Do you understand these charges?"

"I didn't do those things," Ira said.

"That's not what I asked. Do you understand the charges?"

"Don't I have a right to speak with a lawyer?" Ira asked.

Officer Clark turned his phone around and handed the receiver to Ira without saying a word. Ira's eyes began to well up with tears before he shook his head and said, "I don't have a lawyer."

"Then one will be appointed to you Monday morning."

"Monday?" Ira yelped.

"Courts are closed on Sunday."

"I'll be in here till Monday?"

"Yes," Clark responded, picking up the black case, removing a white card, and placing it on the desk in front of Ira. He grabbed Ira's wrist, cut off the zip tie, rolled each of his fingers across the black pad, and dabbed Ira's fingerprints onto the white card. A few seconds later, Clark led Ira to a white curtained-wall, stood him up against it, went to another room for a minute, and came back with a camera.

Clark snapped a few pictures before leading Ira to a small changing room. Inside the room was only an orange jumpsuit on a hanger. Ira took off everything but his tighty-whities and handed it all to Clark, who stuffed it into a large clear plastic bag. Clark scrawled letters on the outside of the bag with a big black Sharpie. Ira felt Clark staring at him.

"Strip," Clark prompted.

Ira looked at him. "I did."

"Underwear," Clark yelled.

Ira let the words sink in before slowly removing his boxers, exposing an unruly bush of curly brown pubic hair covering his shriveled pecker.

"Bend over, spread your cheeks, and cough twice," Clark ordered.

Ira was dimly aware that Clark had gotten on his knees behind him as he bent over, sensing that the man was staring up his anus as he summoned two coughs. Ira felt totally emasculated until Clark handed him an orange jumpsuit and told him to get dressed.

The whole process took less than fifteen minutes. Ira was surprised by the efficiency since NOPD isn't normally known for its competence. Clark offered Ira the phone one more time, but Ira couldn't think of anyone to call. He was certain Lin would have been notified of the situation by then and was probably already on her way to the airport. No one else would have picked up the phone at one-thirty in the morning.

Clark led Ira down a succession of long, drab hallways on a walk of shame that rivaled Ira's exit from the mental hospital on the night Lin was committed. At the end of the last hallway, Clark gave Ira another quick pat-down while they waited for the metal door to open.

He then pushed Ira into a small empty room with a second door on the far wall. Ira was left alone there, an eerie silence enveloping his mind. The door clanged shut behind his back. After a minute, a buzzer went off, the door in front of him opened, and intense clamor smacked into Ira's flushed face. It sounded as if a massive brawl was taking place. In the larger room beyond, thirty or forty orange-clad men stopped what they were doing and stared at the new arrival. Ira looked at the faces, most of them black, then lowered his eyes to the floor and shuffled his feet to the center of the room. There really didn't seem to be anywhere else to go. The walls were all blocked by inmates lying down, passed out, or just stretching their legs. The stench was overpowering: a mixture of fresh sweat and old rank body odor, feces, urine, and what may have been bologna sandwiches. The air was so foul that Ira felt vomit traveling through his esophagus, nearly exploding from his mouth. Instead, he held his breath and forced it back down. Against the back wall, an inmate squatted over a filthy stainless-steel toilet bowl strewn with loose toilet paper. Another wall featured what looked to be a large window covered by a metal rollaway grate. Ira was shocked by what he imagined was a complete lack of supervision until he realized that the ceiling opened to a second-floor balcony from which the inmates might be observed. Two sleepy-eyed guards with tasers and batons attached to their belts hunched over the railing, whispering to one another.

Ira was never comfortable in the company of strangers unless he was under the influence of copious amounts of booze, and he figured this situation wasn't going to be any better. As the hours unfolded, most of the men fell asleep, but Ira just stood in the center of the room with his arms folded across his chest and his eyelids nearly closed. Any time Ira felt close to actual sleep, the buzzer sounded, and a new face entered the throng.

Ira heard the retching sound of someone vomiting near the toilet and smelled it every time he took a deep breath. Several of the new-comers found spots to sit down, but Ira felt the need to stand even as his legs got heavier, his ankle pulsated, and his back began to ache. No one really paid him much attention that night, but unfortunately for him, the daytime would take a turn for the much worse.

21

Throughout Sunday, the dregs kept flowing in, pushing the room to maximum density. The volume of voices grew more intense, the stench of bodies escalated well past the point of simply needing a bath. The heat caused tempers to soar. Fights broke out, men bled, guards yelled. Ira managed to keep to himself for the better part of the morning, skipping breakfast, standing half-awake near the back wall of the cell.

With the space between the men closing faster than the minutes in the day, Ira was forced into some of the most uncomfortable conversations he had ever experienced. Some of the lowlights included...

Guy with shaved head and gold teeth: "Got a sister?"

Ira: "No."

Guy with shaved head and gold teeth: "Got a wife?"

Ira: "Not anymore."

Guy with shaved head and gold teeth temporarily lost in thought: "Got a mom?"

Ira: "Yeah."

Guy with shaved head and gold teeth: "Let me fuck her pussy."

Ira: "She's seventy-eight and has dementia."

Guy with shaved head and gold teeth: "Dam-antcha?"

Ira: "Never mind."

And…

Huge guy with afro: "You can get me out of here?"

Ira, temporarily startled by the man's girth: "How?"

Huge guy with afro: "You got money. I know you got money."

Ira: "I'm broke."

Huge guy with afro: "You gone be broke if you ain't be bailing me out."

Ira: "I'll see what I can do."

Huge guy with afro: "Don't be playin' me, fool. I know where you at."

Ira: "I promise I will bail you out."

Huge guy with afro to the rest of the crowd: "Yo homies, Jew boy gone bail me out."

Ira smiled meekly at the crowd.

And…

Young guy with huge empty holes in his earlobes and tattoos on his fingers: "What you in here for?"

Ira: "Um, DUI."

Young guy with huge empty holes in his earlobes and tattoos on his fingers: "That sucks." Pause. "Got any coke?"

Ira: "No."

Young guy with huge empty holes in his earlobes and tattoos on his fingers: "Any speed? Uppers? Molly?"

Ira: "Who's Molly?"

Young guy with huge empty holes in his earlobes and tattoos on his fingers: "Seriously?"

Ira: "I don't know any Mollys."

Young guy with huge empty holes in his earlobes and tattoos on his fingers: "I can score you some."

Ira: "Some what?"

Young guy with huge empty holes in his earlobes and tattoos on his fingers: "Molly. You know, ecstasy."

Ira: "Are you a drug dealer or something? Is that why you're in here?"

Young guy with huge empty holes in his earlobes and tattoos on his fingers: "No, man. I killed my girlfriend's mother."

Ira, startled by the admission, backed himself into a corner and left the guy talking to himself in the center of the room.

As the afternoon rolled on, Ira felt the effects of missing out on coffee that morning. It started with a tension in the back of his neck, followed by a general throbbing in his frontal lobes. An hour later, his eye sockets felt like they were being sucked out by a vacuum cleaner. By the time dinner rolled into the room, Ira's neck felt like it was carrying the weight of a gold bar and his head was caught in giant forceps. He was so nauseous, it made no difference what food was being served; he couldn't eat a thing.

As the restless Sunday evening came to a close, Ira felt a harsh slap on the back of his neck which sent him scurrying across the cement floor, landing hard on his knees. He didn't turn to look at the benefactor of the crippling blow, but rather managed to crawl the remaining few feet until he squeezed himself between two men, both sleeping and stinking of alcohol and body odor.

Ira spent the night in and out of consciousness. A couple of times he felt a roach crawl across his legs. At one point, when he heard nothing but loud snoring, he judged it safe to get up and take a leak, stepping over a man whose head was resting on the side of the metal toilet bowl. The splatter of piss woke the man, who was clearly still inebriated. He opened one crusty red eye, cursed at Ira, and angrily swatted his ankles, forcing him to cut his piss short.

Without the benefit of a clock or watch or any outside light, Ira could only assume that it was morning when an officer came to the window and started calling out names: Joshua Jones, Maliki Ussam, Curtis Henderson. As names were called, men formed a makeshift line by the front wall until a different officer escorted each to their attorneys and then to stand in front of a judge and await their fate. Boris Dotchinsky, with shaved head and tattoos scrawled across his neck, slept next to Ira. When his name was called and he got up, Ira took his spot on the ground, grabbed the intact toilet paper roll he'd been using as a pillow, and squeezed it behind his aching neck.

As more men were summoned, the agitation grew amongst those still waiting. Ira learned that the men with "real" lawyers went first, while the men with court-appointed attorneys had to wait. With thirty or so still remaining, an officer handed out trays with the day's breakfast. Ira at first waved it off, but the man sitting to his left who Ira thought was sleeping hissed at him, "Take it, motherfucker."

Ira grabbed the tray of oatmeal, toast, and the most liquid scrambled eggs he'd ever seen, along with a small plastic spoon, and returned to his solitary spot against the wall. The man next to him, who hadn't yet moved, slid his hand over Ira's knee and pulled the tray into the small space between the two of them. The motion of the man's hand over Ira's thigh and perilously close to his genitals made him shiver and clutch his arms over his chest. Ira fought back the tears readying themselves in his ducts, knowing full well that any act of emotion might end in the worst beating of his life.

Over the next few hours, Ira sat against the wall half asleep as new men entered and others left. The yelling and screaming kept him mostly awake, but in the brief moments of doze, he had nightmares of the life present and the life to come. He dreamt of his new daily existence as a registered sex offender. For the first time in his life, he even contemplated suicide as a fate more desirable than the other potential ones attacking his brain.

As lunch was served, Ira could no longer bear the pains of hunger that tore through his empty stomach. He stood in line with the other men and warily accepted the cardboard tray: one slice of mystery meat on Bunny bread, a bruised, nearly rotten apple, and a wafer that reminded him of that stuff his Catholic friends ate at Communion. One of the men took a sandwich and threw it against the wall above Ira's head. Everyone looked and waited for it to fall, but it clung to the wall like a squid on the side of a fish tank.

With the day dragging into oblivion, Ira tried his best to keep to himself until a squirrely little guy probably in his mid-fifties came over and asked for a cigarette. He was twitching and itching his arms like a crack junkie, asking everyone for cigarettes, although Ira hadn't seen anyone smoking and wondered what he would do if someone actually did give him a cancer stick. After Ira turned away his multiple overtures, the man asked him whether he was going to make a phone call. Ira hadn't used the phone yet since the line seemed never-ending, not to mention the humungous guy hovering next to it, pushing guys out of their spots every time he felt a violent impulse.

"Why?" Ira finally asked the man after his fifth attempt.

"I want to listen," he said.

"You want to listen?" Ira repeated.

"Your wife. I want to listen to your wife. Is she hot?"

"I'm not married."

"You suck cock?"

Ira paused before continuing, wondering if there was a right or wrong answer. "I do not."

"You got money?"

"I do not."

"I can get you out of here if you got money," the man said, while tearing at the skin on his arm. The arm was full of black and blue marks, skin lesions, tiny holes, and black and white tattoos.

Although Ira doubted the validity of the statement, he didn't feel the need to contradict the man. All he wanted was to not have to talk to him anymore. His nasty hot breath sprayed into Ira's pained face. The man kept the conversation going, every so often getting so close to Ira's face he thought he might get kissed. Ira tried to tune the man out completely until he started grabbing his arm, like a child talking to his deaf father, constantly tapping him to make sure he was being heard.

By the middle of the afternoon, Ira couldn't stand it anymore. When the other inmates started yelling, he yelled too. When a guy checked in wearing a thick veil of makeup, complete with painted eyebrows and lip liner, the group whistled jokingly and Ira hooted along. Despite the mockery, the ladyboy seemed to enjoy the attention, striking sexy poses for the entertainment of the room.

Finally, as pangs of hunger started to overcome his body, a bailiff called, "Silver. Ira Silver."

Shuffling over to the door, Ira tried to regain some sense of composure before saying, "Me. That's me."

"Follow me," said the guard and led Ira back through the maze of cinderblock hallways. Stopping in front of a metal door, the man waited until it opened, greeted another guard, and handed Ira off to him. They were in a room with a half dozen seats, each with a glass partition separating prisoner from visitor.

At an open desk, Ira took a seat and faced a young man who slouched in his chair with his right leg crossed over his other knee and fumbled through a stack of loose papers sitting on top of a leather binder. He wore thick-framed glasses and sported a head full of wavy sand-colored hair that looked like he had just awoken from a nap on a nearby desk.

"Are you my lawyer?" Ira asked.

"No, I'm just a temporary P.D.," he said.

"What's a P.D.?"

"Oh, uh, public defender."

"Where's my lawyer?"

"I'll represent you through the bail hearing and if it's serious, you'll be assigned a permanent public defender," he said.

"Have you done this before?"

"Of course," he said, looking sheepishly at the files on his lap.

"How long have you been doing this?"

"Two weeks."

"Two weeks? How do I get a real lawyer?" Ira asked.

"I guess you pay for one. This is just procedural stuff, Mr. Silver. I can handle this. If you have to go to trial or anything like that, one of the more experienced public defenders will step in. They're really backed up right now on their caseloads. That's why I'm here."

Ira didn't say anything for a minute, just watched his excuse for a lawyer thumb through the stack of papers until finally settling on the one he was looking for.

"Do you have a name?" Ira asked.

"Oh, sorry. I'm Derrick. Derrick Bailey."

"What's the deal here? What am I looking at?" Ira asked.

Derrick looked at the paper in his hand, scanned down it, mumbled, "Mmm-hmm," a few times, lowered it to the table, and said, "This is nothing. Should be twenty-five hundred, at the most."

"Twenty-five hundred dollars?" Ira yelped.

"Is that a problem?"

"I don't have twenty-five hundred dollars."

"You can get a bail bondsman. Do you have any collateral?"

"Like what?" Ira asked.

"Like a car or a house or anything you own."

"I don't have a car and the house is in my mother's name. Is that okay?"

"Yeah, of course. She just has to sign the slip."

Ira had the look of a six-year-old doing a puzzle. "She can't sign anything. She has Alzheimer's."

Derrick returned the confused look and said, "You don't know anyone that will put up twenty-five hundred bucks?"

"I have to think about it."

"Okay, you do that," Derrick said. "Now go stand over there and they'll shackle you to some other guys and march you into court. Probably take about thirty minutes. After you post bail, you'll be out of here in two hours max."

Ira hadn't noticed the line of men standing against the back wall. When he stood up, a guard pushed him next to another orange jumpsuit and handcuffed their wrists together, leaving Ira's right arm free for a few minutes until the next guy was shoved up next to him.

22

Walking shackled to a man twice his size felt to Ira like that little girl must have felt being dragged by her hair through the streets of Shenzhen. Drudging through the courtroom barely able to control the movement of his own limbs, Ira stumbled through the front row of seating until the line stopped and the men turned in forced unison. The guard let out a soft whistle and nodded his head for the men to sit, and they did.

Ira couldn't turn around, but he felt the empty stares of family members, friends, lovers and the like uncomfortably waiting for the fate of their man to be decided. He knew there was no one there waiting for him. What remained of his family were in San Francisco and New York. The rest of the Silver clan had died off years ago. Mother and Father each had one sibling, and neither was lucky in the love department. What few friends Ira had growing up had moved on with their own lives and didn't keep in touch. His staff at the paper—most had never returned from Houston and Atlanta after Katrina. Sitting there, tired and alone, sad and disheveled, hungry and hurt, Ira closed his eyes and silently cried.

Directly in front of the men sat two desks, each holding two microphones and dozens of manila folders piled high with loose scraps of paper. At the desk to the right, Derrick Bailey rifled through the folders, organizing them in a way that made him look like he was just trying to keep himself busy. At the desk to the left, two men and a woman, all dressed in poorly tailored suits, divvied up the folders, scribbled notes, and whispered to each other.

Over the next fifteen minutes, two more strings of inmates filed into the courtroom and followed the routine, the sound of metal chains clinking against the wooden benches. After all the men were seated and the guards hushed them to silence, a bailiff entered the room and asked everyone to rise for the honorable Morton T. Robinson.

As the defendants scuffled to their feet, a tall man with short, curly charcoal hair in a black robe entered the courtroom and seated himself at the altar on a riser above the crowd, while the bailiff motioned everyone to sit. The orange-clad men dropped back to their seats in a motion that looked like the wave at a baseball game. Judge Robinson shifted in his seat, took his bifocals from their case, and adjusted his glasses to scan the stack of papers on his desk.

"When I call your name," Judge Robinson bellowed, "please rise and state your plea for the record."

Ira listened to the list and the litany of charges against these men—all not guilty, at least in the eyes of the public defender. There was little banter between the judge and lawyer, just a few simple yes-or-no questions followed by a set amount of money to post bail. Sometimes the judge offered a reduced property bail while other times, if the crime was heinous enough, he left one large number hanging in the air like a balloon on the dregs of its life support. Most of the guys were already on probation or repeat offenders.

The man to Ira's left was no more than a boy. He could have been thirteen or eighteen, Ira couldn't tell. He was tall and chubby, but there was so much child still in his clumsy mannerisms. When he rose to his feet, the judge admonished him.

"Mr. Anderson, didn't I see you here last month?"

"Uh-huh," Anderson said.

"Mr. Anderson, show the bench some respect."

"Yes sir."

"Didn't I tell you if I saw you here again, I'd throw the book at you?"

"No sir. I mean, yes sir."

Judge Robinson scanned the page in front of his face, looked up once, then back down at the page. "Mr. Anderson, you stole another car?"

"No sir. I is innocent."

"You *is* innocent," the judge mimicked. "Is that your plea?"

"Yes sir."

"I am assuming you haven't gotten a job between last month and today. Is that correct?"

"Yes sir. I mean, no sir."

A stream of sweat floated down the side of the kid's scarred cheek. His entire bottom row of teeth was ensconced in gold which shined through his large puffy lips as he spoke.

"And you are still living with your mom?"

"Yep, my mom and 'dem."

"You are still over at Walter Cohen?"

"No sir. Dropped out."

"You do realize you aren't a juvie anymore? Stealing cars is a felony offense."

"But I ain't steal no cars. I just be riding in them."

"We aren't here to decide whether you stole a car or not," the judge said. "We are here to determine whether you are a flight risk."

"I ain't never flown nowhere."

The judge had the look of a father scolding his two-year-old son, knowing that the latter wasn't going to stop flushing paper towels down the toilet. While shaking his head, he said, "Bail is set at twenty-five thousand. Defendant will be remanded to Orleans Parish Prison." And Judge Robinson lowered the gavel toward the table with a resounding thud. Anderson slunk back down in the seat next to Ira.

"Next up is Mr. Ira Silver. 4238 St. Charles Avenue. Please rise."

Ira stumbled to his feet, tried to raise his hand, but with it shackled to Anderson, he ended up giving the judge a feeble shrug. The judge looked toward Mr. Bailey, who was still fumbling through his manila folders. "Does Mr. Silver have a job?"

"He does, Your Honor."

"And what is that job?"

"He is the publisher of the *New Orleans Jewish Monthly.*"

"Mr. Silver, you are aware that public defenders are for the indigent?"

"No sir. I was not aware of that."

"So, you can pay for your own attorney?"

"No sir, I cannot," Ira answered.

"But you have a job."

"Yes sir, but it doesn't pay very well."

"And you live on St. Charles Avenue?" the judge said, leaning forward and arching his back toward Ira.

"In Mother's house."

"Listen, Mr. Silver. Are you wasting the court's time? The public defenders are very busy. Can you afford an attorney or not?"

"Do you know any that take trade?"

Judge Robinson took off his glasses and rubbed his temples. "Let's just continue. Mr. Bailey, does Mr. Silver have family in the area?"

"His kids are in New York."

"My kids are back in New York?" Ira asked.

Both judge and lawyer whipped their heads over to stare at Ira. "Mr. Silver, I wasn't talking to you."

"I'm sorry, Your Honor. I was just wondering if my kids made it home safely."

"I am not aware of the safety of your children, Mr. Silver. What I am aware of are the charges against you. You are charged with carnal knowledge of a juvenile, indecent behavior with a juvenile, contributing to the delinquency of a juvenile, solicitation of a juvenile, and promoting prostitution. Those are some pretty serious charges. Felonies. With your children in another state, that would make you a flight risk, wouldn't it?"

"No sir. I've never been to New York. If I went anywhere, I'd go back to China."

Derek Bailey groaned loudly and said under his breath, "Ira, shut the fuck up."

"Excuse me, Mr. Bailey. Did you just curse in my courtroom?" Judge Robinson asked.

"I'm sorry. I didn't mean to."

"Look, consider this a warning. If I ever hear you curse in my courtroom again, I will cite you for contempt of court."

"I understand. I am very sorry."

"Now, Mr. Silver, what is this I hear about China?"

"That's where I met Lin."

"Who is Lin?" the judge asked.

"My ex-wife."

"And you will go to China if you make bail?"

"No, I didn't say that. I can't afford to go to China. My parents paid for the last trip."

"Maybe your parents will pay for another one?" Judge Robinson asked.

"Father passed on and Mother doesn't remember who I am."

"What about your home? Can you post a property bond?"

"The house belongs to Mother."

"And where does Mother live?"

"Over at the Lambeth House."

"Do you have any other family in New Orleans?"

"I do not."

"How do you plea?" the judge asked.

Ira gaped at Derek and he nodded back. Ira took a deep breath and let out a muffled, "Not guilty."

"For the record, Mr. Silver pleads not guilty," bellowed Judge Robinson. "Mr. Bailey, I think your client here presents a significant flight risk. I'm setting bail at fifty thousand dollars. Next."

23

"Fifty thousand dollars?!" Ira screamed at the public defender when he entered the room.

"It's really only five thousand cash. The rest is collateral," said Derrick Bailey.

The two men were back in the closet-sized room separated by a glass partition. Bailey motioned for Ira to pick up the phone on the wall.

"I don't have five thousand *or* collateral," Ira pronounced loudly into the phone.

"Nothing? What about your house?"

"It's not my house. It's Mother's house."

"She can sign the bond."

"No she can't," Ira said. "I already told you, she's currently incapacitated."

"Who has power of attorney?"

"Shelly Rubenstein."

"The lawyer?"

"Yep."

"Oh man. How'd you end up with her?"

Ira couldn't help but chuckle at the remark. It was more of a grunt than a chuckle, that is, but the sentiment was the same.

Ira knew that if his fate were in the hands of Shelly Rubenstein, he would spend the rest of his life in prison. Not that she was a bad attorney. From what he knew, he heard that she was quite capable in her job as a family lawyer. But she had had it out for Ira since the day they met. It was at a house party during Mardi Gras back in the early nineties, and Shelly was talking to Father about something Ira couldn't overhear. When the conversation ended, Father gave her a warm embrace that lasted almost a minute. Ira never got a hug from Father like that, and it sparked a fit of jealousy in him.

Later on that evening, Ira and Shelly were alone on the porch when he introduced himself. She was built like a linebacker with hair cropped in what resembled a crew cut and she shook Ira's hand so hard that he had to shake it off when she let go. A pretty young woman with long blonde hair walked out of the front door and introduced herself as Margie as she grabbed Shelly by the elbow. Ira rolled his eyes and said, "You two aren't together, are you?"

Shelly immediately went on the defensive. "Why would you say that?"

Ira stuttered a few inane syllables before spitting out, "No reason."

Shelly repeated more accusingly, "Then why would you say it?"

"I don't know."

"Well, try to have a little more couth next time," she said.

Ira backed his way off the porch and into the house as Shelly kissed Margie on the lips. He remembered little else from that night, but from then on, he tried to avoid Shelly like a coronavirus.

"What happens if I can't make bail?" he asked Bailey.

"First off, we'll try to get the bail reduced. As long as there are no additional charges, I should be able to get it cut in half in a few weeks."

"A few weeks?" Ira cried. "I'll never last in here a few weeks."

"If you don't post bail, you'll be in here a few months."

Ira screamed like a little girl at a horror movie, the pitch a few octaves below an off-key trumpet. "Seriously, Derrick, you have to get me out of here!"

"There must be someone you can call to post bail?"

Ira tilted his head back as far as it could go and stared at the ceiling, lost in thought. When he dropped his chin back down, his eyes were full of tears and his head shook back and forth. "What about the girl? She can prove I'm innocent."

"It's not about proving your innocence at this point. It'll be months before you even get a trial date."

"Can't she drop the charges?"

"She didn't press charges, Ira. The state..." Derrick paused. "The state thinks you're involved in a sex trafficking scheme."

"Sex trafficking?!" Ira yelled into the spit-covered base of the phone.

"They think you're the big man."

Ira started hyperventilating into the phone, his short breaths interspersed with salty tears streaming down his flushed cheeks. "I'm not a big man," he managed to get out in between sobs. "I'm a little man. I'm a small guy. This is ridiculous. I haven't done anything wrong."

"Listen, Ira. This is the kind of case the Feds might get involved in."

"*The Feds?!*" Ira screamed.

Derrick shushed Ira with his lips and a gesture of both his hands. "Interstate sex trafficking is a very serious crime."

"Interstate what? What do you mean, interstate?"

"Your lady friend is from out of state, right?"

"I don't know where the hell she's from."

"Well, she ain't from around here is all I know."

"You don't know her name?" Ira asked.

"All I know right now is that she's sixteen and she's listed as Witness A."

"She's a witness against me?"

"That's not necessarily what that means."

"What does it mean?"

"It just means that she's part of an active investigation."

"How can we find her?" Ira asked.

"When it's time for discovery…"

"Discovery? How long will that be?"

"I don't know. Six months, maybe a year. Depends on the judge. If it goes federal, it might be longer."

Ira started back in with his wheezing, crying, hyperventilating, trying to articulate the dates as best he could. "Six, huh, huh, months… huh, huh, a, huh, huh, huh, year…"

"Look, Ira. You live on St. Charles Avenue. You need to start thinking about who you can call in a favor to. Maybe you can find someone to sublet the house."

"Sublet the what? Oh, no, Mother would never allow that."

"I thought Mother was… what'd you say? Incapacitated."

"I wouldn't feel right about someone living in our house."

"You don't have a lot of choices here. You want to spend the next year in prison?"

Ira just shook his head and stared down at the table. Finally, he whispered, "I'll think of something."

A guard with a flat pug nose that looked like Mr. Frumble came in and announced the end of the conversation. Ira stood up and stuck his hands out for the guard to refasten the cuffs around his wrists. He glanced one last time at the man who controlled his fate. Mr. Bailey was looking down at the papers, lost in thought with his thumb jammed up his left nostril, picking at it.

24

Mr. Frumble led Ira down a series of long, dimly lit hallways. There was only the sound of the officer's boots plodding over the cement floor. It was easily the most frightened Ira had ever been in his whole life. The fear made the hairs on the back of his neck stand at attention. At the end of the maze, Ira stood in front of a video monitor and a steel door that popped open after thirty seconds.

On the other side of the door, his ears were assaulted by a din that reminded him of hell. Shrieking, banging, screaming, and a constant slapping noise enveloped the air like a funnel cloud in a tornado. Ira was led past a series of cells, most of them full of black men staring at the fresh meat walking the plank. Ira stared at one with a word tattooed across his forehead a little too long; the guy's eyes widened and he ran his thumb across his neck threateningly.

Ira was still trying to figure out what the tattooed letters spelled when he realized he was standing in front of an open cell door. Mr. Frumble took Ira's wrists and opened the handcuffs, pushing Ira into the eight-by-eight room. "Be nice, boys," he said, closing the door behind him.

The room held three bunk beds—one against each blank wall—with a metal toilet tucked behind the one on the right, and five men. Five men confined to less than one hundred square feet. And Ira made six.

The most prevalent sensation the room introduced was the mix of feces and body odor drifting into Ira's nostrils. It nearly knocked him off his feet. Two young skinny guys with their shirts off were lying down on the bottom right bunk flipping through a magazine, barely taking notice of the new arrival. A guy with spiky black hair and dark oblique eyes stared down at Ira menacingly from the top bunk. On the bottom left bunk, two older guys were playing cards and cursing at each other. Ira couldn't understand anything they were saying; it was a slang he'd heard before but could never quite figure out.

Ira froze about a foot from the door with his hands covering his crotch and his eyes staring absently at the toilet bowl. One of the two young guys stopped looking at the magazine, glared at Ira, and let a sucking sound slip out of his bottom lip. He rose from the bed, stuck his hand out, and introduced himself as Orphan, or perhaps Orvin, Ira couldn't quite discern.

"Where is you at?" Orphan asked.

Ira couldn't comprehend the question or really figure out an answer that might be appropriate, so he said, "Right here."

The other guy diverted his eyes from the magazine and glanced at Ira before dropping it at the foot of the bed. It was a nudie magazine open to a photo of a dark-skinned woman showing off her large booty in a white thong. "I's Chocolate," he said, sliding out of the bunk and standing up. "You like 'em black? You ever fucked a black chick in the ass?"

Ira had no idea what a right or wrong answer was in this situation. He was about as far out of his element as any human being could be. He let out a half-hearted, "Uh, no."

"You want to look? Go 'head. Take a look," Chocolate said. "It's a'ight."

Ira hesitated, knowing that every eye in the room was now staring at him, waiting for his next move. Chocolate held his palm out, gesturing for Ira to sit on the bed, and that was the only movement in the room besides a large roach crawling up the back wall.

Ira stiffened his aching back, cracked his neck from side to side, shuffled his feet to the end of the bed, bent his knees, and grabbed the tattered magazine in his hands. As his backside struck the thin mattress, one of the guys playing cards bellowed, "Who the fuck you think you are?"

Moving at the speed of a welterweight boxer, the man shifted his body off the bed, flew across the room, and struck Ira with a vicious open-fisted blow across his right ear. Ira was already moving off the bed away from the oncoming attack, so the weight of the slap made him literally fly across the room like a paper airplane and strike the metal bars with such force that his head nearly went through and got stuck like in a *Tom and Jerry* cartoon. Somewhere between hitting the bars and landing on the floor, Ira saw stars. He blacked out and bled on the cold hard cement.

25

Ira had no idea how much time had lapsed between that crushing blow and the officer opening the door and peeling him off the floor. In fact, he barely registered where he was, but he finally realized he was being escorted back out of the cellblock, through the same steel door and long hallway he had traversed earlier.

With his hands cuffed and dried blood stuck to the side of his head, the officer pushed Ira into the little room with the black telephone. He forcefully grabbed Ira's hands and unlatched the cuffs before dropping him into the plastic seat in front of the Plexiglas window.

Minutes ticked off the clock, leaving Ira with nothing to do but contemplate his predicament. He replayed the past three months in his head, oscillating between the moments he'd known that Charlie was nothing but trouble and the memory of the sense of purpose he'd felt in her presence. Wanting nothing more than companionship and hoping that his guidance might lead the poor girl to a better life, Ira had ended up instead destroying his own life.

When the door opened, Ira nearly puked at the sight of the squat woman in the three-piece suit with the closely cropped military 'do. He hadn't seen Shelly Rubenstein since she attacked him on the stairs of the courthouse following his paternity suit with Lin. Though they had known each other for over a decade, Shelly and

Ira always had a contentious relationship, but it hadn't fully blown up until they got into an all-out brawl that left Ira with five stitches above his right eye where a permanent scar now resides. Shelly was heralded as one of the best in the business when it came to family law, and she blamed Ira for botching his own defense. In retaliation, Ira made the mistake of questioning her "unnatural attraction" to the judge. This resulted in a left hook to his face that he was somehow able to dodge before tumbling down the sprawling staircase and landing on his bloodied noggin.

Shelly looked like she would have rather been at her mother's funeral than sitting three feet away from her nemesis, and she avoided eye contact for the first couple of minutes after sitting down. When she finally looked at Ira, her eyes lit up with a smidgeon of empathy at the sight. "You look about the same as when I saw you last," she chuckled.

"That's not funny," Ira said. "What are *you* doing here?"

"I am your legal counsel," she said, shuffling the papers in front of her.

"That's not possible. Who ordered you?"

"I'm not a Big Mac, Ira. People don't order lawyers. They pay for lawyers, and frankly, I am worth every cent."

"Not in my experience," Ira said.

"Would you like me to leave? I'd be happy to."

Ira thought about his alternatives, about the prospect of returning to that repugnant cell and the likelihood of Derrick Bailey botching his defense. Perhaps he waited a bit too long to respond; Shelly rose from her chair, slammed the phone back on its base, and stuck her fat ass in Ira's face as she re-zipped her tote bag and started for the door.

"No, wait. Who paid you?" Ira yelled, banging his fist against the Plexiglas.

Shelly turned, fluttered her eye at Ira, and picked the phone back up. "Howie."

"My son?"

"How many Howies do you know?"

"Where did he get that kind of money?"

"It's Chun's money. Howie just flew up there with his brothers and picked it up. Flew back down this morning by himself with fifty thousand in cash. No surety bond. Very unusual."

"I knew that man was up to no good. Anyone with that kind of cash is up to no good."

Shelly placed both her hands on the telephone stand, leaned in as close to the partition as she could without smashing her nose up against it, and yelled, "*You're* no good, Ira. You're the one who's in jail. Leave it to you to be so ungrateful to the one person who can actually get you out of here."

Ira slouched in the chair, put his hand on his head, and started scratching the scar above his eyebrow. "What now?"

"We posted bail. It's all procedural bullshit now. You should be out of here in a couple of hours."

"Don't let them send me back in there," Ira pleaded with a muffled cry.

"They won't. You'll be in a holding cell by yourself till this all goes through."

"Thank God."

"See you on the outside," Shelly said, straining to smile.

"I didn't do anything wrong."

Shelly put her finger to her lips and shushed Ira, pointing at the video camera. Trying her best to give him a smidgen of empathy, she said, "I know."

26

Three hours later, Ira limped out of central lockup and emerged to darkening overcast skies and a cool breeze. Shelly met Ira at the exit and walked him to her car—a Toyota Prius—where Howie was sitting in the front seat. She opened the back door for Ira and he slid in and muttered, "Hello, son."

Howie didn't say anything. Instead he looked in the rearview mirror at the crusty remnants of dried blood on the side of his father's head. Shaking his own head in disbelief, he whistled.

"Thanks for getting me out of there," Ira said.

"Mom and Dad did it."

That hurt Ira more than anything else that happened that day. He hadn't ever heard Chun referred to as Dad, and until that moment he had shrugged off Howie's previous references to him as Ira. It made a tear drizzle down the side of his face, burning the still fresh cut on his cheek.

Shelly got in the front seat, looked back at Ira, and said, "Man, you smell terrible. I bet you're hungry though."

"I haven't eaten in three days."

"How 'bout Lindy's," she said as a statement more than a question.

"I don't have any money," Ira said.

"Of course you don't. Don't worry about it. I'll buy you dinner."

"You don't have to do that."

"You have got to be the most ungrateful P.O.S. I've ever... Oh, never mind. Just shut up and eat."

The car stopped on a small side street in Mid-City, not far from the courthouse. Lindy's, a popular neighborhood joint with seating for sixty patrons, was nearly empty early that evening. They followed the hostess toward the back, passing the staff—mostly middle-aged male servers—who cringed at the sight of Ira's battered face.

As soon as they sat, Ira excused himself and headed for the bathroom. It was the first time he had looked in a mirror since his frantic calls to the police on Saturday, and what he saw freaked him out more than anything he had seen the past couple days. On top of his bald head were the faint remains of a footprint. The gash on the side of his face looked like it needed three stitches to close. Both of his eyes were black, but he couldn't tell if it was from lack of sleep or the swollen nose. The face that he saw in the mirror looked a decade older than the face he remembered after Charlie's shave and haircut.

Ira lathered a layer of soap over his hands and scrubbed the dirt from his fingernails, then washed his face the best he could, reopening a trickle of blood that he clotted with a piece of toilet paper. Locked in the tight confines of the toilet stall, a cold sweat took hold of Ira, claustrophobia overcoming his fragile psyche. He tried to shit, but only a trickle of diarrhea fell from his anus. The odor of his foul body combined with the stench rising from the toilet nearly made him pass out on the seat, but he managed to finish his duty and stumble out of the bathroom, where he met another patron standing in wait. "Do not go in there," Ira mumbled.

The man didn't listen, and Ira saw him open the door, step inside, and immediately jump back out, close the door, and cover his mouth like he was about to vomit.

Shelly and Howie were still perusing the menu with three water glasses on the table as Ira walked up. "We ordered onion rings," Shelly said.

"I hate onion rings," Ira said.

"Then don't eat them," Shelly said.

Ira grabbed a seat and the waiter appeared. "Can I get a beer?" he asked.

"What kind of beer would you like?" the waiter asked.

"What's your happy hour?"

The waiter looked at his watch. "Just in time. Two-for-one High Lifes."

"Great. I'll take two High Lifes."

"At the same time?"

"You have a cold mug? You can put one in there."

The waiter walked off with Shelly and Howie staring at Ira, slightly shaking their heads. In the center of the table sat salt and pepper shakers, Tabasco, Crystal, and a sugar caddie. Grabbing his water glass, Ira squeezed the lemon and dumped six packets of sugar into it, stirring vigorously with a butter knife. Picking up the Tabasco, Ira opened the cap and wiped the top with a cloth napkin. His OCD was in full effect. Shelly grabbed the Crystal and moved it to the other side of the table as far from Ira as she could.

The waiter brought a chilled glass of beer, a basket of French bread, and some butter. Ira devoured the entire loaf while the others looked on, unable to converse in the face of such childlike gobbling. Shelly took to hiding her face behind the large tri-fold menu.

"Have you all decided?" the waiter asked when he appeared once more.

Shelly and Howie waited for Ira's response, but instead he said to Shelly, "No, you go ahead."

"I think I'll try the Atchafalaya Pizza," Shelly said.

"That sounds good," Ira said.

"Would you like one of those as well?" the waiter asked.

"Of course not. Who gets two of the same pizza? Howie, what are you having?"

"Penne alfredo."

"Penne alfredo?" Ira repeated, raising his voice. "You can get that anywhere. Why don't you eat some New Orleans food?"

"I don't like New Orleans food."

Ira rolled his eyes.

"And you, sir?" the waiter asked.

"I'll have the steak burger with sautéed mushrooms."

"Would you like the regular fries or the sweet potato fries?"

"Both... please."

"I think that was an either/or question, Ira. Are you retarded? When was the last time you ate at an actual restaurant?" Shelly asked.

The waiter was still standing there with his pen perched against the pad when another waiter placed the onion rings in the center of the table. Ira inched the plate away from himself. "I'll have both fries," he said, winking at the waiter, who scribbled in his pad and left the table. "Now what?" Ira asked Shelly.

"Now... you thank me for representing you?"

"No, I mean, now what do we do?"

Shelly placed her fingertips over her temples and rubbed for a second before looking back up. "We try to build your case."

"That shouldn't be too hard. I didn't do anything wrong."

"Are you that naïve? Wait, stupid question. Of course you are. You realize that you are looking at ten years in prison, five years of probation, and you will have to register as a sex offender for the rest of your life?"

"But I didn't do anything. Tell her, Howie."

Howie leaned back in his chair and looked at Shelly, then glanced back at Ira before shrugging.

"You don't believe me?" Ira asked.

"I believe you," he said. "Charlie told me."

"Told you what?"

"That you were the worst sugar daddy ever."

"I never laid a hand on that girl," Ira said with a look of scorn in his beady eyes.

"She told me that too."

"Good," Ira said, "then it's settled."

"What's settled?" Shelly cut in.

"That I'm innocent."

"What about all that Backpage stuff on your computer?" Shelly asked.

"All hers, I guess."

"We are going to need her to prove that, aren't we?" Shelly asked.

Ira looked at Howie and both their shoulders slumped. The waiter brought the food and they ate, all quietly contemplating the situation, with Ira chewing like a drunk cow. With a mouthful of fries, he ordered two more beers.

"Look, Ira," Shelly said, "I can probably plea bargain you out of this with probation, but you are going to have to deal with that sex offender tag."

"Is that a big deal?"

"Of course it is, you idiot. You won't be able to live in your house."

"Why not?" Ira asked.

"Because sex offenders can't live within a mile of a school."

"Sacred Heart's a few blocks away."

"No shit, Einstein."

"I could sell the house and live somewhere else."

"It isn't your house to sell," Shelly reminded him. "I'm sure your sister would have something to say about that."

"Sarah?" Ira asked, rhetorically. "She's got more money than she knows what to do with. Are you going to finish your pizza?"

Shelly shook her head again, her eyes beginning to take on a bit of steam. She picked the last slice up off the tin and dropped it into Ira's outstretched hand. Ira pointed at the Crystal still sitting on the other end of the table and Howie passed it to him. He undid the cap with one hand, drenched the pizza with hot sauce, and started eating before he even put the bottle back on the table, swallowing the pizza in three large bites.

"What should we do?" Howie asked.

Shelly looked at Ira still chewing the remainder of his crust. "Probably find another lawyer. I'm a divorce lawyer, not a criminal attorney. Even if I wanted to represent you, which I don't, you should probably find someone else. But one thing I do know: Whatever you do, do not leave the state of Louisiana."

27

"Howie," Ira moaned.

No answer.

The room was pitch black and Ira was partially covered by a ragged duvet. "Howie," he called a little louder, followed by a prolonged whimper.

Ira tried to roll over, but his foot felt like it had fallen asleep and then had an aneurism in the middle of the night. The pain was so intense, Ira had to bite his pillow and hold his breath while tears and sweat drenched his entire head.

It was the beginning of another gout attack and he knew he would suffer great pain and indignity over the next few days, with little he could do to suppress it. For temporary relief, he had to get to the freezer in the hope that he'd remembered to refill the ice cube tray, but he feared the thought of not making it all the way and getting stuck on the stairs, unable to move.

"Howie," he screamed as loud as he could, hoping to rouse the sleeping teenager in the nearby bedroom, but to no avail.

Ira held his leg in the air as long as he could, hoping the loss of blood would alleviate some of the pain, but he knew that the relief would be short-lived. He rolled his body out of bed and landed hard on the floor on his left foot, quickly hopping to his closed bedroom door. Grabbing the doorknob and twisting with his left hand, trying desperately to massage his foot with his right hand, Ira pulled the door open and screamed, "Help," before slumping to the floor and writhing in pain.

Now wishing he had stayed in bed, he scooched his backside across the floor in the general direction of the staircase, rubbing his foot the entire way. After turning the corner of the railing, Ira pushed open Howie's bedroom door only to find the room dark and empty. Struggling to remember the night before, he was now confused about whether Howie had even spent the night.

At the top of the stairwell, Ira contemplated his choices. He could shimmy himself down the stairs and out the front door, hoping for a stranger to take pity on his wayward body. Doubting his chances of making it to one of the neighbor's houses and the likelihood that they would even be willing to help, Ira thought it probable that only unseemly characters would be walking down St. Charles Avenue in the middle of the night. Choice number two would have been to call an ambulance, but Ira knew those EMTs charged ghastly rates for their services and he couldn't afford to deal with more collection agencies at this point. His third choice was to call someone for help, but Ira felt like he'd already exhausted the help of anyone who would actually answer the phone at this time of night.

He decided that the fourth and best option was to make it to the freezer and hope that either the ice was full or there was a package of lima beans he had forgotten about. He made it halfway down the stairs before the pain became too intense for him to move any further so he laid his body down on the step and squeezed his foot between the railings so that he could get some temporary relief by forcing the blood away from the pain.

And that is how Howie found his father when he opened the front door and walked into the foyer. Rather than rush to Ira's aid, Howie let out a huge belly laugh.

"I'm glad you find this funny," Ira said.

"Sorry. It's the last thing I expected to see. What are you doing?"

"I'm having a gout flare-up."

"What's that?"

"Rich man's disease."

"Then how'd you get it?"

"The burger and beer from last night. I'm not supposed to eat red meat or drink beer."

"Then why'd you have a burger and beer?" Howie asked.

"'Cause it was free," Ira said in a way that made the answer sound obvious. He gingerly righted his body so he could look at his son. "Where were you?"

"On the porch," Howie answered.

"You didn't hear me screaming?"

"I thought it was the wind."

Ira knew the wind was calm that night and his son was lying, but he didn't press him further.

"Should I help you back upstairs?" Howie asked.

"I need to go to a hospital. Need a steroid. It's the only thing that helps."

"I can take you there."

"How?"

"We can call a taxi or an Uber. Touro isn't far, is it?"

"I mean, how will we pay for the hospital visit?" Ira asked.

"I have insurance."

"You're not the one that's sick."

"I can pretend."

"That won't work. They're not going to prescribe a steroid to a fourteen-year-old."

"I'm fifteen."

The pulsating, throbbing pain burned through his ankle again, making Ira screech and take a few deep breaths like a laboring woman in the middle of a contraction.

"I'm calling a cab," Howie said.

"Get the wagon. It's around back."

Howie hurried out the door, leaving Ira on the step punching the inner part of his right ankle. When the boy returned, he was biting his bottom lip, lost in thought.

"Did you find it?" Ira asked.

"Am I supposed to roll you in that little red wagon to the hospital at three in the morning?"

"Is it that late?"

"I won't do it. I'm calling a taxi. Mom gave me her debit card. She knew you'd be like this."

"Be like what?" Ira asked.

Howie hustled into the kitchen and called United Cab. Despite his inclination to protest further, Ira bit his tongue and accepted his son's charity.

28

New Orleans had been without a charity hospital since Katrina. The hulking twenty-story building that once serviced the needy had spent the past decade rotting away in the CBD as politicians and preservationists debated its fate. Instead of rebuilding the old Charity, it was finally decided that the city would clear out a downtrodden part of the downtown corridor and replace it with a biomedical complex. So rather than having to go to Charity, one could walk into any hospital in the city and claim to be indigent, and the staff wouldn't be allowed to turn you away. Ira had tried that numerous times, only to be sent home with a bill when he was unable to convince them that he was too poor to pay. He had stacks of collection letters piled in a filing cabinet collecting dust. He expected his name to show up on some no-fly list every time he rolled into the emergency room, but it never did. He chalked it up to incompetence and accepted his fate amongst the un-credit worthy.

Howie reappeared in the emergency lane with a wheelchair, and the taxi sped off into the night. He rolled his father into the waiting area and went to the window to talk with the receptionist, who looked disinterested with the young Asian boy addressing her in a low voice. The waiting area was half full of mostly elderly patients dozing off in uncomfortable positions on grey plastic chairs. The room smelled like Pine-Sol used as a Band-Aid for recently spewed vomit. The receptionist kept looking over at Ira who was slouched in the chair with his leg curled into his lap and his cane draped over the side. Howie was gesturing wildly with his hands as the heavyset woman continually shook her head.

Howie returned to Ira's side and said, "Shouldn't be long."

"Really? What's that mean? Less than four hours?"

Howie shrugged his shoulders and wheeled Ira to a corner of the room beneath a TV that was showing reruns of *Judge Judy*. A few minutes later, the receptionist called Ira's name and handed a clipboard to Howie.

"I've never been seen this quickly," Ira said, as he scribbled on the forms with one hand and massaged his foot with the other. "Can you get me an ice pack?"

Howie left his father's side, talked to the receptionist for another minute, and then disappeared down a hallway to fetch an ice pack. When he returned, Ira had moved into a regular seat and hoisted his foot on the top of the back of the wheelchair. Howie wrapped a blue ice pack around his ankle.

"Silver. Ira Silver. Through that door," ordered the receptionist, pointing to her right.

Ira's eyes widened and his chin sunk into his chest. He looked at Howie, who helped him back into the wheelchair and rolled him into the emergency room, past an elderly man that was either dead or asleep on a gurney. At the counter, several nurses in light blue scrubs chatted amongst themselves. One of them, a tall thin woman with long dark hair and a comforting smile, pointed down the hall and said, "Room 223."

In the small white room, Ira looked at his son who had a wry smile on his pudgy face. "What did you say to them?"

"Told them you were mugged."

"That's it?"

"And that I was an abused orphan in China, and that you rescued me from a life of slavery in the rice fields."

"Who taught you how to lie like that?" Ira asked.

"If I told them the truth, we'd be in the lobby till the sun rises."

Ira thought about the prospect of sitting in the lobby waiting to be seen, hoping he could convince someone that he required medical attention, waiting through the shift change as the sun rose, begging for pity as the burning intensified, and expecting nothing but nasty looks from heartless wenches in white uniforms.

It wasn't long before a pretty nurse appeared to clasp the blood pressure cuff around his bicep and take his vitals. "Hmmm," she murmured.

"What?" Ira asked.

"Blood pressure's high. One-eighty over ninety."

"It's always that high."

Howie looked at his father with his head cocked to the side.

"Are you taking anything for it?" she asked.

"Can't afford it."

"Why aren't you on Medicaid?"

"Not eligible."

"Why not?"

"It's not important," Ira said.

"Suit yourself," she said, unwrapping the cuff and heading out the door, the scent of apricot body lotion lingering in the room.

Not long after, a young man in a white doctor's coat strode into the room and pulled a chair over to Ira's side. Without saying a word, he took Ira's pulse and looked at the scar on his face. Finally, he said, "You're going to need a plastic surgeon if you don't want a scar on your face."

"Don't care about a scar. That's not what I'm here for," Ira said.

"Says here on the sheet, you were mugged," said the doctor.

"Yes, mugged. But I'm here for the gout."

"Have you filed a police report?"

"No, that won't be necessary."

"You really should," the doctor said. "Otherwise someone else might get hurt even worse."

"OK, I'll see what I can do."

The young man, maybe in his mid-twenties, grabbed Ira's foot, causing him to let out a yelp, and examined the swollen red blotches around his ankle. "Yep, looks like gout."

"It's not my first time."

"What are you taking for it?"

"Nothing."

"Why not?" he asked. "Allopurinol works pretty good, you know?"

"Thanks. I'll try and remember that."

The doctor pulled out a little prescription pad and scribbled on three different pieces of paper, handing one at a time to Ira. "This one's an anti-inflammatory that should give you some immediate relief. This one's a pain reliever in case you can't sleep. This one's a steroid pack that'll get rid of it faster."

Ira took the papers in his hand, looked down for a second, then glanced back up at the doctor. "If you could only take one, which would you take?"

"Why would you only take one?" he asked as Howie sighed next to him.

"Can't afford all three," Ira answered.

"I might have some samples around here," the doctor said and excused himself from the room.

"Ira, why are you so cheap?" Howie asked.

Ira thought about the question. As long as he could remember, being cheap was ingrained in him. His parents never fixed anything in the house, never replaced anything that stopped working, and constantly instilled Ira with a sense of frugality. There was never food wasted nor clothes bought new. This was just how it was, and Ira never knew any different. He also never questioned it. The Silver family came from money and somewhere there was a trust that would keep them going for generations to come; but that didn't mean the trust should be squandered by excess material consumption.

But that was before greed took over. Father was never quite satisfied with living off the virtues of others. He wanted his own fortune and he fancied himself an "investor." In the eighties he invested heavily in savings and loans, in the nineties he bought up public pay phones when they were deregulated, in the aughts he financed a bunch of hot rental properties before the banks collapsed. Even though all of those ended up being abject failures, there was nothing to worry about as long as Bernie Madoff's hedge fund kept up its ten percent return every year.

While Ira grew up with very little reason to be cheap, it was a trait that served him well when his parents lost everything that hadn't already been paid for. They were forced to make reparations to the hundreds of smaller investors who were bilked out of money while the Silvers collected payments for decades. If Father hadn't squandered virtually all that money on his harebrained investments, there would have been plenty to give back. Instead, Father left the world owing more than he was worth and Ira was left to fend for himself, which he was barely capable of doing. As far as Ira knew, the house was all that was left.

While there were reasons that Ira could give his son for why he was so cheap, he thought it better to sidestep the issue. So he asked, "Why do you keep calling me Ira?"

Neither question was answered. The pair sat in silence until the doctor returned with two small packages. "This is a muscle relaxer, Colchicine. Take one right now and then follow the directions until the pain stops. Should be two or three days. These two are for the pain. That's all I have. You will probably need more of these tomorrow."

"Thanks, Doc."

29

Ira spent the next morning icing his foot in the bathtub and wrapping it in a ratty heating pad that was as old as anything else in the house. By eleven, he was getting hungry and it was nearly time to head to Leidenheimer for his French bread. Wrapping his foot in an ace bandage, Ira dressed himself in khaki pants and a Coast Guard T-shirt he had caught at one of the recent parades.

With the aid of his trusty cane, Ira hopped down the stairs calling Howie's name the entire way but hearing nothing but the distant yapping of a dog. He made it to the living room but then had to sit, remove the bandage, and rub his foot vigorously until the flare began to wane. He swallowed the last Oxycodone, gagged, and threw himself into a coughing fit that made him buckle over and steady himself on his knees.

As the coughing came to a halt, Howie walked through the door and stopped in the foyer when he saw his father clutching his chest.

"Are you having a heart attack?"

"Of course not," Ira muttered. "Help me up."

Howie wrapped his arms below Ira's armpits and helped him back to his feet. Spotting the bandage dangling from his ankle, Howie dropped to one knee and re-wrapped his father's foot. "Why don't you go back to bed?"

"Not necessary. I'll be fine. Where were you?"

"Went for a walk," Howie said, lowering his eyes and turning toward the door.

"It's Leidenheimer time," Ira announced. "Help me to the door."

Howie lowered his shoulder to nestle it below his father's armpit and the two struggled out of the house. Ira pointed his cane at the approaching streetcar and the two hustled down the stairs and across St. Charles, the elder screaming at the driver to wait.

"One disability, one student," Ira panted to the driver.

"There's no such thing as a student fare," came the reply.

"Two disability," Ira said meekly.

"No can do. He ain't disabled."

Standing behind his father, Howie said, "I have money. Mom gave me money."

Ira shushed his son, but it was too late. The driver was now standing and ordering them off the streetcar. Finally, Ira succumbed to his demands, swiped his card, and paid the two fares, leading Howie to the last row of empty seats near the back.

They sat quietly, Howie by the window staring at the passing businesses and the trees full of beads, Ira with his eyes closed massaging his foot. As the streetcar screeched to a halt at Euterpe, Ira limped off, leading his son to the lakeside of St. Charles Avenue.

They stopped at the St. Charles Tavern, a greasy spoon diner that served breakfast all day and offered one-dollar bottomless coffee. "You hungry?" Ira asked as he opened the door.

Howie shook his head. "Already ate."

"Really? What'd you eat?"

"Muffalotta."

"Nice," Ira said. "Eating some New Orleans food. I wouldn't peg you for a muff guy. That was Charlie's favorite."

Howie hesitated. "Got it at the Rouse's."

"That's like getting red beans at Popeye's."

"What's wrong with that?"

"Never mind," Ira said, pouring his coffee into a Styrofoam cup and motioning the waitress for more. "Where you think Charlie is?"

"Don't know," Howie said.

"Maybe she's back in Gulfport finishing school."

"Doubt that," Howie said.

"I don't know where else to look," Ira said, waving to the waitress for more coffee and the check.

The walk was painful, but Ira persevered knowing he was running out of time. The last of the trucks would be gone by one and the gate would be locked as soon as the last left the lot.

Ira found that his foot hurt just as much sitting around doing nothing as it did in motion. When they reached the corner of Terpsichore and Simon Bolivar, there were still four trucks idling in the parking lot, each displaying the familiar logo of Vic and Nat'ly sinking their big cartoon mouths into giant loaves of Leidenheimer French bread. Marching up to the will-call window, Ira greeted the petite old woman like a familiar friend. "Ms. Margaret, how are we today?"

"Oh Ira, I was beginning to think you weren't going to make it."

"I would never miss our Tuesday lunch," Ira said, pouring on the charm like a politician at a christening.

Ms. Margaret giggled like a little schoolgirl. "I saved you two whole loaves today."

A delivery driver in blue Dockers and a clean white logoed shirt grabbed the clipboard above Ms. Margaret's head. "Why I always got to go to Mississippi?" he mumbled.

"It ain't so bad, sweetheart. You'll be back by six or seven," she said.

"Biloxi and Gulfport should be one-a-days. Why they need a night run?"

Ira interrupted, "It was good seeing you, Ms. Margaret. We got to get going."

"Who's the boy?" she asked.

"This is my son, Howie," Ira said, lifting his son's hand up to wave as if he were still a four-year-old.

Ms. Margaret had a perplexed look on her wrinkled face. She tried to smile politely, but it looked more like a grimace. Ira tugged his son's shoulder and led him back to the loading dock, where the last truck sat with its trunk open, filled with dozens of racks of white bags.

Ira scanned the dock, but it was eerily quiet. Howie looked at his father and said, "No, no, no, no, no."

"Why not?" Ira asked.

"We're not supposed to leave Louisiana. Remember?"

"You can stay," Ira said. "I'm going to Gulfport to find Charlie." He hurled himself on the back of the truck and nestled his body behind the last two racks against the wall, the smell of fresh bread overpowering his nasal passages.

Seconds later, the door slammed shut. It took Ira's eyes a few more seconds to adjust to the darkness. He could feel the truck shudder as the driver took his seat, revved the engine, and thrust it into gear. Then he heard the faint whisper of his name and realized that his son was somewhere in the darkness nearby.

30

After the initial shocks of riding on the bumpy, derelict streets of New Orleans, the open highway was a welcome respite. Howie moved closer to Ira so they could hear each other breathing, and they talked in a whisper, worried that the driver might hear. They could make out the man singing and talking on his cell phone over the sound of old-school R&B on the radio.

An hour or so later, the driver turned the engine off and opened his door. Ira grabbed Howie by his shirtsleeve and pulled him into the corner behind the racks, where they held their breath and waited for the tailgate to open. But it never did. The driver must have stopped for gas or a snack. In the darkness, they heard the distant sound of cars speeding by and the closer sound of people filling their gas tanks.

Back on the highway for another fifteen minutes, the truck slowed as it reached a series of stoplights and right turns that nearly knocked the stowaways off their feet. They held onto the racks to prevent themselves from falling and occasionally held onto each other on the wider turns. Finally the truck stopped, and they held their breath. The driver's door opened and again the tailgate stayed closed. It was eerily quiet, until a door banged against a wall and two men's voices started conversing. When the tailgate opened, a harsh light spread into the bed of the truck, forcing Ira and Howie to close their eyes.

Squinting with one eye, Ira saw the back of the delivery driver rolling a rack to the edge of the truck, hitting a button, and dropping down the lift until he was on the ground and walking the bread rack into the back door of the business.

"Should we get out?" Howie whispered.

"I don't know. Where do you think we are?"

"How should I know?"

Ira chuckled. "Gulfport comes before Biloxi. I'd guess this is Gulfport."

"How you know he doesn't deliver the farthest point first?"

Smart kid, Ira thought. He really had no idea where he was or where the truck would stop first. The entire ride he had thought about Charlie and walking up to her house and meeting her mom and dad and waiting for her to come home from school. But where was the reality in that? He didn't know her last name or where she lived or anything about her other than the name of her high school and a physical description that must have matched hundreds of girls in Gulfport.

With the extra light coming from the cab of the truck, Ira saw a label on the rack next to his head. "This one says Winn Dixie, Biloxi. What's the one to your left say?"

"Says Ole Biloxi Schooner."

"Can you see any of the others?" Ira asked. "Wait, shush. The guy's coming back."

The lift brought the driver back up to their eye level, and then he pulled another cart onto it. Back down he went, leaving Ira and Howie alone again. They quickly searched the remaining dozen racks and discovered the front four were Gulfport racks. With the lift still at the bottom, Howie jumped to the ground with relative ease. Ira tossed him his cane and dangled his legs over the edge of the truck, and his son grabbed hold and lowered his feeble body to the ground. They scurried away from what they saw to be the back door of a Rouse's Supermarket.

They were on a four-lane road walking past a strip center and toward a Taco Bell. Looked like Anytown, USA. Light traffic passed them heading in both directions. Ira hobbled slowly behind his son as they made for the nearest intersection. A school bus passed, then another, coming from the opposite side of the street.

"You have your cell phone?" Ira asked.

Howie pulled his iPhone out of his khaki trousers and waved it at his father.

"You getting an Internet signal?"

"It's off. Don't have much battery left. Let me turn it on," Howie said.

"Google Gulfport High School."

Howie thumbed his phone for a second, looked up and across the street, glanced back down at the phone, and pointed. "Mile and a half, that way. Should I call an Uber."

"No, no. We'll be fine," Ira answered.

They continued on, Ira's limp becoming more pronounced the further they went. Howie kept looking at his father and shaking his head, but Ira kept moving, trying every so often to grasp his son's shoulder for extra support.

By the time they reached the low-slung brick building on Perry Street, sweat poured through Ira's shirt, his cheeks flushed, and his ankle flared. Howie seemed no worse for wear. It was just past four o'clock and the parking lot was mostly empty. They nodded at each other before making their way to the main entrance.

The doors were locked. Ira rang the buzzer.

And they waited.

Ira rang the buzzer again.

"May I help you?" said the voice over the intercom.

"Umm, yes. My son. We just moved to town and we wanted a tour of the school."

"Hold, please," said the woman.

A moment later, a different woman said, "Ms. D'Angelo isn't in right now. Can you come back tomorrow?"

"Of course," Ira said. "We can come back tomorrow to register. But maybe you can give us a tour now?"

"I'm not authorized to do tours. What is your name? We can schedule something first thing tomorrow."

Ira didn't say anything until the voice said, "Hello?"

"We'll be back tomorrow. Eight-thirty."

As the voice confirmed the meeting time and asked his name again, a group of teenagers came barreling out the door. As it started to close, Ira grabbed the handle, swung it open, and pushed his son inside.

The hallway was long and narrow with lockers on each side, a low ceiling, speckled white linoleum floor tiles, and painted banners hanging on the walls. A few random students muddled about, crisscrossing the hall in groups of two or three. Ira beelined it to the nearest group and asked them whether they knew a girl named Charlie. They did not.

The next group looked a bit older, probably seniors. "Do you know a girl named Charlie?" Ira asked.

A tall, good looking guy with a letterman jacket said, "No."

"What about Charlene?" Ira asked.

A pretty girl with long brown hair said, "Charlene Sawyer?"

"Yeah, about yea big," —Ira motioned with his hand about eye level—"straight blonde hair, blue eyes."

The girl glanced at the tall guy, and then back at Ira. "Charlene has curly brown hair about my length."

The threesome walked off and Ira heard the girl say, "Creep."

They popped their head into the gym and spied a group of boys in gym shorts and T-shirts doing wind sprints. The coach looked at them and barely flinched, and they backed out of the cavernous room.

Back in the hallway, there were just two kids left standing next to a locker, one chatting on a cellphone. Ira and Howie neared them, but as they approached, they heard a deep voice call from behind, "Can I help you gentlemen?"

They turned to face two uniformed security guards. One held a walkie-talkie. The other had one hand on his belt an inch from his gun and the other hand outstretched toward Ira.

"My son is going to be a student here," Ira said, pointing at Howie.

"That's mighty nice," the taller guard said. "But no one gave you permission to be in here."

"We just thought we'd take a look around," Ira said.

The officers inched closer to them, the tension in the air growing with every step. "We take security very seriously here at Gulfport High."

"That's terrific," Ira said. "I want my boy to go to a safe school."

"Would you mind coming with us, Mr...?"

"Silver. I'm Ira and this is my son Howie."

"Let's take a walk to the office and see if we can't get this straightened out," the taller guard said.

31

Ira and Howie were sent to the principal's office. It was a small room cluttered with books and paper, a big desk, and a double set of filing cabinets. No personal pictures on the walls, just a framed diploma from the University of Mississippi. The officers motioned for Ira and Howie to take the two empty seats at the foot of the desk and closed the door.

Behind the beveled glass door, the officers stood guard. Ira spied the filing cabinets and contemplated a brief search, but there wasn't a lock on the door and at this point, he thought trouble might be brewing. A woman peeked her head inside and said, "Ms. D'Angelo is on her way back. Should be here in a few minutes."

"She doesn't need to go through all that trouble," Ira said, rising to a half standing position. "We can just come back tomorrow."

"Oh, it's no trouble at all. She's eager to meet y'all," the woman said.

Ira sat back down as the door closed. Howie looked like a chicken whose head was about to get chopped off. His skin was a pale yellow and his eyes darted back and forth throughout the room, searching for a comfort zone and finding nothing but doom.

The door opened and in walked a tall, wiry woman with short grey hair and reading glasses hanging from her neck. She wore brown pants, a grey turtleneck, and a sports coat that made her look like a gay schoolmarm. She quickly stepped behind her desk, sat down, and folded her hands in front of her. Without a handshake or an introduction, she said, "Who are you?"

"I'm Ira Silver and this is my son Howie. We are moving here from New Orleans and would like a tour of the school."

"Most people call and set up an appointment."

"I'm sorry," Ira said. "We were just in the neighborhood."

Ms. D'Angelo rumpled her nose and twisted her lips back and forth. "What school do you go to, Howie? Do you have any transcripts?"

Howie looked at Ira searching for an appropriate answer, but he knew nothing about the schools in New Orleans and could only think of the one that they passed every day. "Sacred Heart."

Ira stuck his hand over his eyes, knowing that the glare from Ms. D'Angelo was pounding off his face like a featherweight punching bag.

"Would you like to tell me why you're really here?"

"We're looking for Charlie," Howie said.

Ira peeled his hand from his face and grimaced at the angry woman staring at him. "Charlene," he said meekly.

"You think you can waltz into a high school and sneak around until you find some girl. What kind of pervert are you?"

Ira was at a loss for words. He just slunk deeper in his chair as Ms. D'Angelo rose from hers and stuck her head out of the office door. She whispered something to the guards before returning to her seat. "We're calling the authorities."

Ira saw Howie's stricken face. He mouthed the words, "Call Shelly."

Howie fumbled through his pocket, rested the phone on his knee, and dialed Shelly's number. Ms. D'Angelo sat across from them with her arms folded over her chest, glaring at Ira.

Howie whispered, "Hello, Shelly, it's Howie Lee."

"Lee?" Ira cut in. "Since when are you a Lee?"

Howie shushed him. "In Mississippi," he said into the phone. "Looking for Charlie." Pause. "I know." Pause. "I know, but…" Pause. "In Gulfport High School." Pause. "I know." Pause. "They've called the police." Pause. "Okay." Howie hung up the phone.

"What'd she say?" Ira asked.

"That she told you not to leave Louisiana."

Ms. D'Angelo, who was listening intently, said, "Why not?"

Ira looked at the woman across from him and decided that she would be an unlikely ally. Instead of answering, he said to Howie, "What else?"

"She's on her way."

32

Thirty minutes after the phone call, the police arrived: a single unit dressed in black pants and a short-sleeved black shirt. A medium-build balding guy in his thirties entered the room and stood behind Ira and Howie, who were still sitting opposite Ms. D'Angelo.

In a deep monotone voice, the officer said, "Hi Pat. What's going on?"

"Well, Dan. We have a trespassing situation here."

"Got anything else?" Dan asked.

"Seems they're looking for a girl, possibly a student, and they may be in some sort of trouble."

"What kind of trouble?"

"Don't know. Lawyer's on her way."

"You fellas have any identification?" Dan asked.

Ira pulled his wallet out from his back pocket, thumbed through it, and handed the officer his Louisiana ID card.

Officer Dan stepped back out of the room, presumably to radio in Ira's information. They sat in silence for what seemed like an eternity, Ira mumbling from time to time something about the name "Lee." When the officer finally reentered the room, he asked Ira to stand up, patted him down, and ordered him to put his arms behind his back.

As he cuffed Ira, he said to Ms. D'Angelo, "Seems we have a sex offender here."

"Accused," Ira corrected.

"Accused what?" the officer said.

"*Accused* sex offender."

Officer Dan forcefully removed Ira from the room and walked him back to the hallway. Howie followed a few yards behind, shaking his head and sniffling like a lost child at the mall. When they emerged back outside, the setting sun had hidden behind a few dark clouds and four squad cars were lined up at the curb. Several youngsters congregated on the opposite lawn, whispering to each other and pointing at Howie.

Once tucked away in the back of one of the cars, Ira saw three officers talking and gesticulating toward Howie. Ira felt bad for his son, who had done nothing wrong. The boy was full-on crying, unable to control his emotions, his chest heaving in and out. It made Ira's heartbeat quicken and his stomach feel like it was going to jump out of his mouth. He thought he might be headed back to Child Services, and then to New York, where he wouldn't get into any more trouble. Ira would probably never see him again.

Out of the corner of his eye, Ira saw a figure emerge from the parking lot and rush toward the officers like a blitzing linebacker. Rather than tackle them, though, she nestled her big butt between Howie and the officers, who exchanged incredulous looks. She pointed. She hissed. She chomped her teeth like a rabid dog until one of the officers stuck his palms up in a "Who, me?" expression. Even from the back of the car Ira could tell they were on the defensive.

Dragging Howie by the elbow, Shelly hustled back into the school. Ira watched the officers talk to one another. He got the sense they were taking stock of the situation, seemingly deferring to the one officer who must have been in charge. Two of the squad cars peeled away, leaving the head guy and two other officers standing outside when Shelly, Howie, and Ms. D'Angelo came scurrying out the front door.

This time Ms. D'Angelo did the talking, with Shelly hovering over her back shoulder. There was a heated debate with the head officer, who looked about as frustrated as an officer could look. He kept shaking his head and pointing at Ira in the back of the squad car. Howie looked embarrassed, standing a few feet behind until Shelly pulled him closer to the conversation.

At that point, a look of defeat crossed the officer's face and he shut his mouth. Every time he tried to open it, he was quickly interrupted. Finally, he gave up, stalked to the squad car, opened the back door, jerked Ira to his feet, spun him around, and uncuffed his wrists, shaking his head the entire time.

Wanting nothing more from these two women in his face, the officer barely acknowledged them as he hopped into his car and sped away.

Shelly took a business card out of her back pocket and palmed it into Ms. D'Angelo's hand, pulling her in for a brief hug. They smiled at each other, then the principal sauntered back to the low-slung building. Shelly barely looked at Ira as she turned, pulling Howie by his elbow toward the parking lot. Ira stood there for a second not knowing what to do. He decided to follow them and scoot inconspicuously into the back seat of her still-running Prius. Shelly shoved her seat back into Ira's knees seemingly just to make him less comfortable before revving the engine and setting off.

There was no noise in the car, just the faint hum of the engine. The air conditioner and the radio were off. Howie sniffled once or twice. Ira saw Shelly's eyes in the rearview mirror burning with rage.

They were thirty miles outside of Gulfport before Ira worked up the nerve to speak. "How'd you get me out of that precarious situation?"

"Shut the fuck up. Sorry, Howie. Excuse my language."

Another thirty minutes passed. As they crossed Lake Pontchartrain, Shelly said, "You're not going to find that little tramp."

"She's not a tramp," Howie said.

"Sorry… girl," Shelly said.

"How you know?" Ira asked.

"She's already off the grid," Shelly said. "I tried to get her file from the DA, but she went AWOL."

"How will I prove my innocence?"

"It doesn't matter, Ira. They're already offering you probation. I recommend you take it."

"Will I have to register as a sex offender? Ira asked.

"Of course. That's non-negotiable," Shelly answered.

"I'm not taking that deal. You said I'll lose my house."

"It's not your house to lose. As long as your mother's alive, it's her house."

"But I didn't do anything wrong," Ira squealed.

"You don't understand," Shelly said. "If you lose, you'll be looking at a ten-year minimum sentence."

"No deal, Shelly. I'm going to find Charlie."

33

With night settling in, Ira's ankle began to swell again. He left Howie in the kitchen tapping away on his iPhone and submerged his aching body in a tepid bath. Within minutes he was fast asleep.

When he awoke, his penis had shriveled to the size of his thumb and his neck throbbed almost as bad as his ankle. He dried off with a ratty towel and changed into jogging shorts and one of his faded undershirts. Stumbling down the stairs, he headed for the kitchen to grab some ice. It wasn't until he was back out in the living room lying on the couch that he realized he was alone.

He called Howie a few times, but no answer. Clawing his way back to a standing position, Ira stumbled through the house yelling his son's name. The back door was unlocked so he checked the porch, but it was pitch black and he heard nothing but a cricket chirping.

The silence made Ira think it was well past midnight. He went to check the clock on his old PC, but remembered it was now in the possession of the New Orleans Police Department. The grandfather clock said two, but he never knew when the clock was working and when it wasn't. He made his way to the front door and stood on the porch yelling Howie's name until he heard his son's voice beckoning from back inside the house.

They nearly ran into one another near the stairwell. "Were you upstairs?" Ira asked.

"I was out back," Howie answered.

"I looked out there but didn't see you."

"I saw you look out, but you didn't say nothing."

"Say *anything*," Ira corrected. "You're starting to sound like Charlie now. You had me worried."

"Sorry, I didn't mean to."

"What were you doing out there?"

Howie looked down at the ground, then back up at his dad. "Nothing."

"It must be late. Why don't you get some sleep? We'll start looking for Charlie in the morning."

Ira checked the backdoor. It was locked. He opened it and peeked outside but saw only darkness and heard nothing but a few buzzing cicadas.

34

Ira liked the French Quarter best in the early morning when the hustlers and hobos had turned in for the night. Despite the lingering stench of beer and urine, the reality of a functioning city in its glorious nakedness made Ira long for the past. He liked to imagine himself in a top hat and double-breasted frock coat roaming the streets, drinking absinthe and frolicking with the ladies of the evening in the Storyville District.

But this wasn't the beginning of the twentieth century, it was a hundred years later, and this wasn't fantasy, it was reality. At half past ten, Iberville Street was nearly deserted. A sleepy-eyed old man scrubbed the street with bleach and a deck brush. Most of the storefronts were still shuttered, the occasional restaurant welcoming breakfast patrons.

Ira had passed Dixie Divas on numerous occasions in the evening, often unable to avoid running into a half-naked tramp soliciting voyeurs in the cramped entryway. He had never stepped foot in the place. He thought it was too seedy even for him. On that morning, however, the entrance was empty and from across the street Ira and Howie couldn't tell whether it was open or not.

"Stay here," Ira said. "I'll look around and see if anyone's in there."

Howie perched himself against a streetlight, nodded to his father, and folded his arms over his stomach.

Ira crossed the street and paused at the door to read the signs: one about gaming devices, one about underage drinking, one about hiring, and a sheet of loose-leaf paper taped to the blacked-out windowpane advertising the free lunch buffet.

Pulling the handle of the heavy wooden door, Ira was somewhat surprised that it opened. Despite the citywide smoking ban, the cigarette odor was so pervasive that it made Ira's eyes water. A cursory glance around the dark room gave the impression that the bar was not yet open, which was fine by Ira. He didn't want to be accosted by a bunch of skanky hoes eager to swindle him out of the few bucks he had on him. Toward the back of the room was a small stage with a solitary pole lit by harsh spotlights. Along the left wall was a mirrored bar with a dozen stools and a pitiful display of cheap liquors. The sound system pumped a track of dance music with a repetitive base beat.

Just when Ira thought he was alone he saw the black thong of a nearly naked body writhing over two legs on a couch near the center of the dimly lit room. The whiteness of her skin made Ira's heart skip and he nearly turned and ran away. Instead, he slowly advanced on the duo, sniffing like a hound dog attempting to pick up Charlie's scent. But the closer he got, the less familiarity there was, until she whipped her head around, exposing her brutally ugly face.

It was a shocking confrontation for Ira, who peddled his way out of the building as fast as his feet could shuffle and burst through the front door and into the middle of Iberville Street, where he was nearly run over by a passing horse-drawn carriage.

Ira's skin was milky pale, but his cheeks were glowing and sweat soaked through his undershirt. Howie's eyebrows arched, waiting for an explanation.

Ira shook his head. "Thought I saw Charlie, but it wasn't her."

"What should we do?" Howie asked.

"Don't know."

"Want me to go in?"

"That's absurd. You're only fifteen. You can't get into a strip club."

With that, Ira motioned with his hand for Howie to stay where he was and ventured back to the door. This time a man was standing behind the bar eyeing him up and down as he entered. He had one hand on the bar and the other extended below it, as if contemplating what to do with the shotgun hanging from his fingertips.

Ira smiled weakly and slowly walked in his direction. At first glance, the man looked small, but as the distance between them shrunk, Ira realized that the back of the bar was sunken below floor level and that was the reason they were looking eye to eye. The next thing Ira noticed was the man's thick tattooed forearm, which reminded him of Popeye, and then his mustache that curled up in a little twist at both ends. His dark blue eyes channeled a vision of the vast ocean and staring at them long enough gave Ira the feeling that he was lost at sea.

The man said nothing. His stare asked the question, "What the fuck do you want?" Ira got the sense that he needed to proceed with caution, as the slightest provocation would undoubtedly result in him being tossed from the bar. "I'm inquiring about the sign on the door," Ira said.

"Which one?" the man grumbled.

"About the free lunch buffet," Ira said.

"Only on weekends. What else you want?"

At a loss for words, Ira and the bartender stood across from each other, the former staring at the scar on the latter's chin. The heavy base pumping from the speaker stopped, blanketing the room in silence for a few seconds before a slow R&B song—maybe Beyoncé, thought Ira—started up. The bartender didn't move an inch. It was as if he was a figure in the wax museum staring intently with its glass eyes.

"I'm looking for a girl," Ira offered.

The bartender released his grip on whatever he had hidden beneath the bar and waved the back of his meaty hand in Ira's direction. Ira took it as an invitation to take a seat. He watched as the man slid down to the end of the bar, ducked behind a curtain, and disappeared. Then Ira followed to the end of the bar, stepped down two short stairs, and grabbed a seat on an empty vinyl couch with his back to the lone stripper who was still straddling her current victim.

The woman that appeared from behind the curtain was plump in all the wrong places. Her crop top exposed her round, pink belly and her dimpled thighs bulged out of her cutoff shorts. She held a bar tray in one hand and adjusted the strap of her bra with the other as she approached Ira. In a husky voice, she said, "What can I get you to drink?"

"Just a water," Ira answered. "Tap."

She let out an insufferable groan before spinning on her heels and making her way toward the same door the bartender had gone through. Reclining uncomfortably on the couch, Ira adjusted his position a few times, but the couch was so deep that he kept sliding back down so that he looked like a little boy in a giant futon.

A disinterested-looking girl in a Catholic schoolgirl outfit came out from behind the curtain next. A few steps into the room, she kneeled down to adjust the strap on her six-inch pumps.

The outfit looked exactly like the one H. Hanson had pulled out of Charlie's bag, but this girl was nothing like Charlie. From a distance, she looked fine, but as she duck-walked closer to Ira, her face aged a decade every ten feet. When she finally arrived before him, Ira surmised she was somewhere between forty and fifty considering the excess skin rolling from her emaciated frame. Her gaunt eyes and pocked face left Ira the impression that she was some sort of junkie.

Nestling up to his side, the woman stuck her knee between Ira's legs and against his crotch, leaned forward, and whispered, "You want a dance?"

Flustered, Ira stammered, "I—I'm looking for a girl."

The woman seemed temporarily startled by Ira's response. Leaving her hands cupped around Ira's knees, she thrust her hips back, looked into his eyes, and said, "What you think I am?"

"I'm looking for Charlie... I mean, Rose."

"I can be Rose," she said. "Or Lilly, or Iris, or Daisy, or whatever kind of flower you want me to be."

Ira grabbed the woman by her wrists and pushed her back to a standing position. "She works here. 'Bout yea big, blonde hair, blue eyes, young. Really young."

"Oh, you like 'em young?" she asked, squinting her eyes menacingly.

"It's not that," Ira said.

"Why m'I wasting time witchu?" she said, her accent getting more ghetto the more she spoke. She peeled her thin frame away from Ira and backed her way toward the couple still grinding away on the other couch. She whispered something in the woman's ear, then went up to the empty catwalk and started slowly grinding on the pole. She wasn't dancing. She was really just holding on to the pole for support and wiggling her body. She slowly unbuttoned her white collared shirt, exposing a purple bikini top covering shriveled breasts.

Ira tried not to look, but since he was the only one in the room, he felt obligated to sneak glances at the figure on the stage. That is, until the overweight cocktail waitress returned and blocked his view. She took the small plastic cup of ice water off her tray and handed it to Ira. She hovered over him waiting for a tip, but he didn't move an inch. They stayed like that for over a minute until she finally huffed and puffed and left the room.

With the waitress out of the way, Ira had full view of the now-topless blonde-haired dancer on the stage. When she spun around the pole, it showed a back full of colorful tattoos, not an inch of empty skin. From the front, she had stretch marks on her breasts and loose flaps dripping from her stomach. Her thighs were full of tattoos with various script writing. It looked like some kind of poem or the Declaration of Independence, Ira couldn't tell. Her legs were so skinny, it looked as if the pole was her third leg.

Ira wanted so badly to leave, but he hadn't gotten any helpful information. The bartender was back behind the bar staring at him menacingly, so he decided to get up and pay him another visit. Ira knew it was only a matter of time before he was tossed out of the bar, so he decided to be proactive. Marching up to the counter, he declared, "I am looking for Rose."

"You don't look like no regular," he remarked.

"She works here, or she did work here."

"Lots of girls work here. Some for a while. Some come and go. What's it to you?"

"It is imperative that I speak with her."

"Look, asshole, I don't know you from a shit stain on the wall."

As he said those words, the door opened and a stream of sunlight poked through the frame. Ira didn't turn around, but he watched the bartender's eyes follow the figure now striding through the bar area. His double-take compelled Ira to look over his shoulder as the figure hustled into the darkness at the far end of the dance area and took a seat. Without saying a word, the bartender disappeared through the curtain behind the bar and emerged out the other door into the main lounge, leaving Ira unattended.

Ira inched his way toward the curtain as the bartender approached holding Howie up by his shirt collar and dragging him through the bar area. Howie's eyes were like huge bull's-eyes, his mouth in the slightest pinch of a smirk. He gave Ira a quick wink as he stumbled by. Ira ducked behind the curtain and held his breath as the bartender yelled profanities at Howie all the way through the front door.

Ira found himself alone in a hallway dressed with black curtains on each side and a solitary forty-watt bulb hanging from a cord on the ceiling. A heavy smell of baby powder and cigarettes permeated the air. The door to Ira's left was ajar, exposing a room with plastic chairs and make-up cases propped in front of a brightly lit wall of mirrors.

Ira heard the side door kick back open and someone's plodding footsteps enter the hallway. He stepped into the dressing room and hid behind a rack of raunchy robes and lingerie. The bartender opened the door and scanned the room. Ira held his breath. Just as the man stepped inside to investigate, a woman's voice called from the hallway. He grunted, then pulled the door shut, and locked it from the outside.

Ira panicked. He ran to the door and nearly shook the handle, but quickly weighed his options and decided to sit tight and hope for one of the dancers to open the door. He prayed to God that Howie would be able to fend for himself or call Shelly if he had any trouble getting back home.

The room was filthy. Wet towels littered the floor, costumes hung from every conceivable corner. The makeup cases were stuffed with used tissues, half-empty lipstick containers, and crumpled packs of cigarettes. Trashcans overflowed with paper towels and condom wrappers. The mirrors were streaked with fingerprints, while giant mold spots seeped through the dropped ceiling tiles. The room kind of smelled like ass—not rhetorically, but actually like someone's rank asshole after a few days without a shower. The most plentiful thing in the room was a tattered wicker basket overflowing with those miniature soaps, something they must have shared communally like a bowl of after-dinner mints.

Ira was scanning the clothing rack when someone twisted the doorknob and had barely a second to jump behind the rack again and crouch in the corner. Luckily for Ira, it was the emaciated blonde stripper who had tried to give him a lap dance earlier. She was wearing a bra and panties, carrying her white shirt and checkered miniskirt. She hustled to the mirror, grabbed a small purse off the countertop, and removed a pack of Newports. She dropped into one of the plastic chairs, lit the cigarette, took a puff with one hand, and removed her pumps with the other.

Ira would have imagined that peeking through a rack of cheap stripper clothes at a half-naked woman smoking a cigarette would give him a hard-on, but the sight was about as sexy as a bunch of clown midgets hopping out of a VW at the circus. Besides, Ira hadn't been aroused in that way in over a decade.

As the woman blew smoke in the air, Ira's eyes began to water and his nose itched. He contorted his face and swished his nose from side to side, but it only delayed the inevitable. He sneezed.

She was on Ira's ass before he even had a chance to rise from his crouching position. She kneed him in his chin, forcing him to stumble over the rack and crash against the back wall, expunging any remaining air he had in his lungs.

He slid down the wall and landed on his derriere while the skinny stripper stood over him in a *Karate Kid* pose, the cigarette still dangling from her lips. Struggling to catch his breath, Ira stuck his palm up in hopes of checking any further assault. The stripper hurried back to the countertop, grabbed her purse, and took out a small can of mace.

Back in Ira's face, she yelled, "The fuck you doing here?"

"Looking for Rose," Ira screamed back.

"Who the fuck is Rose?"

"My daughter."

The stripper dropped her hand with the mace and offered Ira her other, and he grabbed hold, moving hunched over to one of the plastic chairs in front of the mirror. "I'm Crystal," she said, with their hands still clasped together.

"Ira Silver," he said while coughing twice.

"Listen, man. There's, like, five Roses been in and outta here. What's your girl like?"

"About five six, blonde spiky hair kind of like yours, blue eyes. Nice-looking girl. Young. Really young," Ira said. "Too young to be working in a place like this."

"She got a real name?" Crystal asked.

"Charlene."

"That don't ring no bells, but I'm the new girl. So many hoes running tricks 'round here."

The door slammed open. In walked the other stripper, cursing like a batshit crazy woman on the streets of New York. "Dat motherfucka tipped me a twenty for a suckie. You believe that?"

"Why you letting him play you like that?" Crystal asked, indignant.

Quieting her voice a bit, the other stripper looked at Ira and said, "Who the hell are you?"

"Ira Silver."

"What you doing in here?"

"He's looking for his kid," Crystal said.

"How you know he ain't talking shit?"

Crystal looked at Ira's long face. "You ain't bullshitting me, are you?"

Ira shook his head.

"What this ho look like?" the other stripper asked.

"Blonde spiky hair, blue eyes. Sixteen," Ira said.

The other stripper whistled.

Ira continued, "She has a tattoo of a rose on the inner part of her thigh."

"With thorns or without?" the other stripper asked.

"With."

"Yeah, I know her. Charlie, right?"

Ira's eyes perked up, his teeth slipped from his lips in a semi-grin as he nodded his head.

"She used to come 'round here a lot, but I ain't seen her in a few weeks."

Ira looked defeated. His shoulders slumped so low they practically sunk into his stomach. "If she comes around here again, you can give her my number?"

"What's in it for me?"

Ira glanced at Crystal, who was starting to look disinterested. "Ten bucks. I'll give you ten bucks if you help me find her."

"Woo-wee. Will that be one bill or small denominations?" the other stripper said, baring a mouth full of rotten teeth.

"I think it's time for me to go," Ira said, lifting his beaten body out of the chair and heading for the door. "Here's my card. Call me if you see her."

"Sure thing, Mr. Ira. Can't wait to get me that ten-dollar bill."

35

Howie leaned against the lamppost waiting for his father, passing the time on his iPhone. The menacing bartender saw Ira leaving the bar and called after him, but Ira hurried on. When he finally emerged from the gloom of Dixie Divas shielding his eyes, he was relieved to see his son in exactly the same spot he had left him. Crossing over Iberville, Ira put his hand on Howie's shoulder and said, "Thanks for waiting."

"Where else would I go?" Howie asked. "Find out anything?"

"Not really. They haven't seen her in a few weeks."

Walking down Chartres Street toward Canal, few words were uttered between them. They hopped on the streetcar and headed back toward home. As they passed Lee Circle, Ira said, "You sure are missing a lot of school."

"It's not a problem. I'm way ahead anyway."

"Maybe you should think about heading home."

"Mom already booked a flight for Sunday morning."

"Today's Wednesday."

"That means we have four days to find Charlie."

"This really isn't your problem, son. You shouldn't be getting caught up in my mess."

"Too late for that," Howie said with a chuckle.

As the streetcar approached Marengo, Ira noticed a car parked in the driveway of his house. After disembarking and walking closer, the car became more recognizable. It was a Prius.

Shelly was startled by Ira's knock on the window. At first she rolled down the driver's side window, but after a moment's hesitation, she rolled it back up, opened the door, stood up, and faced Ira with Howie standing just behind him. She had a morose look on her face.

"Good news or bad?" Ira asked.

"I don't know how to tell you this."

"Just give it to me, Shelly. It can't get any worse."

"Your mother has passed."

Ira keeled over as if he was just punched in the stomach. His knees buckled, knocking him backward a step so that he briefly stepped on Howie's shoe. Rather than back up, Howie put his arm around Ira's waist, holding him upright for a few seconds before releasing his grip and letting Ira waddle over to the steps on the porch. Ira sat on the top step with a glazed, faraway look in his eyes.

"Well, I guess that's that," he mumbled.

Shelly and Howie looked at each other and shrugged. Neither knew how to respond to Ira's comment.

"Where is she now? Over at Sinai?" Ira asked.

Shelly sat on the stoop next to him. "I don't have any of the details yet. Do you have a copy of the will?"

"It's at the bank."

"I suggest we get over there as soon as possible in case there's anything in it about funeral arrangements. Also, if you're not on the bank accounts or the box, they can freeze all her assets until a probate judge gets a hold of it."

"How long before they do that?"

"Less than three days."

36

Ira, Shelly, and Howic rushed over to the Chase Bank on Prytania Street with the safe deposit key that Mother had given him years earlier. After waiting fifteen minutes for a bank officer, Ira produced his state I.D. and gave him the family code. Since he hadn't signed the card in fifteen years, the bank officer double-checked his I.D. against the Department of Motor Vehicles on the computer. Ira felt like the bank manager was suspicious of him, but he finally gave Ira back his I.D. and led them to the vault.

Inside the tiny vault, the officer and Ira scanned the metal boxes for #944. Disappointed to see it was one of the smallest boxes, Ira took a deep breath before turning the key and pulling the box out of its slot. The officer ushered Ira to a small cubicle where he sat and lifted the cover.

Inside was a cache of documents, photocopies of bond certificates, loose rubber bands, and medical forms, along with a couple of random old photographs. Ira quickly thumbed through the pictures. Six were of his sister Sarah from different milestones in her life. One was an old black-and-white wedding photo of Mother and Father. One was a picture of a woman that Ira didn't know holding a baby. And the most recent was of Mother and Father on a cruise they took around Europe the summer before Katrina. Ira hated taking pictures, but even so, he was disappointed there were none of him.

Ira dumped the whole pile into a plastic T-shirt Thank You bag and handed the empty box back to the bank officer standing in the hallway.

"Was anything in there?" Shelly asked Ira when he returned to the lobby.

"I grabbed a bunch of papers," Ira said, flashing the full bag.

"What should we do?" Howie asked.

"Let's take it to the park and see what we got," Shelly said.

Shelly drove Ira and Howie to Audubon Park and parked near the pavilion next to the golf course. They found a picnic table, spread the documents across the top, and thumbed through the pages.

"This is the will, alright," Shelly said. "But it's old. Dated 1997. Done by Morton Stern."

"What's that mean?" Ira asked.

"Mort's been dead since Katrina," Shelly said. "Suicide. They might have something newer than this."

"What if there is?"

"This one would be null and void."

Shelly continued scanning the document. It was no more than four or five pages long. She kept "hmm"ing as she read. Finally, she looked up, shook her head, and handed the document back to Ira.

As he looked it over in turn, Shelly said, "This is your father's will. I would guess there's something more recent."

"Why? What's it say?" Howie asked.

"It gives everything to Ira's mother."

"And?" Ira put in.

"You and Sarah are the immediate beneficiaries after that," Shelly answered. "There is also a trust to be divided equally amongst your children."

"Does that mean divided by four and each of my kids get twenty-five percent, or split in half and each of my kids get one-third of fifty percent?"

"Hmmm," Shelly said. "It's a little ambiguous. I think divided equally amongst all four grandkids, but a judge may have to decide that."

"What else is in the bag?"

Shelly thumbed through the documents and let out a soft whistle. "Savings bonds. Ten of them, it looks like. One hundred thousand each."

"Wow. Didn't know they still had that much," Ira said. "Thought Bernie got it all. So each of my kids will inherit two hundred and fifty grand. That's quite a nest egg, Howie."

Howie looked up and nodded to his dad. "Even if it's just a hundred sixty-six thousand, it's still a lot."

"Don't sell yourself short, son. Eden hasn't seen her grandmother in ten years. She doesn't deserve a dime."

Shelly, with eyes still on the savings bonds, started wincing. Ira saw a look in her eyes and said, "What?"

"These bonds were renewed two years ago."

"So?"

"They're all in Eden's name."

"Give me those," he said, ripping the savings bonds out of her hands. "There must be some mistake."

Ira scanned the documents. His face reddened, his eyes widened, his heartbeat raced until he started crumpling the papers in his hand and throwing them onto the ground.

"Maybe it's not what you think," Shelly said.

"What?" Howie asked. "What does he think?"

Ira couldn't speak. He let out small muffled screams, repeating, "Oh no, oh no," between violent shakes of his head.

"What?!" Howie insisted. "Someone tell me what's going on."

Finally, Ira lifted his head from his hands, showing red watery eyes. "Mother gave everything to Eden after Father died."

"Maybe the will takes precedence," Shelly suggested. "It does say everything should be split equally."

"Why would she do that, Dad?" Howie asked.

"Because she hates me."

"She doesn't hate you," Shelly interrupted.

Ira stood up, rubbed his eyes, walked over to a nearby oak tree, and snapped a weak branch in half. "I lived with that woman my entire life. The past few years, I bathed her when Father couldn't. I held his hand when he took his last breath. I was there for them. Where was Sarah? Afraid to fly, bullshit."

Ira's voice grew louder.

"She wasn't afraid to fly to Hawaii last year. She wasn't afraid to fly to India with that stockbroker husband of hers shopping for rugs for their new house. No. She was only afraid to fly to New Orleans. This is because Sarah married a Jew. I'm sure of it. The fucking Holocaust! It's always about the fucking Holocaust." Mimicking his mother, he continued, "'How could you marry a Jap, Ira? The Japanese were on the same side as the Germans.' For God's sake, Mother. The kids are Chinese. Lin is Chinese. They're not Japanese."

Ira stamped his feet as spittle flew off the corner of his lips.

"They don't need her fucking money. Those California assholes have more money than they know what to do with. That kid. That kid Eden is going to Stanford in the fall. What's she going to do with a million dollars?"

Shelly slid over next to Howie and tried to cover his ears, but Howie kept swatting her hand away, amazed at the vitriol emanating from his father's mouth. Ira finally stopped ranting and stalked away from the two of them toward the pond.

Left alone with the boy, Shelly could only offer, "He didn't mean those things. He's just upset."

Howie chuckled.

Finally, Ira walked back over and said, "What about the house?"

"I presume the house and the furnishings are part of the trust."

"So that means we can keep it."

"Or sell it," Shelly said. "I imagine Sarah will want to sell it and split the proceeds. The house will be worth more than the trust anyway."

"Thank God."

"What if she doesn't want to sell it?" Howie asked.

"Then I guess Ira can continue to live in it. I seriously doubt Sarah is moving to New Orleans anytime soon."

"Unless I'm a sex offender," Ira reminded them. "Then I'll *have* to move out and she can do what she wants with that goddamn house."

37

After lunch, Shelly drove Ira and Howie back to the house. She pulled into the driveway and before they got out of the car said, "Maybe we can prove that those savings bonds were changed when your mother had diminished mental capacity."

"What's that have to do with anything?" Ira asked.

"Well, if Sarah forced your mother to change the savings bonds…"

"That devious bitch," Ira yelled. "She would do that, wouldn't she?"

"Do you have any medical records in the house?"

"Yes, of course. There's a bunch of stuff in the filing cabinets," Ira said. "You can come in and look."

Ira got out of the car first, followed by Howie. Shelly shook the car back and forth as she pushed open the door and climbed out, then followed the guys up the stairs. "Well, if they didn't leave you anything, then I'm defending you for free. That ain't going to happen."

Howie was the first to the door, Ira still fishing through his pockets for the solitary house key. "It's open," Howie said, turning to face his father.

Ira stepped in front of his son, pushed the door open wider, and called, "Hello?"

He looked back at Shelly, who stood on the porch with cell phone in hand resting against her hip. She mouthed to Ira, "Should I call the police?"

"Hello," Ira repeated loudly. "Anyone here? Charlie?" Slowly moving into the foyer with Howie brushing against his back, expecting the house to be ransacked, Ira was stunned to find nothing amiss. The filing cabinets were closed, loose computer wires still spread across the desk.

They slowly searched the remainder of the first floor, Shelly hanging by the front door, shifting her body weight from leg to leg, making annoying sucking sounds with her lips. Ira motioned for Howie to stay by the bottom of the stairwell as he fumbled up the stairs and did a cursory search of the second floor. When he came back down, Howie was in the kitchen, peeking out of the blinds on the back door. "Anything out there?" Ira asked.

Howie jumped at his father's voice, sneaked a sideways glance, but said nothing, instead just shrugging his shoulders. When they returned to the front room, Shelly was sprawled across the floor with a large bald figure standing over her motionless body.

Ira took one step forward, then thought better of it. He turned to run, but the stranger yelled, "Freeze."

Ira froze directly in front of Howie, whose feet remained fastened to the floor. "What do you want?" Ira asked, the pitch in his voice rising by an octave or two.

"You left your card at the bar," the man bellowed. "Where the fuck is Charlie?"

"We're looking for her too," Ira said.

"I know she's around here somewhere."

"Not true, not true. I swear she's not here."

"What about you, boy? You seen that ho anywhere?"

"She's not a ho," Howie said.

The man took a few steps forward, his beefy hands outstretched as if he were Bela Lugosi heading for his next victim. "You the one she been fucking?"

Ira's face turned ashen and he tried to step in between the man and his son. "My son had no such relations with that girl."

Howie's head dropped, his chin touching the top of his chest.

"Did you, son?"

With Ira's attention fixated on his guilt-ridden son, the man moved closer to them, lunged forward, and grabbed Howie by the sleeve of his shirt, pushing him against the doorframe. "Where's the girl, kid?"

Howie's eyes darted back and forth between the man and his father, tears flowing vigorously down his puffy cheeks.

"Show me around," the man said, pushing Howie roughly and spinning Ira toward the front of the house. "Lead."

Ira headed for the stairs, Howie behind him and the man last. They took to the second floor, opening each of the kids' bedrooms, scanning the empty closets, rifling through the armoires, and checking the bathrooms. In Ira's bedroom, the man took a long, deep breath as if sniffing for Charlie's scent. His eye twitched a bit when he exhaled, perhaps picking up the slightest hint of her cheap perfume.

Back on the main floor, Shelly's body remained laid out on the floor behind the couch, a trickle of blood streaking her grey hair. The man pointed to the door that exited to the side of the house where they took the trash out. Ira unlocked the door and led them out to the overgrown reeds that blocked the pathway. But the path wasn't blocked. Instead, the weeds had been trimmed back, the reeds snapped, forming a narrow walkway toward the back of the house. Ira turned his head to look up the pathway, then turned back to Howie, who had the look of a rat caught in a trap.

The man must have noticed the trepidation on Ira's face. He pushed past Ira with a brisk stride toward the backyard and smacked the small rusted metal gate open. It looked like the backyard of an abandoned house: dying plants fighting an army of weeds plus a small olive tree for the right to stay alive, and tangled vines winning the battle. The narrow clearing against the left side of the wooden fence was clearly visible. It led straight to the door of the shed.

Rather than use the path, the man forced his way through shoulder-height weeds, beelining straight for the vine-covered wall of the small wooden structure. It had a low tin roof covered in mold and one small window seeped in filth, rotting pieces of wood two-by-sixes lying at the foot of the building. The man reached for the door and shoved it open, crashing against the outer wall and bouncing back into his waiting forearm.

The interior of the shed was long and narrow. On the left, a rusted child's bike, some old tools, rakes, and brooms resting against the wall. A long-abandoned water heater led to an exhaust pipe that rifled through the roof. Straight ahead a naked, crumbling cinderblock wall barely capable of holding up the roof. To the left, a full-size mattress on the floor, a sheet loosely draped over the bottom half, a pillow without its case. Next to the mattress, a round side table overtaken by used candles dripping hardened wax over its small surface.

Charlie's luggage was the elephant in the room. The Louis Vuitton bag sat at the foot of the bed, her stripper clothes hanging over the side. No one said a word. They all just stood there trying to decipher the ramifications of Charlie spending her evenings in this dump, presumably hiding an insidious relationship with Ira's young, impressionable son. With eyes darting across the room, the man finally said, "I want my girl back," then with his voice raised to full force, "NOW!"

With Ira so close to the door and the giant man on the opposite side of the room, he decided to make a break for it. He pushed Howie outside, slammed the door shut, and tried to nestle a two-by-six underneath the doorknob. The man shouldered the door open with ease and chased Ira and Howie back through the side door, through the kitchen, and into the living room where Shelly was now standing with Officers R. Miles and H. Hanson.

Ira was shocked to see his two recent nemeses in his house, let alone that they had appeared so quickly. Shelly stood in the foyer holding a towel against the back of her head. R. Miles had his gun drawn on the three frozen figures in front of him. "On the floor, get down! On the floor!" he shouted.

Ira struggled to his knees, dropping his chest to the floor. Howie followed suit. Ira could not see the bald man behind him, but he heard R. Miles repeat the command. Ira assumed he went unheeded, because the next moment R. Miles hurdled their prone bodies in pursuit of the bald man. Heavy footfalls, then the sound of the back door slamming against the wall.

Ira twisted his head forward and saw Shelly pleading with H. Hanson, who now had his gun fixed on Ira and Howie. H. Hanson temporarily protested back, then started nodding his head in agreement. Moving closer to them until Ira could only see his black socks and scuffed shoes, H. Hanson reached down and lifted Howie off the ground, helping him over to the couch.

The tension in the room was palpable. H. Hanson re-holstered his gun and listened to Shelly explain why Ira should also be helped off the floor. The officer kept nodding and waving his hand to get her to keep her voice down. Apparently, H. Hanson wanted to wait until R. Miles returned before exonerating Ira. When he did return through the back door, he was out of breath, gasping for air, and talking on his walkie-talkie.

"Lost him," he said, looking somewhere between pissed off and disappointed. "Girl's stuff is in the cottage out back."

R. Miles lifted Ira off the floor by the back of his collar so that he stumbled up to a standing position.

H. Hanson said to no one in particular, "How long she been back there?"

Facing Ira, staring straight into his eyes, R. Miles said, "I thought you were told to stay away from that girl."

"He didn't know she was back there," Howie interrupted.

"But you did?" R. Miles asked.

Howie looked sheepishly at the ground.

"You are cavorting with a known prostitute," R. Miles continued. "We can take you in too."

Ira quickly interrupted, "That won't be necessary. This is my fault."

R. Miles didn't hesitate to spin Ira around and slap those hard metal handcuffs back over his wrists. "You have the right to remain silent. Anything you say can and will be used against you in a court of law. You have the right to an attorney. If you cannot afford one..."

"He can afford one," Shelly interrupted.

"One will be appointed for you. Do you understand those rights as I have read them to you?"

Ira nodded.

Despite Howie's and Shelly's protestations, R. Miles led Ira out the front door and to the squad car with flashing lights parked in front of the house, pushed him forcefully into the back seat, and slammed the door shut.

38

Ira sat in the back of the squad car with his head resting against the window as the air grew stuffy and still. Two other cop cars pulled up, making a total of six officers in his house, presumably discussing what to do about Howie. Four streetcars passed in both directions. Joggers flew past his peripheral vision. He wondered whether Howie would lead the officers to Dixie Divas, though he figured he was trying his best to protect his girlfriend.

How was Ira to explain to Lin that their son was dating a prostitute? Was Howie even using protection? Ira didn't know. He'd figured the birds and bees conversation was still a few years away. He had also assumed that someone else would be giving that speech, himself being so ill-equipped to supply advice on dating. The only talk he remembered with his own father was about the class guinea pig that gave birth during his junior year in high school and ate all its babies. "That's what females do to males," Father said. That advice stuck with Ira through most of college. It was pretty much why he still never wanted a woman's mouth anywhere near his own genitals.

Ira must have been daydreaming, because he was startled to see R. Miles's outstretched hand suddenly pulling him out of the back seat. He removed the cuffs from Ira's wrists and led him back into the house where an EMT was removing a sphygmomanometer from Shelly's bicep.

Shelly snarled at Ira as soon as he entered the room. "Who was that guy? Howie won't say."

Ira looked at the four officers who were waiting for his reply. Howie was leaning against the wall, sniffling with his arms folded and his head down.

"Don't know," Ira answered. "He came sniffing around here last week…"

"When?" R. Miles interrupted.

"Oh, ah, I guess it was Ash Wednesday. When I fell out of the tree."

The room erupted in laughter, breaking some of the tension strangling the air. "Go on," R. Miles said.

"That's it, pretty much," Ira said. "He came around, pounding on the door right after Charlie got home."

"You know anything else about him?" R. Miles asked.

Ira glanced at Howie, who was now staring back at him. Ira looked back at the officers and shook his head.

"Will you need anything else from my client?" Shelly asked.

"You mean you're not arresting me?"

"We're going to give you a pass this time, Mr. Silver. You look like you've been through enough."

"Thank God," Ira said. "I'm not really cut out for OPP."

The group laughed again. As the officers started for the door, Ira asked, "Does this mean you're going to drop the charges?"

"Quit while you're ahead, Ira," Shelly advised.

"But you saw that guy! He's the real pimp."

"Shut up," Shelly yelled.

R. Miles waited for Ira to say something else stupid, but after a few moments of silence, he closed the door behind him.

Ira tried to comfort his son with an awkward hug. Howie left his arms at his side, but he did lean his head slightly onto Ira's shoulder. It was the first time Ira realized that his son had outgrown him. They stayed embraced for nearly a minute until Shelly interrupted the silence. "That's sweet, guys, but are you going to tell me where the whore went?"

"Charlie!" Howie and Ira snapped back.

"Whatever. She's obviously been sleeping here," Shelly said. "Are you going to say anything?"

Howie mumbled something incoherent.

"Speak up, son," Ira said.

"She has nowhere else to go," Howie yelled.

"Why didn't you say anything?! Why'd you make us go on this wild goose chase? We went all the way to Gulfport for nothing?"

"I guess I didn't want you to find out," Howie said.

"You guess?"

"I knew you'd act like this."

"Act like what? What are you talking about? I'm just trying to get myself out of trouble. I thought you were trying to help."

Howie went back to mumbling. Ira looked at Shelly, who was giving him the head bob. Ira's eyes narrowed. Shelly's eyes narrowed. She bobbed her head to the right twice and Ira slowly made his way after her into the foyer.

"What?" Ira asked in a low voice. "What's the matter with you?"

"Listen, Ira. I'm not the motherly type. In case you hadn't noticed. But my brother Bob, he's got three kids. My nephews. Little pricks they are. I've seen them all go through puberty. Your son. He's got nothing on those kids."

"What are you trying to say?" Ira interrupted.

"I'm trying to tell you that you're not going to figure that kid out. Not tonight and probably not tomorrow either. You might as well drop it."

"Drop it? I can't drop it. I've got to find Charlie."

"Fine. I get that. But you're not going to find her by badgering your son."

Ira finally took a breath. He'd been all hopped up but the nervous energy was finally starting to dissipate. That's the moment he realized the gout was back and he immediately needed to grab Shelly's hand and find the nearest seat. She led him back into the front room, where Howie was still sulking in the corner.

"Howie, get my medicine, please. It's in my bathroom."

Howie ran up the stairs while Ira lay on the couch massaging his foot, which was now elevated above his knee.

Shelly pursed her lips and said, "I forgot all about your mother's medical records. I'm not really up for searching through your filing cabinets. If you don't mind, I'm going to head home, take some Tylenol, and crash."

"What should I do?"

"Start making funeral arrangements," she answered.

"Why me?"

"Who else is going to do it?"

39

Early Thursday morning, the doorbell started ringing. Apparently, an email blast had been sent out to all the members of Temple Sinai. First came the Pearlmans. They brought the strudel. Then Father's old driver Mr. Hopper, who seemed like he would have stayed the entire day had Ira been a more welcoming personality. Shirley, Mother's favorite salesclerk at Perlis, brought a sandwich tray. The Stones brought a fruit salad, the Ornsteins brought an Asian noodle salad from Whole Foods, and the Danzygers brought a cheese plate.

By mid-afternoon, Rabbi Maisel paid his visit. He noshed on the food, gulped lukewarm coffee, spewed condolences, and discussed the funeral. Ira was relieved to find out that Father had arranged and paid for everything in advance. He offered to get food from the Louisiana Pizza Kitchen, but the rabbi assured him that it wouldn't be necessary. The bigger problem was the whole twenty-four-hour rule. The funeral really should be tonight, but that would be impossible. Since the Sabbath was a little over twenty-four hours from then—and Jewish law prevented burial on the Sabbath—they would have to squeeze the funeral in on Friday morning.

"That's fine, Rabbi. I'll call everyone this evening," Ira said.

"What about Sarah?" Rabbi asked.

Ira rolled his lips and let out a whinny before shaking his head back and forth.

"You haven't called Sarah?" Rabbi asked.

"Not exactly."

"Would you like me to call her for you?"

"Very much so, Rabbi. We haven't talked in years."

"That's too bad, Ira. Sometimes tragedies like this bring families together," Rabbi said. "She's all you got now, you know?"

Ira looked at Howie who was sitting on the arm of the sofa, halfway paying attention to the conversation.

"Yes, I understand," Rabbi said. "You have your kids, but there will be a time when your kids have their own families to worry about. They may not have time for an old mishigas."

"Are you implying that Sarah would have time for me?" Ira asked.

"You never know. Crazier things have been known to happen."

"Not in this family," Ira answered. "Not in a family that will hold a grudge until the day they utter their last word."

Rabbi dusted off his pants, scattering crumbs to the floor. He gave Ira a final sheepish look, shrugged his shoulders, and headed for the door. As he crossed the threshold, he turned and said, "Let's push the funeral back to one o'clock. That should give Sarah enough time to get here."

"That's fine. I'll start making some calls right away. Thank you, Rabbi."

As soon as the rabbi left, Ira got out an old phonebook and started calling the numbers. Many of them were home landlines long since forgotten, but he left a dozen or so messages and spoke to three or four people from out of state who bid him condolences but passed on flying in on such short notice. Ira thought it barbaric to follow this persnickety ritual. Four thousand years ago, it probably wasn't too difficult to round up the tribe for a backyard burial on the fly. These days, with families spread throughout the continent and sometimes the world, Ira had no idea how he was supposed to plan and execute a funeral in the same amount of time it took to send an overnight FedEx package across the country.

Lost in the innocuous phone calls was everything else going on in Ira's life. He forgot about his upcoming court date, his son's budding romance, the prospect of losing his home and his livelihood. It had been a few days since it dawned on him that every article, every ad, and the entire layout for the *New Orleans Jewish Monthly* were sitting in an evidence room somewhere at Orleans Parish Prison. Not to mention the manuscript that Ira had spent the past ten years working on. It was finally complete and just needed the attention of a proper editor and a literary agent. When Ira had begun working on it, there weren't ten million self-published books every year. Back then, he expected dozens of agents would be knocking down his door. The reality was that over the past two years, the forty query letters he had sent hadn't lured even a single response.

When he finished the monotony of the phone calls, he made himself a plate of food and sat in his rocker silently thinking about his inauspicious destiny. As the shadows darkened in the old house, Howie emerged from the second floor and headed for the front door. "Where you going?" Ira asked.

"To look for Charlie," he answered.

"The hell you are."

Howie's eyes narrowed and twitched, and he grumbled under his breath. Without replying, he continued out the front door and didn't look back.

Ira jumped up from the couch and tried feebly to give chase, but his balky ankle gave out before he even reached the foyer. He crawled the remaining few feet onto the porch and watched his son scurrying down the block toward the French Quarter.

40

gain, Ira had a weighty feeling of solitude. There was no one he could call for help. He crawled back to the couch and stared at the wall for a few hours. A couple of times, he tried to stand and walk outside, but his inflamed ankle made each journey through the house more and more difficult. At some point, he must have dozed off because he was surprised to wake to the sound of whippoorwills serenading the sunrise.

Ira shook off the arthritis, stretched his back, and slowly rose to his feet. He called Howie's name, but got nothing more than the echo of his own voice. While he searched the backyard, Ira heard pounding on the front door. He rushed through the house, stumbled to the door, and thrust it open.

Before him stood Sarah. She wore a blue patterned wrap-around day dress with ruffles around the neckline. Ira hadn't seen her since their brief encounter at Father's funeral. He wondered if she always wore clunky oversized sunglasses or only when in mourning. She had her arms folded over her chest and there was something in her posture that made Ira feel that she was bracing for a fight.

Sarah was nine years younger than Ira. She was the darling of the family. Everything Ira was, Sarah was not. She was smart, played piano, stood three inches taller than her brother, had friends and feelings and wit and charm. From the very beginning of their lives together, there was a distance begotten by age and then kindled by jealousy. Ira felt like his parents treated Sarah like she was a do-over. There was a sense that she was. From Ira's childhood through third grade, Mother and Father always talked to people as if they never planned on having another kid. It was a distinct memory for Ira, one of the dozens of early memories of childhood misfortunes: burning his hand on a firecracker; breaking his elbow falling down the stairs; sitting in the closet hiding from Father after a parent/teacher conference; overhearing through the hangers of pantsuits, "Maybe we should try again."

From her birth through the day Ira left for college, the doting never stopped. Sarah was pampered, given everything she ever wanted, anything she ever asked for. During his four years at Tulane and the following five years before she left for college, he had bitter memories of her blossoming into a beautiful woman. She graduated from Newman High School, studied at Stanford, and never looked back. When it was time to marry, she forced the family to fly across the country so she could consummate her marriage at an exclusive chateau in Napa Valley.

"Are you going to let me in, or what?" Sarah demanded.

Ira lowered his arm from the door and Sarah pushed her way past him into the foyer. She dropped a small bag onto the sofa, then picked the bag back up, brushed the dust off the sofa, and returned the bag to her shoulder. Without looking at Ira, she tried flicking on all the lights and sighed after each fruitless attempt. Finally, she took off her shades and said, "Why is it always so fucking dark in here?"

"Good to see you too," Ira responded.

"Shut up, Ira. I'm going upstairs to wash up. I'll be staying in the master. I brought my own sheets."

Ira didn't have a chance to respond. She was going to do as she damn well pleased. She couldn't care less that it was Ira's room now. For all intents and purposes, it was her room until she decided it was time to leave New Orleans.

While Ira stared up the staircase sullenly, the handle of the front door shimmied back and forth. When he crossed back into the foyer, he saw his son with a tired, dreary look in his dark eyes. Ira reached out to hug Howie, and for the first time in as long as he could remember, one of his children actually hugged him back. He fought back the propensity to scold him or slap him in the face. Instead, they held their embrace for a minute until Howie let go. It had never been in Ira's skill set to read his children's minds, but somehow, he knew that Howie's search had come up empty.

"The funeral's in a few hours," he said. "Go upstairs and get some rest. And stay out of your aunt's way."

Howie walked over to the bottom of the staircase, held the banister for a second, looked back at his father, and said, "Charlie's gone."

"Gone? Like dead gone?" Ira asked.

"No. Like left town gone."

"How do you know?"

A tear rolled down the side of Howie's cheek. He sniffled and said, "She left a note in our spot."

"You two had a spot?" Ira said with a bit of a chuckle.

"It's not funny," Howie said in an elevated voice.

He took a crumpled piece of paper out of his pants pocket and handed it to his father. Ira looked at his young son and tried to wipe the tear from his cheek, but the boy turned away. Ira perused the scribbled note.

Dear Chunky,
To much trubble in Nawlins.
Dont wanna hurt yall. Desided to take off.
Please thanks Ira for me. C u when I c u.
Luv, Charlene

Ira was flabbergasted. He finally said, "Where'd she go?"

Howie shook his head. "I've been at the bus depot all night. She never showed up."

Ira paced around the room on his bum ankle, clasping his fingers around his temples. "For Christ's sake, what if she'd showed up? Were you going to run away with her?"

"No."

"No?"

"I don't know what I would have done. I wanted to bring her to the police station. I've been trying to get her to go all week."

"She's a prostitute, Howie. There's no way she's going to the cops on her own."

"Then how are we going to get you out of jail?" Howie asked.

"Out of jail?" Sarah parroted, appearing at the top of the staircase.

Ira let out an "uggh" that sounded like a balloon deflating.

"Out of jail for what?"

"Nothing!" Ira yelled. "It's none of your business."

Sarah seemed taken aback by Ira's tone of voice. She cocked her head to the side and submitted a fake smile to her nephew. "Hello, Howie. So nice to see you. My, how big you've gotten."

Howie returned the fake smile.

"Is someone going to tell me what's going on?"

Ira and Howie both looked up the staircase and screamed in unison, "No!"

41

About three dozen people showed up for the funeral. Rabbi Maisel must have been expecting a bigger turnout, because he held the ceremony in the large sanctuary. A fresh coat of beige paint covered the walls; the stained glass windows reflected the light off the forty-foot arched ceiling. Twenty people, mostly elderly, sat toward the front right near each other. A few solitary souls were scattered throughout the rest of the pews.

Ira and Sarah were locked in the rabbi's office for about an hour as the other mourners trickled into the sanctuary. The rabbi spent fifteen minutes offering his sympathy to Ira and his sister, discussing the process of the imminent ceremony, the eulogies, and the walk to the gravesite.

Ira reminded the rabbi that they had been through it all with their father less than two years prior. With that, the rabbi left them alone again and they spent the better part of the hour shifting uncomfortably in their seats, Sarah pecking away at her cell phone. As the wall clock ticking towards one, Ira looked at his sister, who by now had put her phone away and was tapping her nails against the mahogany desk. "Where's your wedding ring?" he asked.

Sarah looked down at her hand and the tan line where a ring had once sat. "Left it at home," she said. "Never know when you might get robbed in this town." She returned her hand to her lap beneath the table. "You have a chance to look at the will?"

Ira instinctively pounded his fist against the table, startling Sarah. "I did."

"The most recent one?"

"You have a recent one?" Ira asked. "Let me guess, she left everything to you?"

"Essentially," she responded.

Ira's hands balled into little fists and shook so fervently that Sarah moved to the other side of the couch.

"Whoa, easy there. I thought we could make this a little less difficult," she said.

"Why, why, why?" Ira hissed.

"Oh, Ira, for God's sakes. If you can't figure it out, I'm not going to help you."

Ira paced around the room rubbing his fists like he was ready for a fistfight. "Well, let me see it."

"The will? I didn't bring it. Besides, it'll be up to the executor to interpret what's in it," Sarah said.

"Who's the executor?" Ira asked.

"Shelly Rubenstein," she answered, shaking her head, rolling her eyes, and twisting her lips. "Who else would it be?"

Ira paced around the room. He was about to speak again when a light knock came at the door. The rabbi poked his head in and said, "Would you two like to follow me?"

Sarah jumped up and followed the rabbi without even looking at her brother. Ira waited for the door to close before walking over to the bookshelf and punching his fist into a row of textbooks. He flexed his hand a few times to dull the pain, then opened the door and caught up with Sarah, the rabbi, and the cantor just as they were entering the sanctuary.

Ira and Sarah took seats on opposite sides of the front row. Howie got up from his seat a few rows back and joined his father. The rabbi began the sermon with a few prayers in Hebrew followed by a hymn sung by the cantor. Behind the two clergymen sat Mother's pine casket raised on a metal stretcher.

Cantor Cohen, who had been at Sinai for nearly two decades, spoke first. "The Silver family have been important members of the Sinai community since its inception one-hundred-forty-five years ago. We owe a huge debt of gratitude to this family who have worked so tirelessly to keep our community alive. I have stood on this pulpit and looked out at the faces of both Stanley and Lettie for many, many years. They both sat up here on this very stage, serving as president of the board of trustees and heads of the Brotherhood and Sisterhood. I don't know where this congregation would be without the dedication of people like Stanley and Lettie. So we gather here today to pay our final respects to a wonderful wife, mother, daughter, sister, grandmother, woman. Her legacy will remain a part of this congregation for as long as this building stands here on St. Charles Avenue."

The cantor stopped and Rabbi Maisel asked everyone to bow their heads in silent meditation. Then he continued, "Sarah Bronstein has asked to speak next. Sarah is the daughter of Lettie and a longstanding member of our community. We thank her for her generous donations all the way from San Francisco. Her husband Dan and daughter Eden could not be here today, but I wanted to acknowledge their generous gift of the Oneg Shabbat following tonight's service. You are all welcome to join us this evening for services beginning at six-fifteen p.m. Sarah." The rabbi extended his hand toward her.

Sarah traversed the stairs, kissed the rabbi on both cheeks, and took her place behind the podium. Ira was fuming beneath his exterior smile, yet he was also relieved he wasn't called upon since he usually clammed up in front of an audience. He had scribbled a few notes on a piece of paper the night before but hadn't fully committed to giving the eulogy. He must have missed the communication between the rabbi and his sister, because he seemed a little stunned that she had been called up before him.

"My mother," she said, choking back a sob, "was a wonderful person, as you all know. She was a wonderful mother too. She gave me the courage to be the person I am today. Her support, both emotional and spiritual, was invaluable. I admired her for her dedication to this congregation and to the entire Jewish community in New Orleans. We had a unique bond that only a mother and daughter can have. We spent countless nights talking on the phone, gossiping as girls tend to do, and it pains me to know that I will never hear her…" Sarah cut herself off right then and started bawling. Rabbi came to her side and offered her a tissue, which she grabbed and used to dab her eyes. "…never hear her voice again."

"Oh, stop with the fakery," Ira yelled from the pew. He could tell when his sister was putting on a show, and this was just way too over the top. Sarah walked down the stairs without taking her evil eye off her seething brother. Rabbi Maisel asked if anyone had anything else to add, but Ira couldn't bring himself to say anything about the woman who had essentially written him and his kids out of her will. The more he thought about it, the more livid he became. He was lost in his head for the rest of the service, recalling those subtle hints Mother had dropped over the past few years. She never mentioned phone calls with Sarah, but she sure did harp on the lack of communication from Howie, Sammy, and Yang. Sarah must have put those thoughts in her head. Even if she didn't orchestrate the name changes on those bonds or the will, she must have insinuated that it was the proper thing to do.

Ira didn't remember the service ending. He couldn't recall rising from his seat nor leaving the sanctuary. It wasn't hot nor cold, raining nor sunny. Everything was just hazy. He vaguely recalled the brief ceremony at the gravesite where he shoveled the first scoop of dirt onto the submerged casket. Before the rabbi could recite the mourner's Kaddish, Ira had turned his back to the other ten people paying their respects and headed for the exit.

42

Reformed Judaism had gone so far to assimilate in American society as to make its tenets nearly unrecognizable. As Rabbi Benjamin once said to Lin, "You just pick and choose which parts you like and as long as you believe, that's good enough for me." Ira had a problem with that concept, and he went through immeasurable pains to make sure his father had a proper burial and a thirty-day Shiva.

Mother's Shiva was going to be something less however, far less. First off, Sarah insisted that it begin that evening because she had a return flight to San Francisco on Sunday night. That was blasphemous to Ira, who tried to insist that Shiva couldn't be called on the Sabbath. Then Sarah made sure that everyone knew when she was leaving so that things would wrap up in three days rather than the traditionally minimum seven.

Ira tried to put the will out of his mind until after the Shiva. Instead of sulking, he returned home to set up the house. He placed a pitcher of water and a basin on a small table outside the front door for guests to wash their hands. He draped natty old blankets over the mirrors and placed a huge mourning candle that someone had brought over for Father's Shiva on the mantle.

Sarah returned while Ira was moving the trays of leftover food and spreading them onto the dining room table. "I'm going upstairs to change," she said to no one in particular.

While Sarah was upstairs, a representative of Temple Sinai brought two special metal folding chairs for the family members to sit on, just above floor level, and set them up in the living room. Ira imagined they were better suited for a Sunday school teacher in a classroom full of four-year-olds.

People began trickling in. First Howie, Shelly, and Rabbi Maisel, then most of the people who had been at the Temple. Rabbi lit the candle and said a few prayers as Ira took his rightful spot on one of the metal chairs. Thirty minutes later, Sarah came downstairs and chatted with guests. She looked as if she had just showered and put on a fresh coat of makeup. When she finally took her spot on the folding chair, Ira snickered. "You're wearing makeup? You know you're not supposed to wear makeup or a fancy dress at a Shiva."

"Shut the fuck up," Sarah whispered under her breath.

Ira folded his arms over his chest and bit his tongue. They spent the next few hours inching their chairs further away from one another while receiving guests. Most of the funeral worshippers left within the first hour, but others arrived bearing fresh platters of food and fruit. Many of them were old friends of Mother's or Sarah's, with the exception of some of the temple board members who served with his parents over the years.

Most people had the sense and sensibility to refrain from asking about the estate, with the obvious exception of Sarah's old college sweetheart. He was a blonde-haired blue-eyed former member of the swim team from the great state of Alabama. He looked exactly like he had in college, except his hair was a little greyer at the temples and his belly had a bit of a paunch. He smacked a wet kiss on Sarah's lips and embraced her in a bear hug. Strangely, Sarah didn't seem to mind. She actually kept her hand on his shoulder far too long, and they ignored Ira throughout their pompous conversation.

"Hey sweetheart, how's it going?"

"Alright, Tommy. How are you?"

"Grand, baby, just grand. You planning on moving back into the old house?"

"Don't think so," Sarah said. "Can't really see myself moving back to New Orleans."

"My sister's got her real estate license if you want some help selling it."

"You have her number on you?"

"Sure, baby. I'll text it to you."

That was the first clue Ira got of his sister's motives, and it made him want to kill her. Not metaphorically, either. The rest of the day, not a word was uttered between them. All Ira thought about was the multitude of viable ways to end his sister's life.

As if Friday evening wasn't bad enough, it wasn't until early Saturday morning that the shit really hit the fan.

Shelly woke Ira just after eight. She brought Ira a coffee from PJ's and they talked on the front porch.

"Sarah's got the new will," Ira told her.

"She say what's in it?"

"No. But she did tell me that you are the executor."

"That's it? That's all she'd tell you?" Shelly asked.

"She said something about me knowing why Mother would write me out of the will. I thought about it all night. I really have no idea," Ira said calmly.

Shelly sighed. "Look, Ira. I feel really bad about this. I know your Mother entrusted me with the will, but…"

"But what?" Ira asked.

"But I'll do what I can to help you."

"Why?"

"I don't like that girl. Don't like her one bit," she said, pointing at the door. "Let me take Howie for the day and we'll get out of your way. Just try not to fuel the fire with your sister. She can make things very difficult for you. Right now, she holds all the cards. Remember what I said, though—diminished capacity. That's going to be your best hope."

Just after nine, Ira poured himself another cup of coffee and took it to his seat on the metal folding chair. No one showed up for over an hour as he sipped his coffee and massaged his ankle. Finally, a well-dressed, grey-haired woman wearing a knee-length skirt and black stockings and holding a clipboard arrived. She smiled at Ira when she entered the living room and immediately thrust out her hand for a cordial handshake.

She was about to walk away when Ira asked, "Are you a friend of Sarah's?"

The woman tilted her head to the side, seemingly unsure how to answer. She finally said, "Sarah invited me. Who are you?"

"I'm her brother, Ira."

"Nice to meet you, Ira."

"Would you like some coffee?" Ira asked, as he heard his sister bounding down the staircase.

The woman didn't answer. She turned her attention to Sarah, tucked the clipboard beneath her armpit, and introduced herself.

"Nice to meet you, Liz. So nice of you to come on such short notice."

"Not to worry. I'll be out of your way in no time."

As they were talking, Mr. Hopper and his wife arrived. They walked straight up to Ira and handed him a fruitcake. Mrs. Hopper couldn't say enough good things about Mother. She spent the next fifteen minutes telling Ira about the time she was in the hospital with ovarian cancer and Mother paid a visit. And when the Hoppers' only son graduated from high school, Ira's parents generously gifted him a fondue set. If that wasn't enough, after Father passed away, Mother bequeathed them the title to the old BMW. Unfortunately, the Hoppers could never afford to pay for the new transmission, so it had been sitting in their garage collecting dust for the past two years.

Another four or five guests arrived as Ira finished his conversation with the Hoppers. One of them brought bagels, and Ira could see his sister cutting the bagels and setting up the rest of the food in the dining room. Liz was kneeling in the foyer looking at the underside of the rug and scribbling notes on her clipboard. Ira kept glancing around the Hoppers at her.

When she removed the blanket from the mirror above the fireplace, Ira interrupted Mr. Hopper. "Um, excuse me, Liz. What are you doing?"

"Looking at the mirror. It's quite a piece. Too bad it has such a big chip on the corner. Do you have any idea why it's covered?" Liz unraveled the corner of the blanket and dropped it back over the face of the mirror as she spoke, then shrugged her shoulders.

Struggling up from his low seat, Ira shuffled forward to confront Liz, who hugged the clipboard against her chest at his approach. He poked the clipboard with his pointer finger and said loudly, "It's to prevent the mourners from showing their vanity."

Liz cowered a bit and said, "I'm so sorry. I had no idea. I will try to be more careful with the rest of the stuff."

"What in God's name are you doing with my *stuff*?"

"It's not your stuff," Sarah interrupted.

Ira faced his sister who was standing beneath the door frame into the dining room with her arms folded over her chest. "It's Mother's stuff," she reminded him with an obvious sense of entitlement.

"What do you mean?" Ira asked, with his voice rising. "What're you doing?"

"We're having an estate sale," Sarah answered.

"An estate what?! What are you talking about?"

"What else are we going to do with all this junk?" Sarah asked rhetorically. "You think I want any of this at my house?"

Ira's face glowed like a Bunsen burner. He breathed quick and heavy through his nostrils, feeling the fury rise though not really believing what he was hearing. He wanted to wring his sister's neck, but she was in much better shape than he was, and he feared a colossal beatdown in front of their guests, who had now peeked their heads into the room to see what was going on. Ira finally growled, "These are family heirlooms. Don't you care about any of them?"

Sarah didn't even take a moment to think about it. She shook her head and said, "Not really."

"*You fucking bitch!*" Ira screamed while the recently arrived guests became recently departed by scurrying out the front door. Liz was the only one who stuck around, still standing with her mouth open and her clipboard attached to her chest. "You don't need the money. Why are you doing this?"

"You don't have any idea what I need. All you think about is yourself. That's all you ever thought about."

"Me? Me?! Don't make this about me," Ira yelled, stomping his foot.

"It's not about you, you stupid fool. Dan moved out and left me with nothing but a house full of furniture and an upside-down mortgage. He hasn't even paid the child support. This crap gives me another six months to a year."

Ira didn't know what to say. He stood silently seething, still too disoriented and angry to provide any meaningful retort to Sarah's admission. Instead, he punched the clipboard out of Liz's hands and grunted before storming out of the room and stumbling up the stairs.

43

Ira and Howie were roused Sunday morning by loud voices outside the front door. By the time Ira had dressed and peeked his head outside, a small crowd was jostling for position on the porch. Liz and two other women, all holding clipboards, were pushing their way through the crowd, admonishing everyone to hold their horses.

Ira stepped out of the way and let the three women into the foyer. They immediately went about their business, stamping every item in the house with a price sticker. They moved about the room with the swiftness of fairy princesses, brandishing their pens like magic wands, calling out numbers as they went. Liz never thought to introduce her assistants or to ask Ira about the history of any of the items in the room; to her, everything was just a dollar sign and it was her job to make Sarah as much money as she could. When Liz started up the stairs, Ira smirked and said, "The sleeping Chinese kid is not for sale."

At eight a.m. sharp, Liz opened the door to a crowd that snaked down the entire walkway, all the way to St. Charles Avenue. Faces lit with excitement as they crossed through the threshold of the front door. They were from all walks of life: some black, some white, some young, some old. The only things Ira felt they all had in common were their ugly faces and an affinity for cheap clothing. They fanned out across the house like a wildfire in the California wilderness, staking claim to everything they could get their grubby hands on, practically ripping items out of each other's hands.

Ira sat in one of the Shiva seats, shaking his head incessantly as he watched the hustle and bustle of strangers scooping items into their arms and shouting over each other. Numbers and negotiations flew across the room like spit at a rodeo. Somehow Liz and her cohorts tracked the prices on their clipboards and collected money, halting some of the snakes as they tried to leave without paying. They all looked like shysters to Ira, and he was about to storm off when two of his mother's oldest friends appeared at the front door holding a casserole dish.

The two women, who were built like small refrigerators, wore headscarves and girdles, looking as if they had just gotten off the boat at Ellis Island. They pensively approached Ira and held out the dish. He pointed toward the dining room where the twelve-foot table was in the process of being lifted in the air and carried out the front door. These women had known Ira all their lives, but other than a few words of Yiddish, they hadn't said much to him over the years. He had never understood their coldness toward him but assumed it was just a generational gap, and that was how they treated everyone. They looked perplexed by the commotion around them, and it took Ira a few moments to realize that they were sneering at him with a "How could you?" look.

Ira insisted that it was his sister's idea to sell all the stuff, but since Sarah wasn't around to defend herself, it made him seem even weaker. He thought they were about to leave, but instead they took the casserole to the kitchen without another word to him. A few minutes later they reappeared with a couple of Mother's glass bowls and their casserole dish, now clean and empty. One of them, Mrs. Berkowicz, took a five-dollar bill out of her purse and shoved it into Ira's palm, shaking her head the whole time. They said nothing else before leaving.

Howie followed two men carrying the twin bed and box spring down the stairs, holding his suitcase in his arms. He sat in the empty Shiva seat and stared at the random faces walking around the house. "Dad," he said, "this sucks."

Ira laughed and looked at his son, nodding his assent. They sat in silence for the better part of an hour watching the furnishings disappear with alarming speed. Around lunchtime, Shelly stormed into the house with an angry, contorted face. "What's going on?" she asked.

"Sarah's selling everything," Ira answered.

"What? Why? She can't do that!"

"She just did."

"I am the executor of the will. I could've gotten an injunction or something," she cried. "This has to go to a probate judge first. You can't just start liquidating shit. Why didn't you tell me last night?"

Shelly stood over Ira like a scolding schoolteacher. He really didn't know what to say to her. "She said she really needed the money," he said meekly.

"So do you, you stupid fool," Shelly spat.

Howie interrupted. "That's not nice."

"Sorry," Shelly said, before moving out of the way of two men carrying a dresser heading toward the front door. She turned back toward Ira and said, "Fine. If this is the way you want it, why don't you pay me for some of my time? You owe me at least ten grand in legal fees."

Ira choked up a cough. "Ten grand?"

"That's a conservative estimate."

"I don't have that kind of money. Sarah's not giving me any of this."

"The hell she isn't. If y'all want to sell everything before probate, then you're entitled to half. This isn't her stuff yet." Shelly looked at Liz, who was cowering in the corner, and pointed at her boldly. "You hear that, missy? Half is his. Howie, come with me. I'm taking you to lunch. You don't need to be here. Man up already, Ira."

Ira slouched back onto the Shiva box and whimpered. A few minutes later, he put his hand over his eyes and shook his head repeatedly for the better part of the rest of the afternoon, as nearly every item that wasn't affixed to the floor or wall disappeared from the house. When he went to the bathroom, he was flabbergasted to see the toilet seat cover missing. The only things left in the kitchen were a broken water filtration system and the old green refrigerator. The coffee pot was gone, but the creamers and packets of Sweet'N Low were scattered across the countertop. An elderly woman walked in carrying the Shiva basin that she had scooped up from the floor next to the front door. Ira yelled at her to put it back, but he noticed it was gone when he walked outside an hour later.

Sarah never even bothered to show up for the Shiva that day. Just before the last of the treasure hunters left, she stopped at the house with Tommy, who was sitting out front in his idling Camaro.

Liz and her cohorts greeted Sarah with fake European kisses as soon as she entered the house. They smiled phonily as they talked in a corner of the front room. Ira wished for the balls to walk up and smack the shit out of all of them. Instead, he sulked in his chair. Thirty minutes later, Sarah shoved a bag full of cash into Ira's chest. "Liz told me I had to give you half."

"You only came for the money?"

"Of course not," Sarah answered. "I loved Mother more than you will ever know."

"Are you kidding me? I'm the one that's cared for them the past ten years. You going to tell me why she wrote us out of the will or what?"

"No. No, I'm not."

"So that's how it's going to be?"

"Maybe if your kids ever called, this might not have happened. Eden called her grandmother every Sunday for the past—"

"Every Sunday?" Ira interrupted.

"Yeah, every Sunday. Even last Sunday, when Mother had no idea who she was."

"At least my boys came to visit once a year. A fucking phone call a week gets you a million dollars, huh?"

"That's it?" Sarah asked. "Even with that fucking Madoff scam, I thought there would've been more."

"You're just a greedy bitch."

"Oh no, this isn't about greed. It's about getting what we deserve. Enjoy your bag of cash 'cause that's the last you're going to see of it. I'll be back next month for the house."

"Over my dead body."

"What you going to do? You can't stop me. You don't have the balls."

Ira finally got the nerve to look his sister in the eye. He got as close to her as he could without their toes hitting and said, "I won't give up this house without a fight. Shelly says you tricked Mother when she was sick."

Sarah gave a harrumph, stiffened her arms at her sides, and hurried to the front door. She stopped on the porch and glared back at

Ira, her eyes squinting into little almond slivers. "No. No tricks, just mistakes. You were just a big fucking mistake," she shot at him before slamming the door behind her.

Ira was in the middle of counting his money on the floor in front of his Shiva seat when Shelly and Howie returned. Large piles of cash were strewn in front of him. Ira's face flushed at their appearance, and he tried vainly to pull the money under his arms and cover some of the cash with his body.

Realizing his attempts at discretion were futile, Ira finally pulled five piles of bills off the floor, put them back in the bag, and handed them to Shelly. "Here's your money. Ten thousand dollars, exactly."

Shelly took the bag and held it under her armpit. "You know, Ira, a 'thank you' would be nice too."

"What'd Sarah mean by 'mistakes'?" Ira asked.

"What you talking about?"

"She said, 'no tricks, just mistakes.' What'd she mean by that?"

Shelly looked at Howie, then rolled her eyes.

"What?" Ira asked. "What are you not telling me?"

"Can you give us a minute?" Shelly asked Howie, who walked straight to the front door and let himself out.

Shelly and Ira sat down in the two metal chairs. She tried to reach out and grab his hand, but he awkwardly pulled his back. "I don't know how to tell you this," she began.

"Shit, Shelly, just give it to me. My day can't get any worse."

"I really loved your father and I promised I would never tell."

Ira got out of his chair and paced the room. "Why'd you love my father so much?"

"Oh, Ira. You're such a fool, aren't you?"

Ira banged his fist against the seat of the chair, turned to Shelly, grabbed her shoulders, and shook her violently. She tried to tug away but couldn't get out of his grip. "Tell me!" he screamed.

Shelly slunk to the floor near Ira's feet and looked up. She was crying. "Your father was a serial philanderer."

Ira failed to understand the implication. "You mean philanthropist, right?"

She couldn't help but laugh. "Do I have to spell it out for you? He was a cheater. And your mother always stayed by his side. That's the way it was back then." Shelly sighed. "Mother wasn't your birth mother. Your birth mother ran away after she had you. Left you in an orphanage. You were about a day away from adoption before Father came and got you."

Ira was stunned, his eyes and ears and mind unable to process the information together. His whole body burned with rage.

"They weren't bad people, Ira. They did the right thing. They took you in and cared for you. They gave you a proper education and a roof over your head."

"But they never loved me." Ira scrambled over to the desk and shuffled through the papers from the bank. He grabbed the pictures and stared at them again. Facing Shelly, he held up the picture of the woman holding an infant.

Shelly nodded.

"That's my mom, isn't it?" Ira asked through streaming tears. "Where's she now?"

Shelly, through tears of her own, whispered, "She's dead. Died a couple of years after you were born. Heroin overdose. You know, it was the seventies."

"How did you know? How do you know all this?"

Shelly tried to hold back her tears, but she was breathing heavily through her mouth. "I didn't know Father till I was seventeen, when my mother passed. Did he love me? I don't know. Put me through law school, though."

"And Mother never knew?"

"About me? No. I don't think so. She just thought I was the family lawyer."

"Wait, that makes us half…"

"Don't say it," she yelled through tears. "Let's just pretend this conversation never happened."

They both laughed.

44

Ira woke Monday morning wrapped in an old crocheted blanket, lying across the two metal Shiva chairs. A cool front had moved in overnight and he was shivering beneath the natty blanket. He crossed the room and closed the window, shutting out the wind. The cold weather and the uncomfortable makeshift bed brought out all the cricks and creaks in Ira's bones. He took quick stock of his aching body: the gout in the ankle was finally starting to dull, but the knuckles on his hands throbbed and his upper back flared, causing him to walk with a hunch. The sciatic nerve in the back of his left leg was pinched so that every time he tried to stand up, a flame shot through his entire spine.

Ira fell to the floor and attempted a few stretches that a physical therapist once showed him, but as soon as he rolled onto his back, he could barely move. He stayed motionless for thirty minutes before slowly and methodically crawling toward the steps. Pulling down hard on the banister allowed him to ascend the staircase. He made it to the bedroom, where the only things that remained were his worn-out and faded clothes, all of which truly looked to have been continuously washed in a bathtub full of cold water with little bars of hotel soap. He wasn't surprised that no one wanted to buy his clothes, but he was surprised that someone had actually picked out most of the linens and towels.

He managed to find one of those complimentary towels from the JCC in a small pile of dirty laundry to dry off with after a long, cold shower. He dressed in his usual khaki Dockers, a faded undershirt, an old pair of his father's once-lavish Italian loafers, and white socks. Then he found a plastic bag under his sink and stuffed it with the remaining cash from the estate sale that he had hidden under a broken floorboard in the dining room. He concealed the bag under his T-shirt, tucked into his waistband, and set out for the day.

Ira made his way to the closest banks on St. Charles Avenue. The first two, Chase and Iberia Bank, wouldn't help because he was not an account holder, but he was happy to secure himself a free cup of coffee at each stop. The third bank, First NBC, told him it wasn't a problem and they counted all his money three times before issuing him seventy-five one hundred-dollar bills. Ira cut the stack in half, wrapped the cash in rubber bands, and deposited them into the two front pockets of his pants.

Ira joined the tourists waiting at the streetcar stop. The wait seemed excruciatingly long and Ira couldn't help pacing about with his arms crossed over his stomach, his shoulders hunched over, and his face contorted in an angry grimace. When the streetcar finally arrived, he pushed ahead of the other riders in order to board first, but when he swiped his card, the driver informed him, "Out of money."

Ira's eyes widened. The driver shook his head. Ira stuck his short arms into his deep pockets and a heat flash took over his entire body. "Um, do you have change for a hundred?" he whispered.

"You know we don't carry cash," the elderly driver said loudly enough for all the passengers to hear.

A young guy with rotting teeth in the front row smiled and said, "I gots change. How much ya needin'?"

Ira was completely flustered. He rarely, if ever, carried more than a few dollars in his pocket. In order to get change from this man, he would've had to pull out the entire stack of bills in one of his pockets. There was no way he was going to do that, so instead he pushed his way back through the boarding passengers and jumped off the streetcar.

He decided to walk. He slowly made his way toward the French Quarter, shuffling his feet down the middle of St. Charles Avenue between the two streetcar tracks, nervously glancing from side to side at every passerby for fear of getting mugged. It wouldn't have been the first time. Ira could count over a dozen times that he had been held up in New Orleans. Ten of the twelve times, the robber left with little more than a buck or two, and once a crappy Seiko watch. The other two times, Ira left with a black eye and cuts on his face and head because he had nothing to give. Ira never put up a fight. He just put his hands high in the air, closed his eyes, and shut his mouth. What else could he have done? He was certain that if he had ever carried a gun the mugger would have easily overtaken him, and there would be one more illegal gun on the street and one more dead body in the morgue. But this time would have been different. Ira assured himself that if he were confronted today, he wouldn't go down without a fight. He would make sure no one took this money from him if it was the last thing he ever did.

Although pangs of hunger were attacking Ira's stomach, he vowed to march on. Several other streetcars passed, but he just kept inching forward. The three-mile walk took nearly three hours, and before the end a slight drizzle had begun to patter off his bald head. By the time he crossed Canal Street, his T-shirt was soaked through and his socks were full of dirty sludge from the puddles in the street.

Ira ended his walk on the opposite side of Iberville Street across from Dixie Divas, hoping he might catch a glimpse of Charlie heading to work. Instead, he saw the big bad bouncer dude holding a Subway sandwich bag enter the strip club, followed by two or three customers and one stripper over the course of the following hour. Ira paced back and forth down the sidewalk checking out the rest of the quiet block: Chez Joey, a hole-in-the-wall strip club next door that catered to bikers; the back of Jimani, a gritty dive bar that fueled the service industry personnel; and Country Flame, a greasy Latin restaurant that served up cheap tacos and Cuban sandwiches. Behind him were the facades of three nondescript buildings and a small alleyway for deliveries through a back entrance of the Hotel Monteleone. There weren't too many blocks in the French Quarter with more character and less charm than the one Ira was standing on.

After a long stretch of nothingness, two older men walked past the entrance three or four times and nervously peeked into the covered windows before finally sneaking into Dixie Divas. Most of the men that entered did so discretely. Ira wondered at how many went in while no one ever seemed to leave. He imagined creepy guys spending all day, every day drinking cheap domestic beer and scoring dates with skanky strippers. Ira knew what it was like to be lonely and desperate, but not to the extent of wasting away his time and money in a two-bit joint like the one he was about to reenter.

Ira was afraid to confront the bouncer. Every time he took a step toward the front door, he pulled himself back. He wished for some liquid courage, but he hardly ever paid for his own drink. Despite the stacks of hundred-dollar bills lining his pockets, he couldn't bring himself to buy a full-price drink in a strip club, so he walked another two blocks down to Bourbon Street in search of a decent happy hour special. He bypassed the signs for "Huge-Ass Beers" and the annoying doormen hawking tourists with obnoxious bullhorns. In a little alcove between two bars, he found a sign advertising three-for-one cocktails and bought a triple rum and Coke for five dollars. Sipping his drink through a cocktail straw, he made a lap around the block, came back up Royal Street, and finally beelined it into Dixie Divas.

The smell of Bourbon Street was only slightly worse than the odor inside the bar. The darkly lit room juxtaposed with the natural light outside made Ira a little wobbly when he entered. The bartender was serving two men at the bar and didn't pay him much attention. A stripper stood between two grey-haired men, rubbing the backs of their necks. She wore a see-through red robe and black panties with ripped fishnet stockings. She was standing profile. At the top of her panties, a belly the shape of a football jutted out, and resting atop that, huge droopy boobs with star-shaped pasties attached to them.

As Ira made his way a little closer to the dance floor, the bartender grumbled, "No outside drinks."

Ira slurped down the rest of his rum and Coke, found a trash can by the front door, and threw out his cup. He turned back around and teetered a bit, grabbing hold of the railing on the wall so he didn't fall. Ira wanted to confront the bouncer right away, but he was nowhere to be seen. So he scanned the room looking for Charlie, but all he saw were two strippers occupied with their marks and a third pole dancing on a small stage near several black faux-leather couches. He tried to discreetly check out the strippers, but it was so dark in the club, he could barely see.

Ira moved in closer. He was facing the bare back of a woman who was riding the lap of a man like she was straddling a toilet seat that she didn't want to sit on. Her arms were behind her holding his thighs or maybe his dick, Ira couldn't be sure. She was small and blonde like Charlie, but with her back to him, he couldn't be sure. She grinded over the man slowly, methodically, moaning slightly under her breath. Ira bent down below the couch and lightly tapped the woman on her elbow. She turned her head but not far enough to lock eyes with Ira. What he saw was her nose, a giant hooked nose that reminded Ira of a caricature of that *Sex in the City* woman.

Ira was about to straighten up, but instead he got the swiftest, hardest kick in the ass imaginable. His forehead smacked against the back of the couch and his entire body bounced backward into a waiting knee. Ira crumpled to the floor, writhing in pain. He looked up and saw nothing but blinking stars and Christmas lights, one of which were probably on the ceiling of the club, the other a figment of his newfound nausea. Before Ira even knew who was performing the aggressive ass-whooping, he was dragged off into a dark hallway by the back of his pants with his underwear riding up into his crack. Still staring at the ground, vomit began to swell in the bottom of his throat, and he tried to hold it in, but to no avail. He puked out the coffee, the rum, the coke, and whatever bile had built up in his empty small intestine.

Ira received another swift kick in the ass that made him fall right into his own vomit puddle, completely drenching his neck and T-shirt in brown sludge. He now smelled like the inside of one of those broken Katrina refrigerators that littered the landscape after the storm. Splayed out across the floor on his belly, he heard the voices of two men talking quietly to each other. He couldn't hear much of the conversation, just bits and pieces that sounded something like:

Guy 1: "Fuck… fucker… fuckball… motherfucker."

Guy 2: "Kill piece of shit… kill him… kill… kill… kill."

There was probably more to it than that, but that was the gist that Ira got and he could do nothing more than turn his head from side to side because one of the men had his giant boot affixed to the middle of Ira's back. He could barely breathe, and he felt as if his ribs were cracking one by one. He was finally lifted by the seat of his pants and thrown into a small, dark windowless bathroom where he sat up and leaned against a dirty toilet bowl.

Ira was left alone for a while, wheezing for breath between cracked ribs. There was no way to tell how long he was in there, but it felt like hours. The room was hot and stuffy, and the odor of his vomit clung to the air like the smell on Bourbon Street at four a.m. After a while, he finally took off his shirt, wiped the crust off his neck, felt around in the dark for the sink, and washed his shirt with hand soap and hot water.

As the day turned to night, or so Ira imagined, he heard the voices of strippers and men in the hallway. It sounded like the women were escorting the men to some kind of VIP room for sex or blowjobs. There were definitely some negotiations and transactions going on, he was sure of that. He thought about calling out for help but doubted anything good would have come from it. Perhaps it would have led to another beating. So he lay against one of the walls, faced the door, closed his eyes, and dreamed about food. Bacon, specifically.

.

45

There was no way to tell how much time had passed between when Ira fell asleep and when he woke up. Only two things had changed during that indiscriminate period. One was that his wet T-shirt was now dry and the other was that there was no sound outside the room. The annoying dance music had stopped blaring and the voices of strippers and their marks had turned silent. Ira checked the handle on the door, but it was still locked. He went back to thinking about bacon. If he tried hard enough, he could actually smell some from a nearby greasy spoon diner or hotel buffet. It almost hid the lingering stench of vomit. Almost.

"Hello," Ira yelled. He waited a few minutes and tried again. "Hello, anyone out there? Charlie? Crystal?"

There was no response. Ira figured that whoever kicked his ass had gone home for the night. He hoped the man had forgotten that he left him there, doubtful as it seemed. He shouted louder and louder until he was out of breath and his ribs felt like they were hit with electric shock therapy. The only saving grace at that point was the fact that Ira still had thousands of dollars of cash lining his pockets. He hoped to use that money to get Charlie and himself out of this precarious situation.

His stomach growled. Again, he thought of bacon. Not thick-cut bacon, not that flavorless pork belly bacon, not turkey bacon, and certainly not fakin' bacon, just good old crispy, deep-fried Oscar Meyer bacon that turned up in every breakfast buffet that Ira had ever been to. His daydreaming ended when the door whipped open and a bright light blinded him so that he never even saw the person that grabbed him by his shirt and dragged him out of the room. By the time he could see anything at all, the man was shoving him in the back down a long corridor, heading toward a black door below an emergency exit sign.

Ira slammed against that door and out into a small courtyard containing a dumpster and enclosed by a chain link fence with barbed wire at the top. He was alone, facing the back of an abandoned building on one side and a high-rise with a black garage door that looked like it was never used. The sky was grey and overcast, or maybe it was just the dawn breaking over the horizon. He stood there blankly for a few minutes until the door crashed open against the wall again.

Charlie flew toward Ira so fast that he could do nothing but turn his body so that he ended up kneeing her in the crotch as she crumpled to the ground. She was on her knees, out of breath and crying when Ira tried to lift her. She looked up at him with her bloodshot blue eyes full of tears and her makeup smeared so that she looked like a goth heading to a Nine Inch Nails concert. He realized at that moment that it was the first time he had seen her in over a week, and though he felt like he had just gotten hit by a delivery truck while riding a bicycle at thirty miles per hour, he was glad he came.

While lifting her to her feet, the giant galoot bouncer lumbered into the courtyard. He was holding some rope in one hand and a baseball bat in the other. Charlie yelped. Ira put up his hands and yelled, "Stop, please! I'll pay you."

The man stopped, leaned his weight on the barrel of the bat, dropped his other hand to his side, and cocked his head to the right.

"I'll pay you for the girl," Ira said.

"You want to fuck the girl," the man said. "Why didn't you just say so? We could have avoided this whole mess to begin with."

"No," Ira said, looking down at the top of Charlie's head. "I want her for good."

The man looked Ira up and down like a father inspecting his teenage girl before she headed out for an evening on the town.

Ira wasn't good at waiting for answers. He also wasn't good at negotiating. These were tactics for suave men who could get themselves out of these kinds of situations. Instead, Ira just blurted out, "Seventy-five hundred."

"You're full of shit, little man."

"No, I swear."

"You swear? I should just take your word for it?"

Ira fumbled in his pockets. The man lifted the bat off the floor, thinking that Ira might have brought a gun, but he put it back down when he saw the two packs of hundred-dollar bills emerge from his pocket. The next thirty seconds were like a blur to Ira. First the man started toward him. Then Ira threatened to throw the money over the fence. The man barely paused. He lunged for Ira, who weakly attempted to heave the cash over the barbed wire. One pack smacked off the fence and dropped straight to the ground. The other escaped from the rubber band and rained down on the man, who grabbed the bills out of the air like in that giant chrome ball on that stupid game show.

Ira took the opportunity to run. He tried to pull Charlie to her feet, but she was like dead weight, still hunched over like a dog staring at the concrete beneath her. When the last of the bills hit the ground and the man looked at Ira again, he gave up pulling on Charlie, flew through the door, down the long corridor, past the bar, and smacked straight into the locked front door. His chest felt like it almost exploded. His adrenaline was on full tilt, his cracked ribs reverberating through his skin and down the sides of his arms. The music was so loud and the bass so heavy that he couldn't tell if he was being followed. He pushed the door again, but it didn't budge. Finally, he looked down and saw the sign that read, *Pull*. He needed both his shaking hands to grab the knob and twist before pulling the door open and shoving his body through the frame.

Ira's weak little legs dragged behind the rest of his body so that he nearly fell over face first as he rounded the corner on Decatur Street. As soon as he hit Canal Street, he doubled over in pain, clutching his chest. A homeless guy sitting on the sidewalk with his back to the Audubon Insectarium asked Ira if he was okay. He nodded in the affirmative but could only take another few steps before he crumbled to the ground a few yards from the beggar.

The guy looked to be in his mid to late thirties, had a small, scraggy-looking mutt on a chain leash, and wore a black backpack. On his head, he had dirty blonde dreadlocks poking out from underneath a black conductor's hat. He stared at Ira with mild concern until a group of young girls came over and read his sign. They laughed and dropped a dollar bill in his plastic cup. Ira couldn't read the sign from where he was sitting, but he could see the look in people's eyes when they passed the homeless man. About half had scorn written on their faces and sped up their gait or swerved closer to the gutter to avoid him. The other half chuckled or laughed, and a few of them even gave him a dollar or spare change. From what Ira could tell, his cup overflowed with cash, and at that moment, Ira was a little envious. He would have done anything for something to eat and a cold drink, but he never imagined himself begging for money. Fortunately for Ira, he didn't even have to try. He looked so pitiful that two women in business suits dropped a dollar bill in front of his folded legs.

"You'd do better with a sign," the homeless guy advised.

Ira looked at him but didn't say anything. He sort of half smiled and tried to stand up, but he couldn't even roll his back off the wall. For better or worse, he was stuck right there on the corner of Canal and Decatur Streets wondering what was happening to Charlie and powerless to do anything about it. The building to his back, built in 1848, originally housed the customs offices, the post office, and the federal courthouse. It said all that on a little plaque above his head. For the past eight years, it had been the home of the Insectarium, the only museum in the country dedicated to bugs. Ira had taken the boys one day after it opened and a week before they left for New York. It was the last place they went together before Lin stole them from Ira.

Across the street was one of those cheap T-shirt abominations that littered the French Quarter. A few doors down on Canal, Ira could see the neon marquee for Arby's, and though he hadn't had a roast beef sandwich in years, he longed for one as if it were a filet mignon.

"I have an extra piece of cardboard," the homeless guy offered.

Ira continued to ignore the man as he rifled through his meager belongings and tore off a piece of a cardboard box. He slid it over to Ira, where it stopped against his leg, and then tossed a black Sharpie that hit Ira in the chest and gave his ribs a jolt that ran through his body to the bottom of his feet and left his toes tingling. Ira held the pen to the cardboard for a few minutes, unable to think of anything to write. As he pondered the message that might buy him lunch, another group of young girls came over to the homeless guy and asked if they could take his picture. He smiled widely as the girls produced a selfie stick and shot off a few photos of one of New Orleans' finest. When they started to walk away, the man flashed the sign at Ira: *Even Losers Need a Beer.*

Ira decided to be a bit more pragmatic. He scribbled his own sign: *Hungry. Lost Everything. Please Help.* Almost immediately, a man dropped a quarter at his feet, but it was pretty slow after that. Ira watched the faces of the people who did everything they could to avoid eye contact. He felt beneath them, not physically or even metaphorically, but more in reality, as if his life had no value at all. He caught sight of a woman from way up the block walking toward him. He recognized her from back in the day, maybe from temple or college, he wasn't sure which. She did look at Ira. She did a double-take, glancing between the two homeless men on the ground, but she too walked past without stopping. Ira wondered if it would have been too much trouble for her to take a moment out of the day to see if she could help. He would have much preferred the charity of one to the ignominy of the masses. No such luck. She shook her head back and forth the entire way across Canal Street as she most likely examined her distant recollections of the man now lying on the sidewalk.

"You need a cup," said the homeless man. He ran across the street, searched through a trash can on the corner, and pulled out a plastic go-cup, one of those big ones from Pat O'Brien's that was once filled with a twelve-dollar hurricane. When the man left, his pitiful-looking mutt scampered over to Ira and sniffed around at his legs. He didn't stay long, as Ira's odor was so foul as to turn off even a dog. The homeless man handed Ira the cup and returned to his makeshift home.

Before long, Ira's cup began to fill with loose change. A family sitting in a horse-drawn carriage threw a slew of quarters at them; a child tugging at his dad's overcoat gave him a dollar; a young guy with a buzz cut dressed in a Coast Guard uniform gave him two quarters.

"My name's Donnie," the homeless man said.

"Ira."

"Please to meet you, Ira," Donnie said. "Where you from?"

"Uptown."

"Uptown? New Orleans? What you doing down here?"

Ira thought for a moment about the previous two weeks. He had a comfortable life just a short time ago. His wants were few and his needs were even fewer. How had he fallen so far? How did he end up here? "Run of bad luck, I guess."

"I'm from Tupelo," Donnie said. "That's in Mississippi."

"I know where Tupelo is," Ira said. "Birthplace of Elvis."

"Right on, right on. I'm staying up over at the Mission. You know where that's at, right? I'll be heading over there right quick. Surprised the police haven't run us off yet. Usually they on us like brown on rice." Donnie chuckled. "You best move quick when they do, 'cause they haul your ass down to OPP in no time."

Ira took the warning seriously. The last thing he wanted was another night in jail. Struggling to his feet, he bid Donnie farewell and staggered over to Arby's to get himself something to eat. It was only a half a block, but the walk was arduous and painful. Ira literally felt like he had gotten run over by the streetcar. When he finally made it to the Arby's, it was closed down. Ira guessed it couldn't keep up with the inflated rents in the French Quarter, and it would soon become another daiquiri bar or souvenir shop.

He counted his money. He had a total of four dollars and twenty-six cents, which wasn't enough for a po'boy or even a Lucky Dog. It was barely enough for a Big Mac or a slice of pizza in the Quarter. Bourbon Street was just a few blocks away, and Ira figured his best bang for his buck would be found at Krystal Burger, a half block from Canal Street.

There was a flurry of activity in the fast food joint. It was as if the bustle of Bourbon Street continued uninterrupted inside. Everything was loud, from the bad music on the speakers to the employees shouting profanity at one another. There were several homeless-looking people asleep in booths.

LaQueesha, the counter girl, sized Ira up as he approached. The special was two double Krystals, a small fry, and a small drink for $3.99. Ira was just a few cents short so he smiled at LaQueesha, turned around, and stepped back out to Bourbon Street where he shook his cup in front of tourists until someone was kind enough to drop in a quarter. LaQueesha leered at him as he sidled back up to the counter and ordered his value meal.

"Where's the restroom?" Ira asked.

"You ain't usin' no bathroom for a shower, is you?" LaQueesha asked loudly.

"I just want to wash up."

"You needin' more than a wash-up, mistah. I don't want to clean up after your ass." She had a hand on her hip and made this statement like she meant it. Ira wasn't up for a fight, so he just cowered in the corner next to the ketchup stand until his number was called.

The burgers went down quick and easy. Ira refilled his Sprite three times and the second he finished eating, the food was ready to come back out. He burped loudly, held his stomach, and rushed toward the restrooms, hoping LaQueesha wouldn't see him run by.

An older man was exiting the bathroom as he walked up. He held the door open for Ira, but he had a look on his face that seemed to be warning him not to go in. It was even more disgusting than he had imagined. It smelled like someone had already puked in it that morning. The walls were smeared with ketchup or diarrhea or a combination of the two. Two of the three overhead lights were burnt out and graffiti was scribbled on most of the walls. He hurried into the stall and tried to clean the remnants of puke from the toilet seat, but he couldn't wait any longer, so he braced his arms against either side of the stall and squatted over the seat as a stream of diarrhea splattered into the bowl. It was like a volcano, slowly simmering until it exploded like a gusher and likely ripped some of the lining out of his small intestine. When the volcano finally stopped spurting, Ira looked down and noticed two things. One was that the entire toilet was covered in excrement. The other was that there was no fucking toilet paper in the stall.

Ira duck-walked to the sink and luckily found a few hand towels to wipe with. He threw them in the toilet and flushed, watching as the bowl filled with brown sludge which oozed up the sides. He could hear it overflowing and crashing to the floor as he ran from the bathroom and out of the Krystal, back into the fading sunlight on Bourbon Street.

46

Ira was so tired and sluggish, he could barely keep his eyes open. His body ached from head to toe. He wanted to go back and rescue Charlie, but there was an insurmountable fear that prevented him from going anywhere near Dixie Divas. He thought it best that he return home and ask Shelly to help get Charlie out of that stinking hellhole. But there was no way he could walk all the way home in his current condition. He thought about begging for more money, but the idea of going to jail frightened him more than the alternative. Instead, he headed for The Mission, the homeless shelter on Baronne Street.

Ira had to walk through the homeless encampment underneath the I-10 overpass to get there. The city tried to clean them out every few months, but slowly they reappeared with their tents and sleeping bags, forming little pockets of depression. Ira remembered an article he read in the *Times-Picayune* that said the tent city was infested with drugs and rats, and sure enough, he saw a rat scurrying over the legs of a passed-out man.

The Mission was a place Ira had passed hundreds of times. Though it was known as a shelter for men and women, Ira remembered seeing only the former congregating around the street in front of the big brick building on Baronne Street. Most of the men were middle aged and black and looked as if they had a long history of drug and alcohol abuse. It looked pretty much the same that day as Ira hesitantly crossed Calliope Street and wandered over to the front entrance.

No one said anything to him. He stood in front of the door for a few minutes until a man walked out and held it open for him. There was a woman at the front desk staring at Ira as he entered. The room felt like a hotel reception, except without the bags and the bellhop. The woman was heavyset with bad skin and dark facial hair, and she breathed so loudly through her mouth that it sounded like snoring.

"Name," she yelled at Ira once he seated himself about three feet away from her in a plastic chair in front of the desk.

"Ira Silver."

"Have you been here before, Mr. Silver?" she asked, writing his answers on a paper attached to a clipboard.

"No."

"Then you will need a consultation with one of our counselors."

"I just need a place to sleep," Ira said.

"That's not how it works, Mr. Silver. We have to do an assessment first. Beds are five dollars a night. It's almost seven. You can join the others for chapel. Evening praise and worship service starts in a few minutes."

"But I'm Jewish," Ira said.

"Don't matter what you are. If you want to stay here, you go to chapel."

Ira slunk in his chair. There was nothing he hated more than being forced to swallow others' religions. He once got free tickets to a Hornets game—before they were the Pelicans—and was forced to sit through the pre-game sermon. By the time the players took the court, Ira no longer had a taste for basketball. And the six-dollar hot-dogs and nine-dollar beers didn't help either. He left before halftime.

The woman, who never introduced herself, handed Ira the clipboard to finish filling out the questionnaire. He took it to a nearby couch and started writing but gave up halfway through and left the clipboard on a small table by the front door. Back on the street, the sky had darkened, the wind swirled, and Ira was shivering and scared. There were still men—shady men—congregating on the street corner. It looked as if drug deals were going down. Ira managed to make it to a cement riser underneath the overpass. He propped his back against the wall and slid his body to the ground. The stench of urine was overpowering. He wanted to use his shirtsleeve to cover his nose, but the smell from the shirt was even worse.

Despite the abhorrent conditions, Ira fell asleep a few minutes later. It was a cold, restless night. He was in and out of sleep, constantly shivering and feeling as if someone were next to him. At some point in the night, his loafers were stolen from his feet. He didn't feel them being taken off, but he felt the coldness on his toes afterward. Every hour or two, a cop car rolled up and turned on its siren. Ira guessed he was trying to run off the addicts, but all it did was make his sleep more restless.

He woke just before dawn to the sound of people having sex nearby. At first he thought someone was choking, but then he heard heavy breathing and a few loud grunts. It was close by and startled Ira so much that he hopped to his feet fairly quickly for someone who was in such bad physical condition.

With nowhere else to go, he figured his best option was to try to head for home. He stood on the corner of Calliope and St. Charles Avenue hoping for some spare change so he could take the streetcar, but not one person even lowered their window to acknowledge him. He had left his sign on Bourbon Street, and though he looked pitiful, he wasn't aggressive enough to garner much attention. Instead, he walked in his holey socks, dirty pants, and filthy T-shirt. His empty stomach was tied in knots and his throat was as dry as the herbs in an unwatered garden.

With his shoulders stooped and his feet burning, he trudged up St. Charles Avenue. At each public trashcan, he stopped to look for a half-drunk beer or bottled water but found little more than pizza crusts, which only scratched his parched tongue. The journey was slow and tedious. People stared at the shoeless man with the bruised head and grubby clothes. The streetcar riders pointed and sneered. Through the window of Houston's restaurant, the employees avoided eye contact, piling shame on the shipwreck passing by.

Twice Ira thought he was going to pass out, but both times, he sat on the curb and breathed heavily through his mouth until the nausea passed. From far up the block, he could see several cars parked in front of his house. One he recognized as Shelly's; the others looked like unmarked police cars. He was too tired and beaten to hide any longer. He was going to have to face whatever awaited him inside his home.

Shelly was on the porch talking with Officers R. Miles and H. Hanson as Ira approached. They were in a heated debate, which stopped short as soon as Shelly saw Ira. In unison, their three heads shook back and forth, and Ira gleaned a look of pity from each of their eyes. He made it to the bottom of the staircase without any of them moving, then stopped and stayed there until one of them spoke.

"A body washed up along the river," Shelly said.

Still nobody moved. Ira guessed they were waiting for him to respond, but he still had no idea what they were getting at.

"Young woman, blonde hair, tattoos, crushed skull," H. Hanson said, interrupting the awkward silence.

As the words were coming out, Ira grabbed his stomach, lurched forward, and dry-heaved until his broken ribs could no longer handle the pain. When he finally straightened his body to its upright position, he was full-on crying—heavy, gasping sobs that made Shelly reach out to hold him until he finished his emotional outburst on her shoulder.

"They want you or Howie to identify the body," she said. "We don't know where Howie is. You don't have to, you know? We can go straight downtown for questioning. They have the pictures at OPP."

Ira stared at the two cops with their menacing eyes. "They think I killed her? Oh my God, I didn't…"

Shelly interrupted, "Ira, don't say a word. You are under no obligation to say anything."

"Shelly, I didn't do anything."

"Shut your damn trap," Shelly yelled. "Read him his rights."

"You have the right to remain silent. Anything you say can and will be used against you in a court of law. You have the right to an attorney. If you cannot afford an attorney, one will be provided for you. Do you understand the rights I have just read to you?"

Ira nodded.

"With these rights in mind," R. Miles said, "do you wish to speak to me?"

"It was the bouncer from Dixie Divas."

"Shut the fuck up. This is not the time or the place to defend yourself," Shelly yelled.

"But, but—"

"No buts, just keep your mouth closed until we get to the station."

47

Ira remembered little about that ride to OPP. He cried the entire way, thinking about that poor girl and the rough life she led. Under different circumstances, he was sure she could have turned it all around. Deep down, she had a good heart and she meant well. And yet, all that had happened to him over the past two weeks was directly or indirectly attributed to her. As for Ira, there was no turning back now. He was sure of that. He was going to spend the rest of his life in Angola Prison, as he'd feared he would.

Soon he was in a sparse interrogation room with white walls on three sides and a glass wall on the fourth, two chairs and a small metal desk. Ira tried to move his chair closer to the desk so he could lay his head down, but it was affixed to the floor. Still, he was so tired that he nodded off for what he thought was a few seconds. A man he had never seen before startled him awake. He introduced himself as Detective Roussel, pronounced French Cajun like "roo-sell."

Detective Roussel was tall and thin, wiry some might say. He had light hair receding at the top and small lips, wore grey slacks and a blue blazer. Sitting on the edge of the desk, he crossed his arms and smiled nonchalantly at Ira. He smelled like cheap cologne, although it did little to hide the odor emanating from Ira.

"Would you like something to drink?" Roussel asked.

"I would love a scotch," said Ira, "but a water will do."

Roussel laughed long and smoothly, like he was trying to make Ira feel more comfortable. He excused himself from the room and returned a few minutes later with a small cup of water.

"Your attorney is on her way," Roussel informed him before returning to his imposing seat on the corner of the desk, two feet above Ira's head.

The silence made Ira uncomfortable. He squirmed in his seat and changed positions a few times, slowly sipping the lukewarm water. The room was warm and stuffy, and Ira couldn't believe that Roussel wasn't sweating in his heavy blazer. Ira's sweat started at the small of his back and worked its way up his body until a sliver of perspiration glistened at the corner of his eyebrow and finally dripped into his eye. He wiped his face with the back of his hand.

They heard two light knocks on the door followed by a short pause before Shelly stormed into the room, looking like an angry football coach walking into the locker room after a blowout defeat. She was perspiring like she had just been running and was a bit short of breath. She sat down heavily in the empty seat across from Ira, while Roussel stood up and rested both hands on the top of the table.

"Thank you for coming, Ms.—?"

"Shelly Rubenstein."

"Thank you for coming, Ms. Rubenstein. As you are aware, the body of a young woman was recovered from the banks of the Mississippi this morning."

Roussel paused for affirmation, and Ira and Shelly both nodded.

"We are in the process of identifying the body. Her face was completely bashed in, but we should be able to use dental records. We believe Mr. Silver might be able to save us some time in identifying the body."

Ira looked at Shelly, who was now shaking her head.

"I am giving Mr. Silver the opportunity to come clean here and save us all a lot of time and trouble. Would you like a few minutes to discuss this with your client, Ms. Rubenstein?"

"That would be very helpful, Mr.—?"

"Roussel."

The detective left the room. Ira and Shelly said nothing to each other for a minute. Shelly made her way over to the mirrored wall and, keeping her back to Ira, said, "You are under no obligation to say anything. You understand that, right?"

"You don't actually think I killed Charlie, do you?"

Shelly turned around from the mirrored wall and looked Ira straight in the eye. She folded her arms. "It doesn't look good."

"For Christ's sake, I would never hurt that girl," Ira yelled. "I loved that girl."

Shelly made the motion for Ira to zip it, crossing her two fingers over her lips. As she was doing that, Roussel returned with a plastic Ziploc bag. He tossed the bag on the center of the table. It was easy to see the remains of a dead body in the picture at the top of the bag.

Ira felt like he was going to puke again, but there was nothing in his stomach that could possibly come up. He tried to push the chair backward but remembered that it was nailed to the floor.

"You don't have to do this," Shelly said, covering the pictures with her hand.

"She's right," Roussel said. "We have enough already to make an arrest."

"And I'd have to go back to central lockup?" Ira asked with fear in his voice.

"Oh, no, Mr. Silver. We don't put murderers in central lockup."

That threat hung in the air like a helium balloon on its last legs. Ira grabbed the pile of pictures and thumbed through them swiftly, expecting the gruesomeness of the naked body to give him heart failure. First, he saw the close-ups of the head and face. Though the head was matted with dirt, the hair looked short and blonde. There were bruises on the neck and upper arms and most of the skin had peeled away from the face so that Ira could see the bones of her nose. When Ira saw the full-body photos, he took a long gasp.

"It's her?" Shelly asked.

Ira shook his head back and forth and looked at her with his eyes full of tears. "No. It's not her. It's Crystal."

Shelly and Roussel both looked shocked, their eyes bursting out of their sockets. At the same time, Shelly said, "What?" and Roussel said, "Who's Crystal?"

Ira glanced back and forth between the two of them. He wasn't sure if he should answer, but Shelly looked so disoriented that he figured he might as well continue. "One of the other strippers at Dixie Divas."

Shelly immediately smacked the palm of her hand against her forehead.

Roussel asked, "How can you tell?"

Ira answered, "I recognize the script tattoos on her thighs. It isn't Charlie. She has just a rose near her…"

Roussel and Shelly waited for Ira to finish his sentence.

"Near her, you know, thingie," Ira said, pointing at his own crotch.

"Are you sure?" Roussel asked.

"One hundred percent."

"Is my client free to go?" Shelly asked, rising to her feet and pulling on Ira's shoulder without waiting for an answer.

48

Shelly refused to let Ira ride in her car, worried that she'd never be able to get rid of his stench. They argued about it from the moment they walked out of the interrogation room until they were sitting across from each other on the red streetcar rolling down Canal Street. There was no debate where they were headed, though. It took nearly thirty minutes to arrive in the French Quarter, and they were astounded to see a dozen cop cars already parked in front of Dixie Divas.

Decatur and Chartres Streets were both blocked off, but it wasn't hard to walk around the barricade. A raid was in full effect on the tiny club. Women in all stages of undress scurried out the front door. Old, drunk men wobbled behind them. Ira was surprised to see over twenty people taken into custody. He had never seen that many people in the place. Perhaps those VIP rooms got more use than he'd imagined.

Then the street went silent, eerily silent. Several officers drew their guns and stood behind their squad cars, facing the front door. Ira and Shelly made their way to the alleyway behind the Hotel Monteleone where they would have a better view of the commotion. Four other officers entered Dixie Divas with their guns drawn. Bystanders began crowding the street behind the cop cars until one of the officers shooed them away.

Ira was barely able to look. He held both hands over his eyes and squinted through his fingers, as if that would have made any difference. The tension hung in the air like on one of those *CSI* episodes. This was the part of the show when eerie music would foreshadow the climax, but this drama was for real and Ira could only pray that Charlie would come out alive. What he saw next was the big bouncer dude, the bartender, and another man he had never seen before escorted in handcuffs out of the bar and into the back of three different police cars. Behind them, a female officer escorted a girl draped in a white sheet.

Ira yelled, "Charlie!" and the girl stopped. She broke free from the grip of the officer, dropped the sheet to the ground, and ran toward Ira, falling into his arms and collapsing into his chest.

The female officer tried to restrain Charlie and pull her off Ira, but Officer Roussel stepped in and let them hold their embrace. Sounding like a TV cop, he said to Shelly, "We got there just in time."

Charlie was crying on Ira's shoulder, heaving her chest in and out and uttering gibberish. "Take me home," she whispered.

"My sister took all the furniture," Ira said.

"There's also the sex crime charges you still have to deal with," Shelly put in.

"No," Charlie said, "my real home."

49

The motor hummed, the wheels spun, and the silence stifled the air in the small car. Shelly's eyes remained focused on the highway. Charlie slept under a blue felt blanket that Officer Roussel had given her, still wearing nothing more than her bra and panties and an oversized T-shirt that Ira found in his closet. Ira fidgeted in his seat, nervously bobbing his knee up and down.

They were heading north on I-55 toward Utica, Mississippi, where Charlie said she lived. According to the map on Shelly's dashboard, Utica was about thirty miles west of Jackson. Though only two and a half hours from New Orleans, the backwoods of Mississippi were as unfamiliar to Ira as the streets of Guilin.

Shelly followed the GPS, exiting the highway, making several turns onto smaller and smaller roads until there was nothing but blank space on the Google map at the end of a gravelly road. Ira and Shelly sat there for a minute or two, kind of waiting for a sign from God, but nothing happened. Shelly rolled the window down and they listened to the squawking of a lone chicken.

Ira turned to the sleeping beauty, whose face was twisted in a grimace and eyes were twitching as if she was having a nightmare. He looked once again at Shelly, but she just gave him the head nod and waited for his next move. Ira gently tugged at the blue blanket, but nothing happened. He tugged again, this time calling her name in a voice just above a whisper. Nothing. Shelly was staring into the rear-view mirror, her beady eyes fixed on the space between Ira and Charlie.

Ira turned his entire body around, got on his knees, and reached across the console, stretching as far as he could until his arms reached Charlie's shoulders. He shook her twice and then twisted back around, plopped in his seat, and gave Shelly a nod as if to say, "That ought to do it."

They turned their heads in unison only to see Charlie's eyes still closed and her head now a foot lower and leaning against the door. Shelly slapped her palm to her forehead, shaking her head back and forth in disbelief. She unlocked her door and shuffled her weight back and forth, finally pushing her way out and into the warm stale air of the Deep South. With the driver's side door still open, Ira could hear Shelly tugging on the back door and yelling, "Fuck, fuck, fuck. Open the fucking door, Ira."

Ira looked around for the unlock button, taking way longer than was warranted, according to Shelly's cursing. He hit the button at precisely the same time Shelly pulled the handle so that poor Charlie halfway collapsed out of the opened door on top of Shelly, who tried her best to hang on beneath her armpits.

As Ira scrambled between the front seats to grab hold of Charlie's bottom half, a loud car horn blasted from behind. It scared the living bejeezus out of both of them, and they let go of Charlie, who had now regained consciousness and was falling further toward the ground. Neither had noticed the loud grumble of the pickup truck approaching, but they heard it kick up dirt as it drove by. The driver yelled, "Assholes," as he passed and turned right.

Charlie had fallen completely out of the car, mostly landing on top of Shelly, who now had the look of a scorned sailor at a whorehouse. Or maybe it was more of a look of wanting to kill someone.

That look made Ira turn around and reflexively lock the doors. Shelly wobbled off the ground using both her hands to brace against her knees and rise to a standing position. But she hadn't yet gotten her balance, so her butt backed against the car door, slamming it shut. She pulled against the driver's side door handle and her eyes widened to the size of golf balls when she realized it was locked. She hustled to the other side of the car and banged against Ira's window with both her fists.

Ira kept shaking his head back and forth with his arms crossed over his chest like a little boy refusing to eat his oatmeal. "Calm down," he said.

Shelly looked irate, tossing every curse she could Ira's way. Ira slid into the driver's seat, but the car beeped, and the dashboard flashed, "Key not in ignition."

Looking through the front window, Shelly held a key chain in one hand and a snide smirk on her fat face. It was as if the light went off in both their heads at the same time. Shelly twisted her body to look down the driver's side of the car, while Ira tilted his head and eyed the side mirror up and down. Shelly shuffled around the back of the car with Ira following her every move in the rearview. She had made it completely around the car before gazing back at Ira and shrugging her shoulders. Charlie was gone.

Shelly took a huff of breath and walked back to the end of the road where it made a T. With both her hands clasped above her waist, she stared down the block, first to the right, then to the left. Then she shuffled back to the car and squatted to inspect the dirt road where she and Charlie had crashed to the ground.

Ira heard the muffled sound of Shelly's voice saying something like, "Footprints." They evil-eyed each other through the window until Shelly apparently determined that Ira was not getting out. Staring at the ground, she walked down the dirt road and took a left behind a bank of trees which hid her from sight.

After a few minutes, Ira looked in each of the mirrors, unlocked the door, and quietly got out of the car. He did one lap, bent down to look at the same bare footprints that Shelly had seen. Then he took off in the same direction as Shelly. He rounded the corner and saw her stocky silhouette about a hundred yards ahead. Past her, about another two hundred yards up, was a small house near the top of a slight rise in the road.

They walked that same way toward the house, separated by distance and a lingering hatred for one another. Finding out that they had the same blood hadn't made much of a difference. They were still two vastly different people and it would take more than a fleeting admission to fix years of animosity.

Ira purposely made up no ground on Shelly, keeping sure to slow down when she slowed down. She stopped at the top of the hill and turned toward her right. Ira followed and then saw what she saw— that it wasn't really a house. More like a battered RV with a cement block in front of it.

He kept walking until he was a mere twenty feet from Shelly, who hadn't moved any closer to the front door of the RV. As Ira neared, he could now see torn screens covering the windows and the broken stairs leading to the top of the cement block. Only when he got close enough was he able to notice that the whole structure was tilted toward the back left, and not just a little bit; more like you'd imagine it would if it were missing wheels on one side and had giant wheels on the other. But this trailer had no wheels at all.

They stood in front of the sad domicile for what seemed like an hour but was probably closer to ten minutes, until finally the front screen door flung open and slammed against the outside of the trailer. No one came outside to greet them. It was as if the inhabitant was saying, "Come in or go the fuck away, I don't really give a rat's ass."

Ira and Shelly both took fake steps toward the trailer, but neither made the full-fledged effort, kind of daring one another to go in first. Finally, they both succumbed to the curiosity and made their way to the front door, Shelly just a few feet ahead of Ira. She held one hand against the wall of the RV and the other against her knee as she shimmied her way up the broken stairs.

The odor hit them before they even entered the room. It wasn't as if they weren't bracing themselves for something foul. It was as if the atrociousness of the smell was beyond imaginable. It reminded Ira of a Port-o-Let at the end of a festival that hadn't been cleaned in three days. Though it was the middle of the day, there was a veil of darkness over the room, the only light coming from the screen door. The back windows were covered with plywood.

The room was cluttered with crap. Newspapers, old tin cans, and rotten bananas sat on a small counter swarming with flies. Two metal folding chairs leaned up against the counter. A green shag rug covered the floor. Trash covered the shag rug. To the left, a small closet jutted out halfway to the middle of the room. Behind the closet was a bed that stretched nearly across the entire back wall. Something was spread out across the bed, but it was really dark on that side of the room. Above the bed looked to be a loft of some sort.

Ira and Shelly held their noses and looked at one another. They didn't see Charlie and thought maybe they had the wrong house. Walking backward toward the door, however, they picked up the muffled sound of someone crying.

"Charlie? Is that you?" Ira asked.

More crying.

Ira slowly squeezed his way past Shelly, who was now halfway out the door. He inched closer to the back of the room, past the closet—which turned out to be the bathroom—and saw Charlie sitting at the corner of the bed, hugging her legs and rocking back and forth erratically.

The bedspread moved and moaned, stopping Ira in his tracks. He was only a few feet from Charlie, his arm reached out to comfort her. Through her streaming tears, she whispered, "Mama, don't get up. It ain't nothing."

The bed shook back and forth with Mama trying to shift herself into a reclining position. But it was no use. Mama's arm rolled out from underneath the cover. It was rolls of skin upon rolls of skin. She was one of those thousand-pound women that Ira had only seen on TV, confined to a bed and languishing in this godforsaken hovel. "Did you bring me my medicines?" Mama asked.

"No Mama," said Charlie. "I ran into a little trouble, that's all."

Mama groaned.

Charlie sniffled.

"Where's your lil' sister at?" Mama asked. "She was supposed to be fetching me a bologna sandwich and I'm starving."

"Don't know, Mama. I'm just getting home."

"Who's here?" Mama asked.

"My friend Ira," Charlie answered.

Shelly sort of cleared her throat.

"Oh, and Shelly."

"You the one been sending us all that money?" Mama asked.

Ira didn't know how to answer. He obviously hadn't been giving Charlie any money. What money she had came from her Johns.

Shelly said, "That's right. Ira's been looking after Charlie while she goes to school."

"That's mighty nice of you, Mr. Ira," Mama thanked him. "Where's your damn sister?"

"I'm right here, Mama."

Ira turned to see a girl standing behind Shelly. She looked no more than ten or eleven years old, a smaller, younger version of Charlie. She was wearing a dirty wifebeater and tight pink shorts, maybe hand-me-downs from her sister. She held a rolled-up white butcher's paper with masking tape on it. Shimmying past Shelly, the girl started toward the back of the room, until she noticed Charlie scrunched up against the side wall. "Charlie!" she screeched.

The little girl grabbed hold of her sister and dropped the sandwich at the foot of the bed. They hugged each other tightly and the little sister said, "Where you been so long?"

"Got stuck in the city, you know?"

"Guess I been missing you, that's all."

"Hand me that sandwich, girl," Mama yelled.

The little sister broke free of Charlie's embrace and grabbed the sandwich off the bed. She unrolled the butcher's paper and laid it across Mama's chest, then climbed a little ladder against the back wall and disappeared for a moment. She returned holding a pillow, which she propped up behind Mama's head so she could eat her sandwich.

The sound of Mama slurping down her food made Ira gag. Charlie let out a sad little giggle and asked him, "You want to talk outside?"

Ira tripped down the broken stairs, nearly falling on his face. But he righted himself and gasped for fresh air, practically hyperventilating as he did. Shelly was already outside, getting her phone out of her front pocket. Charlie and her sister followed down the stairs.

"Who are you calling?" Ira asked.

"Child Protective Services. Who do you think?"

"They won't do nothing," Charlie said. "Hustle back inside, Amber."

Amber faced her sister and scrunched her nose at her, folding her arms over her chest and shaking her head.

"What do you mean, they won't do nothing?" Shelly asked.

"They been here many times," Charlie answered, "but they ain't got nothing to do with Mama so they leave us here looking after her."

"That's absurd."

"It's true," Amber piped up. "They been here last year and the year before that. Seeing as I go to school and all, they ain't been bothering with us."

"Well, Charlie can't come back to New Orleans. It's no good for her over there," said Shelly.

"Only way I can pay the landlord," said Charlie.

"Don't you get disability checks? Social Security?" Shelly said.

"Mama needs lots of food," Amber answered.

They kind of chuckled and then stood there silently. A fly swarmed around in the air, jumping from person to person. Inside the trailer, the TV flicked on to a commercial for Popeye's fried chicken.

"Guess y'all can go now," Charlie said. "We ain't your problem." She walked over to Ira and gave him a hug, then turned to Shelly and hugged her too. Ira could barely lift his arms to hug her back. Shelly looked even more dejected.

The pair looked at each other, waiting for the other to come up with an idea. But realistically, what could two middle-aged loners do for a morbidly obese woman and her two teenage kids trapped deep in the sticks of Mississippi?

EPILOGUE

"*Why is this night different from all other nights?*" Amber read slowly and methodically. "*On all other nights we eat leave-it bread...*"

"That's 'leavened bread,'" Ira interrupted, raising a piece of matzah hidden beneath a cloth napkin.

Amber swished her lips and glanced at her sister.

"Go on, Amber, you're doing fine," Shelly insisted from across the table.

"*But on this night, we eat only...*" Amber paused as Ira lifted the giant cracker again. "*Matzah,*" she said, pronouncing the As like in *cracker.*

"Matzah," Ira repeated with the correct pronunciation.

"*On all other nights we eat all kind of herbs, but on this night we eat only...*" This time she looked directly at Ira for help.

"Maror," he finished, pointing at the parsley on the seder plate, then nodding at the girl to continue.

"*On all other nights, we do not dip even once. On this night we dip twice.*" Amber made a sour face and looked at her sister again.

"I can't stand dip," Charlie said. "Cooter spits that stuff everywhere."

"Dip is gross," Amber agreed.

Shelly and Ira couldn't stop laughing. "Dip is what the salt water on the seder plate is for," Ira said. "We dip the parsley in the salt water."

"That sounds gross too," Amber responded.

"It is," Howie said with a laugh.

When the table returned their focus to Amber, she was gazing up from the book at the fraying curtains and the chipped paint on the ceiling in the same way her sister once had. It made Ira a little embarrassed. So did the plastic folding table covered by a vinyl tablecloth in his empty dining room. He longed for Mother's china, which she used to bring out just once a year on Passover for the family seder. It had disappeared at the estate sale. Tonight, they were eating off paper plates.

"On all other nights, we eat sitting upright or reclining, but on this night we all recline."

As Amber finished the reading, the irony didn't escape her listeners. They all looked down instinctively at the metal folding chairs beneath their butts. The laughing started with Shelly, but soon they were all overcome with hooting and howling. It was a sound that hadn't been heard in the old Silver home in as long as Ira could remember. Once they all caught their breath, Shelly and Ira went to the kitchen to fetch the first course.

"Thanks for bringing the girls," Ira said.

"No problem," Shelly answered. "They wanted to come."

"How are they getting along over at Sacred Heart?"

Shelly rolled her eyes. She'd gone through a lot of trouble getting the girls into her alma mater. Usually you had to test in, which was problematic because Charlie and Amber were far behind in the academic world. But Shelly's always been a big donor at Sacred Heart, and in return, she gets all kinds of referrals for parents with marital strife. Apparently, the Catholic administrators figure it's best to turn a blind eye by letting the Jewish lawyer handle the divorces. The girls tested a year behind, so Charlie was placed in tenth grade and Amber in sixth.

"Charlie's doing fine," Shelly said. "Amber's having a bit of trouble though. Got called down for a meeting about some fights. But she made the soccer team, so there's that."

"Soccer, huh? Howie used to play soccer."

"He told me he's thinking about Tulane."

"He told you that?"

"Yep. Said he wants to live here with you."

"No kidding," Ira said, and tried to hide a grin by changing the subject. "Charlie's braces are a nice touch."

"Yeah. Figured she'd have more trouble going back to stripping with braces."

"That Catholic school girl uniform makes me cringe though," Ira said with a chuckle.

"School rule."

"I like the pink pearls," Ira said. "They look nicer than the Mardi Gras ones I gave her."

"That's because they're real pearls, dufus."

For a second, Ira and Shelly sounded like brother and sister, giggling in unison and rolling their eyes.

Shelly finished ladling the matzah ball soup and together with Ira carried the five Styrofoam bowls to the table, placing one on each paper placemat. The girls looked at each other from the corners of their eyes. They had no idea what to do with the giant ball floating in broth.

"Howie, do you remember the prayer over the matzah?" Ira asked.

"Seriously?" Howie asked.

"Come on, Howie. I know you remember the hamotzi."

"Ahh, Dad, come on."

"Please?" Ira pleaded. "Just this once." He handed Howie the Passover Haggadah, who sighed and scanned the lines for the English pronunciation. With his elbow on the table and his cheek resting on his hand, he mumbled, *"Baruch atah, Adonai Eloheinu, Melech haolam, asher kid'shanu b'mitvotav, v'tziavanu al achilat matzah."*

"Now the English," Ira demanded.

Howie groaned again but continued, *"Blessed are you, Adonai our God, Sovereign of all, who hallows us with mitzvot, commanding us regarding the eating of matzah."*

"Good job," his father praised him.

"You want me to do it in Chinese now?" the boy asked sarcastically, gleaning laughs from around the table. The girls were still staring at their soup hesitant to start, so Howie said, "Watch," and used his plastic spoon to cut a slice out of the dense matzah ball. The girls imitated him.

"How's your mom?" Ira asked the girls.

"We saw her last Saturday," Charlie said. "She's doing fine, I guess. She's lost almost a hundred pounds already."

Ira and Shelly had left the trailer that March afternoon but returned the following morning with Child Protective Services, a gaggle of reporters, the chief of police, and the entire Utica volunteer fire department. A crane was brought in from a nearby factory to slice the back wall off the RV. It took eleven men to extricate old Mrs. Tuohy from her dilapidated confines. She moaned and groaned most of the way out and onto the flatbed.

The reporters did their job. Shelly made sure the entire state of Mississippi knew how much this family had been neglected by the system. Charlie's mom was sent to a rehabilitation center in Jackson where they prepped her for stomach bypass surgery as soon as they could get her blood pressure under control. With the mere threat of a couple of lawsuits, Shelly made sure the state was responsible for Mrs. Tuohy's operation and aftercare.

"She's dying for a bologna sandwich," Amber said with a giggle.

"Speaking of bologna," Ira said as he rose from the table and carried his empty bowl to the kitchen.

Ira struggled to open the jar of gefilte fish, but after a few whacks on the Formica countertop he finally got the top to twist off. He used some tongs to grab the beige-colored fish dumplings and place them on the small paper plates, careful not to spill too much of the gelatin while doing so. Then he spooned small amounts of red horseradish next to each one and carried the plates to the table.

The girls looked astonished by the food sitting in front of them, and both bent their heads down to smell the congealed fish. Ira wasn't surprised by their sour-faced reactions. "It's better than it looks," he urged.

Howie chuckled. "No it's not."

"You just got to smear that red stuff all over it," Ira said, waving the comment off.

The girls bent down again to smell the horseradish but popped back up instantly, holding their watering noses.

Charlie poked the slimy flaccid fish with her plastic fork. "It looks…gross," she grimaced.

"Ira, I think you need to go a little slower with the Jew food. Not too many people like gefilte fish," Shelly said.

Ira shrugged and sliced into the rubbery mix of carp and pike, slathered it with horseradish, and downed it in two bites. All four of his guests stuck their plates out across the table, offering him their servings of gefilte fish. He chuckled, though feeling a little disappointed. He took each plate and lined them up next to his own while Shelly went to the kitchen to prepare the next course. Between forkfuls of fish, he asked, "How do you girls like living with Shelly?"

"It's alright, I guess," Amber said.

"She's pretty hardcore," Charlie complained. "My curfew's nine."

"And so much homework," Amber added her grievance. "I never did homework at home."

"Well, that's alright girls. I think this is best for both of you right now. You can't live here, that's for sure."

"They dropped the charges, though, right?" Howie asked.

"Well, they did," Ira nodded, "but they made me promise not to allow any minors in my house." He saw the trepidation on their faces. "We'll keep tonight between us."

Shelly appeared, heavily laden with two platters of chicken and mashed potatoes and a bowl of peas. They passed the food around the table and started quietly eating.

"Chicken's pretty good," Shelly commented. 'Did you roast it yourself?"

"Me? No. Don't have a roasting pan anymore. Got it at Winn-Dixie. They were having a special, two for $9.99."

"With the can of peas, the matzah ball soup, potatoes, and the gefilte fish, this meal must have set you back a pretty penny," Shelly remarked with a raise of the eyebrows.

"Over twenty bucks," Ira agreed. But with a secret smile he added, "I got some good news today."

They all stared at him as he laced his fingers behind his head and leaned his metal chair back as far as it could go without tipping.

"Well?" they demanded in unison.

"I got an advance on my book."

Shelley: "No way."

Howie: "That's awesome!"

Charlie: "Oh my gawd."

Amber: "What book?"

Ira's book—the one he had been working on for the past ten years—was about a father and son who embark on a journey to Jupiter. During their flight through space, the son ages and, mysteriously, the father does not. By the end, the son ends up on his deathbed being cared for by the father. It was a love story, and for a man who knew so little about love, it was quite a brilliant one.

"How'd you get an advance?" Shelly asked. "I thought you didn't even have an agent."

"It's actually a funny story," he answered. "Remember when they took my computer downtown? You know, when Charlie got picked up?"

"Yeah," all but Amber said in unison.

"Well, the guy who did the diagnostics on the computer is also a guest writer for *NCIS*. He found the story and had to read through it in case there was any incriminating evidence in it. There wasn't, of course. But he told me he loved it. He showed it to his agent and next thing you know, I'm getting offered a ten-thousand-dollar advance."

"Holy shit, Ira!" Shelly exclaimed. "That's fucking awesome. Excuse my language."

"Maybe they'll make a movie of it one day," Amber said.

A chorus of compliments followed. Ira hadn't felt so lauded in years. He had nearly given up on the book, figuring he'd just self-publish and hope to sell a couple of dozen copies. Maybe he'd get to do a reading for the men's club at Sinai. Then at least he'd have something to be proud of, something that might live past his own ignominious existence. Or at the very least, something his children, and their children, might read and admire one day. Something to be remembered by.

But now. Now, Ira had something to look forward to. He'd finally proven something to himself. He looked around the table at the faces of his new family. Maybe life wasn't so bad after all.

ACKNOWLEDGEMENTS

My heartfelt gratitude to my wife Courtney and both of our parents for sticking with me when the going got tough. And to my kids, Drew, Remy, and Cole, may you always reach for the stars and follow your dreams and be the best version of yourselves that you can be.

This book took many years to write. Sometimes it was a labor of love; other times, it was a creative outlet for escaping reality. Writing is an all-consuming activity and it can be hard to balance with other responsibilities. But I am finally happy with this story, and sometimes you have to let go of your babies and let them stand on their own two feet. The value of the effort won't be seen until they're out in the world and others can judge them for what they are.

About the Author

Shane Finkelstein is originally from Valley Stream, New York. After majoring in English at the University of Maryland, he spent nine years in Atlanta as publisher of *University Reporter/ Insite Magazine*. He wrangled his girlfriend at the time, Courtney, to travel around the world in Y2K before settling down with her in their favorite city, New Orleans. Together, they opened four locations of Nacho Mama's—a popular local Mexican restaurant chain—produced festivals, and had three wonderful kids. Shane continued his passion for writing with entertainment articles in local publications like *Where Y'at Magazine, New Orleans Levee, and Le Monde du Merde*. In 2013, he published his first full-length novel, *Finding Gordon Lipschitz*, which went on to become an Amazon Best Seller in the humor category. He's currently living and self-quarantining in the Broadmoor neighborhood of Uptown, New Orleans.

Made in the USA
Columbia, SC
02 June 2020